Kelly Elliott is a *New York Times* and *USA Today* bestselling contemporary romance author. Since finishing her bestselling *Wanted* series, Kelly continues to spread her wings while remaining true to her roots and giving readers stories rich with hot protective men, strong women and beautiful surroundings.

Kelly has been passionate about writing since she was fifteen. After years of filling journals with stories, she finally followed her dream and published her first novel, *Wanted*, in November of 2012.

Kelly lives in central Texas with her husband, daughter, and two pups. When she's not writing, Kelly enjoys reading and spending time with her family. She is down to earth and very in touch with her readers, both on social media and at signings.

Visit Kelly Elliott online:

www.kellyelliottauthor.com
@author_kelly
www.facebook.com/KellyElliottAuthor/

Entice Me

NEW YORK TIMES & USA TODAY BESTSELLING AUTHOR

KELLY ELLIOTT

piatkus

PIATKUS

First published in Great Britain in 2019 by Piatkus

1 3 5 7 9 10 8 6 4 2

A CIP catalogue record for this book is available from the British Library.

ISBN 978-0-349-42241-1

Printed and bound in Great Britain by Clays Ltd, Elcograf S.p.A.

Cover photo: Lauren Perry, Periwinkle Photography
Cover design: RBA Designs, www.rbadesigns.com
Interior Design & Formatting: Christine Borgford, www.typeaformatting.com
Developmental Editing by: Elaine York, www.allusiongraphics.com
Editing & Proofing: Hollie Westring, www.hollietheeditor.com
Proofing: Callie Hamilton

Papers used by Piatkus are from well-managed forests
and other responsible sources.

Piatkus
An imprint of
Little, Brown Book Group
Carmelite House
50 Victoria Embankment
London EC4Y 0DZ

An Hachette UK Company
www.hachette.co.uk

www.littlebrown.co.uk

Entice Me

One

NASH

THE MOMENT I walked into Sedotto, the bar my best friend Tucker owned, I was wishing I had opted to stay home. If it hadn't been for my younger sister Morgan's birthday celebration tonight, I would have done just that.

"Nash!"

I had barely walked into the door when I heard her call out my name. I smiled when I saw Morgan rushing over to me.

"I was worried you wouldn't come."

"And miss your birthday? What kind of a brother would that make me?"

Her smile had me returning the gesture. "Even if you had decided to stay home, I would still say you were the best brother ever. Did you work today?"

"I did, but I'm actually supposed to be on vacation, but Dad wasn't having that."

"You deserve it and just need to take one."

She was right. I did deserve it. After busting my ass along with my crew, we finished Tucker and his wife Charlie's house in four months—a feat that would normally take nine months to a year. The damn thing was more than nine thousand square feet. It was a miracle we got it done when we did. It was worth the hard work to see how happy they were. There wasn't anything I wouldn't do for Tucker though. Or Charlie. Any of my friends, for that matter. We all went to college at the University of Texas and had remained friends since. Over the years, it had been a roller coaster of emotions with this bunch. After years of denying their feelings for each other, Tucker and Charlie finally tied the knot last December. Terri and Jim, another couple from our group, had been dating for years and were finally getting married in December. Blake, the wild one among us, had moved to New York City but came back to Austin last year. Tucker's sister and my ex—Lily—was also part of the group. Of course, when she admitted to cheating on me and getting pregnant by another guy, she quietly stopped hanging out with us.

"Dad's pissed I gave up a job to build Tucker and Charlie's house, so he's had me busting my ass the last few months."

Morgan rolled her eyes.

"So, who else is here?"

She glanced over her shoulder. "A few friends of mine from college and work. Oh, and Kaelynn."

With a frown, I replied, "Kaelynn?"

"Yeah! She's the girl I met last year on my mission trip. I've talked about her a lot. We really connected and have become good friends. She moved here to Austin to help me with my start-up."

My eyes widened in surprise. "She moved here to help you?"

Laughing, Morgan wrapped her arm around mine and led me toward the private room that Tucker rented out to groups.

"Yes! It's her job, Nash, and she loves Austin, so it was a no-brainer for her to move here. She's from Utah, not Mars, for crying out loud."

"Very funny, Morgan. So she's a consultant of sorts?"

"Sort of. She helps with start-ups, setting up foundations, scholarships, things like that."

"Morgan, can you afford to hire someone like that? It's not a good idea to get in over your head before you even make the first dollar."

Her smile faded some, and I felt like a jackass questioning her judgment. I didn't want to see my sister get in over her head with this new venture she had going on.

"I appreciate you worrying, but she isn't charging me. She owns her company and it's a nonprofit organization. She mostly deals with people who are doing something associated with veterans. So when she heard what I was wanting to do, she offered to help. For free, as a friend."

I frowned. "Wait, so she isn't getting paid to be here? She's helping you out of the kindness of her heart? That doesn't sound suspicious at all."

She sighed then looked away for a moment before steeling her eyes back on mine. "I'm not stupid, and I actually know what I'm doing. Like I said, I'm not paying her; she owns her own company. When we talked last year and I told her my plan, she was the one who really helped me get things going. She has already helped me so much, Nash. I couldn't have gotten this far without her help and encouragement."

My heart dropped knowing that I had made my sister think I doubted her business acumen. Pulling her into my arms, I hugged her and spoke against her ear over the loud music.

"I know you've got this, sis. I'm so proud of you for doing something you love and making it come to life. You're going to do great."

She drew back, tears in her eyes as she replied, "Thank you for your support. I know Mom and Pop want me to keep working for Barrett Construction, and Dad never really knew why I chose the career I did, but I can do this. I will make this a success and help people in return."

"You will. I know it."

Throwing herself back into my arms, she squealed. "Oh my gosh! I can't believe I'm going to be helping people while doing something I love!"

With a smile, I hugged her tighter. My parents had given Morgan a hard time when she went to school to become an art therapist. She had finally earned her master's degree after busting her ass working for my father and going to school full time, nearly year-round. I was proud as hell of her. My folks were as well; they just never got why Morgan picked the path she did. What they didn't know was that Morgan had fallen in love in high school, and her first love, Mike, went off and joined the army. He was in special forces, and once he came home after serving a few years, he had changed, Morgan said. He committed suicide at the end of Morgan's freshman year of college. That was the catalyst for her to go into art therapy. It was also her way of dealing with her grief over his death. She was determined to help veterans like Mike.

"Morgan! We're doing shots!" someone called out. My sister jumped back and grinned from ear to ear.

She knew exactly what my raised eyebrow meant. Years of me brainwashing her over the dangers of drinking in public must have worked because she immediately started parroting to me the same things I've told her over and over and over again.

"I've got a designated driver, I won't drink too much, and yes, I will not take any drinks from anyone."

I kissed her on the forehead and replied, "That's my girl. Go have fun. I'll be in there in a second. I saw the gang when I walked in."

"Don't be long!" she called out as she rushed into the private area.

As I made my way toward what was known as the boss's friend's booth, I smiled when I saw everyone here. Terri, Jim, a very pregnant Charlie, and Tucker. The only one who wasn't there was Blake. He was probably working, because the man was the definition of workaholic. Or he was screwing a girl in the restroom. It was either work or sex with Blake and was a toss-up to where he could be at this very moment.

"Hey, y'all," I said, extending my hand to Jim and then Tucker.

"I was wondering when you were going to show up," Tucker stated.

Sliding into the booth, I gave everyone the same smile I had been plastering on my face the last year. The one that said everything was perfect in my world.

It wasn't though. Not since the day I found out the woman I loved, Lily, cheated on me. She got herself pregnant by another man and basically left me because my wallet wasn't big enough. It had been hard seeing her the few times she showed up to hang out since she was Tucker's younger sister and had been a part of our group since college. She had slowly backed away from the group lately. Her life soon became cocktail parties and high-society dinners, not hanging out at her brother's bar.

Once I got into the booth and really looked around the table, I couldn't help but notice how everyone stared at me.

"What? Do I have something on my face?" I asked with a chuckle.

Tucker glanced over to Charlie, who rested her hand on her belly. The only reason Tucker let his wife be at the bar was because there was no smoking allowed. That, and he watched her like a hawk.

It was Charlie who cleared her throat and then took in a deep breath before speaking.

"Lily texted and said she needed a night out and is on her way here."

My entire body stiffened and I tried like hell not to let anyone notice. I had gotten so used to Lily not being around, so when she showed up, it felt like a kick in the gut.

It was Tucker's turn to talk. "I guess she and Mark needed some time together, and they felt like it would be good for them to go out. My mom's watching the baby."

I had yet to even ask if Lily had a boy or a girl. I honestly didn't give two shits, but a small part of me still believed that baby should have been mine, not some rich asshole's.

"Maggie is adorable and plenty old enough now at five months for Lily to be leaving her with a sitter," Charlie added.

My chest ached slightly knowing Lily had a little girl. I knew in my heart Lily wasn't the one for me, my soul mate, but that didn't mean it still didn't hurt. When Charlie saw my pained expression, she reached across the table and squeezed my hand.

Charlie and Lily had been best friends since college and had remained friends after we had broken up. Terri had tried with her, but she wasn't as close to Lily anymore. Even though I tried not to let it happen, our friends sort of picked teams, with me coming out the victor. Charlie and Tucker really were Switzerland. With Lily being Tucker's sister and Charlie's best friend, they remained close to both Lily and myself. Jim and Terri, on the other hand, made it known from the get-go they were Team Nash. Terri was pleasant to Lily, but their friendship had been strained after Lily cheated on me. Blake, well, let's just say Blake hates cheaters. He has yet to even acknowledge Lily when she's around, which isn't often.

"I'm glad she's happy."

Terri laughed. "Yeah, I don't think she's happy."

"I'm going to have to agree with Terri," Tucker said with a sigh. "My sister seems far from happy."

I shrugged. "Some women experience depression after the birth of a child, and I'm sure not having your dad here plays a part in that. It would make sense she might seem a bit sad."

Everyone stared at me before Terri shook her head and wiggled her finger in front of me. "See, this is what I mean. She leaves you for a dickhead like Mark. It doesn't make any sense. Any woman would be lucky to have you."

Charlie nodded. "I agree."

"She's unhappy because it's called karma. Sorry, Tucker, I know it's your sister and all."

He gave a halfhearted grin.

"Listen, y'all, it's over and done with, so no sense in going down that road. Honestly, it worked out how it was meant to. Let's just change the subject," I asked of them.

"Too late," Jim said as we all turned to see what he was looking at.

The feeling in my stomach was somewhere between sickness and anxiety. Lily was heading toward our table. Mark was next to her, his arm around her waist.

She looked good. You would have never known she had given birth to a baby a few months ago. Knowing Lily, though, she probably hit the gym right after she gave birth.

"I need to get going. Morgan is waiting on me," I said, sliding out of the booth.

"Nash, dude, you don't have to go just because . . ." Tucker's voice trailed off when Lily and Mark came to a stop.

"You're not leaving because of me, are you?" Lily asked, giving me a smile that said she really hoped I was leaving. No one wanted that awkward feeling that would surely be thick in the air if I stuck around.

"No, Morgan is having a birthday party and I need to get to it."

Her smile faltered some. Turning my attention to Mark, I reached out my hand for his. For a quick second, he debated shaking my hand.

Dickhead.

"Nash, it's good seeing you." He shook my hand firmly. Probably under other circumstances, I might have actually liked the guy.

"Yeah, congratulations on the baby. If you'll excuse me."

With a quick glance over to Tucker, I asked, "Is it okay if I use your office to make a quick call?"

"Sure, of course. You know the code."

I nodded, then moved my way around Lily and Mark. The faster I got away from them, the better.

It wasn't two seconds before my phone buzzed in my hand.

> Lily: *Can we talk?*

Letting out a scoff, I replied to her.

> Me: *We don't have anything to talk about.*
>
> Lily: *Nash, please.*

Not looking at where I was going, I ran right into someone. My phone dropped and I bent down to pick it up, only to see two phones on the floor. I picked them both up.

"Damn, I'm sorry about that!" I shouted over the loud music. The band Tucker hired had started playing right at that moment. When I stood up, I handed the person back their phone.

When the most exquisite hazel eyes captured mine, I froze. Then she spoke and it felt like the ground had rippled underneath me.

"Oh gosh, thank you. I'm sorry, I wasn't looking where I was going! I guess that's why they say no texting and walking."

She let out the cutest giggle, and I actually felt my stomach drop.

What in the hell? That feeling hasn't happened in a long time.

When I was finally able to find my voice, I chuckled and said, "Looks like we would both be fined then. I'm guilty of the same thing."

Her teeth bit into her lower lip, and I couldn't help but let my gaze move down to her mouth. Jesus, this woman was beautiful. Her long brown hair was pulled back into a low ponytail and she wore a T-shirt that said *No cheesy pick-up lines . . . I'm taken.*

Pointing to her shirt, I asked, "Boyfriend buy you that?"

For a second, she didn't move. Her gaze was locked on mine until finally she replied.

"What? No! No . . . I, um . . . I don't have a boyfriend . . . um . . . it was a bet. I lost."

Lifting my brow, I asked, "Why would you bet to not wear this T-shirt? Seems like it would keep the creeps away."

Her mouth turned up into the cutest, crooked grin. Then she held up her finger in a *wait for it* moment and turned around.

The back read, *Just kidding. Tell me your best pick-up line. I'm horny as fuck.*

I laughed, you know the kind that you almost choke because that wasn't what you were expecting kind of laughter, as she faced forward again. "See! That's why I didn't want to wear it. I just went to the restroom to put it on."

My eyes scanned her quickly. Her curvy body fit her jeans and showed off her figure, while the tight T-shirt showed off her upper body. Her *ample* upper body.

"Explains why the shirt is so . . ."

"Tight? Yeah, my boobs are suffocating."

This time I laughed harder. I couldn't remember the last time I actually laughed. It felt good. Really fucking good. I even had to bend over to catch my breath because I laughed so hard.

She tilted her head and regarded me as I let it all out. It hadn't been that funny, but I clearly had needed the release.

"Thank you! I needed that laugh."

Her cheeks blushed and she glanced down to the floor, a shy smile playing across her face.

When she looked back up at me, her mouth parted slightly, as if she wanted to say something else.

"Am I interrupting?"

The sound of Lily's voice made my smile fall.

The woman looked over my shoulder, and deep lines appeared on her forehead before she glanced back up at me and spoke. "Well, it was nice talking to you. Enjoy your evening." She walked around me and headed down the long hallway.

For the first time in months, my body actually felt something when a woman talked to me, looked at me. I'd had a few one-night stands, nothing that meant anything. Just enough to keep the edge off and keep me from making my dick raw from my hand.

My gaze followed her down the hallway, not paying any attention to Lily standing there.

"Jesus, could you stare at her any harder?" Lily spat out.

Turning away, I made my way to Tucker's office. Unlocking the door, I walked in, Lily right on my heels.

"Lily, what do you want?" I asked in an annoyed tone as I turned around to face her.

Before I could even process anything, she wrapped her arms around my neck, kissing me. It took me all of two seconds to realize what in the hell was happening.

Lifting my hands, I pulled her arms from around my neck and pushed her gently away.

"What in the hell are you doing?" I asked, wiping my mouth.

"I missed you."

"Your fucking husband and the father of your kid is out there, Lily."

She rolled her eyes. "Mark hasn't acted much like a husband the last few months. He's hardly even touched me."

I screwed up my face and stared at her. Terri was right; Lily was most likely getting served her full dose of karma, and why she thought I would care baffled me.

"What's wrong, Lil? Things not going so great with your knight in shining armor? I often wondered what happens with a cheater . . . I mean, do they stop after only one time, or once they get bored do they find their next target? I guess I got my answer."

She pressed her lips together.

"This was what you wanted, wasn't it? Him. Not me. So now things aren't going so well and you think you can just show up and kiss me? Like get a redo on your fuck-up?"

"We were in love once, Nash."

"Yeah, once. You cheated on me. You gave up what we had. Ironically, that has a way of making you fall out of love really quick."

"I thought Mark was what I needed, but he isn't. It's you, Nash. I *need* you. Please. *Please* forgive me."

Closing my eyes, I took in a deep breath and slowly let it out before focusing on Lily.

"You know, it took me a long time to forgive you, Lily. I can't even begin to explain to you how much you hurt me."

Her eyes filled with tears. "I know, baby. I'm so sorry. I'm ready to be a real couple now. You and me."

I shook my head. "I forgave you, Lily, but I'll never forget what you did. Ever. For months I've been walking around with a hole in my damn heart, so fucking afraid to let anyone in or even dare to let myself be happy. Why? Because I trusted you, and you stole that trust from me. You never cared enough to even be honest with me. I wasn't enough for you then. I know now that I will never be enough, and I won't make that same mistake twice."

She went to reach for my hand, but I backed away.

"Let me make it up to you, Nash. I know now what I had in you. I was stupid and young, and I thought I needed a bit of excitement in my life."

I bellowed out and stared at her in disbelief. She wasn't getting it. Any of it.

"I know how to make you happy."

"No, Lily, you don't. You never did. All those months I spent hiding because I was afraid to let someone too close to me after your betrayal. Then something happened tonight. That shit got knocked right out of me, literally. I'm sorry you're not happy with your husband, I really am. But you made your bed, sweetheart. Lie in it."

I walked around her and she grabbed my arm.

"No! Don't do this, Nash. Don't walk away from what we had."

Withdrawing my arm from her grip, I smiled as I looked down at her defeated face. The last bit of anger I held toward her felt as if it was finally fading away. I felt sorry for her.

"Just a reminder, you were the one who walked away, Lily. And finally, I've seen it was the best damn thing to ever happen to me."

As I made my way to the door, I heard her start crying. I balled my fists and did my best to ignore it as I pulled the office door open and walked out. I'd go make my call somewhere less crowded.

For the first time in months, it felt like the dark cloud that had been over me was gone. And the girl I had ran into was the reason. When I got back out to the bar, I scanned the place looking for her. I had no idea what caused the instant spark I had felt when she smiled at me. Or the way her voice made my body feel warm and in need of something I hadn't let myself want in months. But I needed to find her, to see if the connection we had was a fluke. I had to know.

Damn it. She's gone.

"Who you looking for?" Charlie asked as she walked up to me.

"I don't know. Someone I ran into a few minutes ago. Lily interrupted us and I didn't have a chance to get her information."

Charlie laughed. "Figures Lily would cock-block you."

I rolled my eyes. "Yeah, right?" I replied with a chuckle. "Well, if it's meant to be, I'll see her again. I better get to the party."

"And I better get to the ladies' room before this baby makes me pee all over the floor."

Lifting my hands, I moved out of her way as she made her way past me. It was hard to believe Charlie was the CEO of a billion-dollar consulting firm in Austin. Her parents had died in a car accident a year ago, and she had been thrown into the position and had to fight to keep herself in the position.

The bar was packed, so it took me a minute or so to get across and back to the private room Morgan's party was in.

Stepping into the room, I felt an instant change. A surge of electricity felt like it made every single nerve ending in my body come to life. *What the hell is happening with me tonight?*

Sweeping my eyes across the room as I looked for Morgan. I stopped searching when *her* gaze caught mine from the far back corner.

A slow smile spread over my face when her cheeks blushed. Did she feel the connection between us? I needed to find out who she was, even if that old familiar feeling of fear—or maybe it was excitement, it had been so long that I couldn't distinguish between the two—had begun to creep in.

Forgetting everything that had happened with Lily, I made the decision that it was time for me to move on. It was time to trust again and let down the wall I had built up around my heart. The woman who currently held my attention was the cause of that decision.

Two

KAELYNN

MORGAN PULLED ME from one person to the next as she introduced me to both family and friends. A few members of her family, namely her mother, asked a ton of personal questions. It was a subject I had always guarded and answered short and sweet. Not that I had done anything wrong or came from a shady family. Just the opposite actually. My family was one of the wealthiest families in the state. Second wealthiest in Utah, where I was from. That was the problem. Once people knew who I was and how deep my pockets were, I was treated differently. I never really had true friends growing up. And all of my boyfriends were never really interested in me, only the money or what knowing my father could do for them. After college I stopped telling people who I was. They didn't need to know I was an heiress to a billion-dollar fortune. Most of it old money from the railroads and investments my family had made many years ago. My father didn't even have to work, but he continued to do so every day. His job was to make more money, like his father, and his father before him. Even with that, my parents did so much for our community and other programs. I was proud of the way they helped others, almost always keeping their generosity anonymous.

The sound of Morgan's voice pulled me from my thoughts. "Rich, this is Kaelynn. We met last year on a mission trip and have been friends ever since. She's helping me get my new business off the ground."

Rich lifted a brow as he let his gaze roll over the stupid shirt I had on. "Nice shirt."

I sighed and looked at Morgan. "Morgan and I had a bet and I lost. Hence the silly shirt."

He stared at me for a moment before speaking again. "So you're *helping* Morgan get her business going? How much are you soaking her for? You know she's just getting started and really can't afford a consultant who probably isn't going to be of help anyway."

My eyes widened, and I felt Morgan tense next to me.

"Rich! Holy crap, are you out of your mind?" Morgan shouted. A few people who heard her outburst turned our way.

With a smile, I extended my hand to him. "It's nice to meet you, Rich. I actually own the company, so that allows me to help Morgan without charging her the crazy fees that some consultants charge. We're a nonprofit, and everything we raise helps go toward helping individuals, as well as companies, who work directly with veterans. We do a variety of things from offering simple support to helping find resources to start nonprofits, as well as assisting people like Morgan who are starting a new business geared toward helping our veterans get the help they need. And although we do charge people for our assistance, it is at a much lower cost and goes right back into the system to help others. In this case, though, I'm offering my services to Morgan pro bono. One friend helping another. I'm sure you get that."

He had the decency to look embarrassed. Then he looked at Morgan. "Mike?"

Morgan swallowed hard and nodded.

"Makes sense he's the reason you're doing this."

I felt the tension between the two of them. I knew who Mike was, Morgan's boyfriend who had committed suicide after suffering from PTSD. It was something that was also very dear to my own heart, the reason for my own business.

Morgan seemed to snap out of her pensive state and jabbed her finger into his chest. "You owe her an apology, now."

I lifted my hands and said, "None needed, really."

Rich looked to Morgan. "You didn't mention she was doing it for free; that would have been helpful."

"It was none of your business," she spat back, a look of disappointment on her face toward the gentleman standing in front of us.

Glancing between Morgan and Rich, I arched a brow. "Am I missing something here?"

Morgan shook her head and forced a smile. "No. Rich and I used to date, but I thought we could remain friends. It appears he thinks he can interject his opinions into my life still. If he's going to act like a dick . . ."

"Morgan, I'm sorry. I shouldn't have said anything. It's only . . . well, I worry about you. I worry what feelings this type of venture might bring up for you."

Her body relaxed a bit while my heart melted some. I made a mental note to question Morgan about Rich later. It was clear he still cared about her. I was curious about how long they had dated and why I hadn't heard her mention him at all before tonight.

"Listen, I'll let you get back to introducing Kaelynn around. Again, I'm sorry, and it was great meeting you. I look forward to seeing Morgan's business take off with your assistance."

With a quick lift of my hand and wave, I replied, "You as well."

As Rich walked away, Morgan sighed. "I'm really sorry. First my brother and now Rich. I need to let everyone know you're working for free, I guess. Care to walk around wearing a sandwich board or something? Seems like no one has any confidence in me."

"That's not true. They're simply worried about you. That's a sign of people who love and care for you. And I'll happily wear a sandwich board if that's what it takes. Plus, it'll hide this shirt I'm wearing, right?"

She chuckled, then glanced to her right. "Let's see . . . Who else do I need to introduce you to? Maybe you can meet someone and get lucky tonight! After all, your shirt advertises how horny you are."

We laughed when she nudged me with her elbow because we knew how unlikely that would be. Not that I wasn't down for a good night of sex—I wasn't a prude—but I was picky. And picky meant I hadn't been with anyone in a while. A really, excessively long while.

The moment he stepped into the room, though, I sensed him. It was the oddest sensation and one I had never experienced. Scanning the room to see who had my hackles raised, it was right when our eyes met that he smiled and I couldn't help the heat that built in my cheeks. I'd been attracted to men before, of course, but something about *this* man was different. His smile and those dimples. Lord, they made my knees weaken. Not only was he handsome, but there was something different about him. There was goodness in his eyes, something you didn't really see too often anymore, especially in men around my age.

Before he had a chance to make his way over to me, though, Rich walked up and slapped him on the back. They were soon lost in conversation. I watched him intently. The way he grinned at the man, nodded his head, and really seemed to be focused on what Rich said. He wasn't letting his eyes wander the room at all. His entire attention was on his friend. Well, I assumed they were friends.

"So, who do you have your eye on?" Morgan asked, bumping me on the arm yet again, and this time using a teasing tone to her voice. "You're practically undressing him with those bedroom eyes."

"What?" I asked, letting out a chuckle. "I don't know what you mean."

"Uh-huh. You have a lustful look in your eyes, Kaelynn. One I've never seen before. Who is it? Show me!"

I gave her a slight push. "Shut up! I do not. I have, however, spotted the hottest guy I've ever seen. We actually ran into each other outside the bathrooms earlier. Seems like a really nice guy. You must know him if he's at your party."

"Point him out to me," Morgan demanded, standing up on her tippy toes.

My eyes went to the last place I had seen him. He was still there, still deep in conversation.

"There. The guy talking to Rich."

Morgan's face erupted into a full-blown grin. "The one in the blue shirt?" she asked for confirmation.

"Yep. Mr. Hottie McHot. I feel like I need to break out into a version of Janet Jackson's 'Nasty' with the thoughts I had after I bumped into him earlier. Don't judge me; it's been a while."

Morgan covered her mouth in an attempt not to laugh.

I sighed. "Geesh, listen to me. I sound like a pathetic woman who has gone way to long without sex. But I think I could get on board for sex with Mr. Hottie McHot."

"It's been that long, huh?" she asked.

I rolled my eyes. "You could say. He's good looking, though, isn't he? You should see his dimples. Lord, I'm a sucker for dimples. He has to be too good to be true, though. He was so sweet and kind, then add the good looks on top of it. He has to be either gay or married."

Morgan focused back on him and shook her head as she finally let out the laugh she had been trying to hold in. "He's not either. He is, however, one of the sweetest men I have ever known."

My interest was piqued. "Spill it. Who is he and how do you know him?"

Morgan grabbed my arm and we started making our way through the crowd. She walked over to introduce me to him. A part of me wanted to stop her; I'd already had my dreams crushed by the last guy I dated. I made the mistake of taking him to meet my parents. Three days later, he dropped to one knee to ask me to marry him. His speech was one of a kind, definitely one for the keepsake books. He stated he hadn't fallen in love with me *yet*, but he was pretty sure a trip to Europe, just the two of us, obviously financed by my resources, would surely do it.

Jerk.

The other part of me, however, liked the way this guy made my entire body tingle. The way I felt a fire deep inside my soul when he smiled at me. No man had ever made me feel that, and it sort of scared me. But not enough to keep from meeting him, though.

What was one more encounter with him anyway? We'd meet, talk a few minutes, then he would probably go after one of the women in here who were throwing themselves at guys like this.

"I can't wait to introduce you!" Morgan shouted over the music, a giddiness in her voice I'd never heard. I couldn't help but grin at her.

It didn't take long for Mr. Hottie McHot to see Morgan pushing her way past people to get to him. As a matter of fact, they seemed to understand why she was trying so hard to make her way through the crowd, and they moved out of her way—think of Moses parting the Red Sea as a helpful visual—once they caught sight of who she was heading toward.

Oh no. If this was an ex of Morgan's, I was going to hit myself.

"Hey, long time no see," Mr. Hottie McHot said to me, and then looked over at Morgan with what? A look of adoration passing between them? "Same goes for you."

When he leaned down and kissed her cheek, I tried not to feel jealous. Damn, I knew it. I pushed away that nagging feeling in my stomach that screamed I didn't like that he kissed my best friend and not me.

"Nash, I understand you already met near the bathrooms, but now I'd like for you to officially meet my best friend Kaelynn."

My mouth dropped open as my shocked look went from Morgan to Nash and back again.

Nash?

Nash as in the brother Morgan always talks about?

The brother who had his heart broken by a woman who cheated on him, and from what I could tell from the stories, cared more about money than him.

With a smile that made my knees tremble yet again, Nash extended his hand. His dark hair looked messy, like he had run his fingers through it a lot since the last time I saw him. His eyes were so dark, and they danced with a little bit of mischief. It made me smile even bigger.

I placed my hand in his and he shook it. Why had I been secretly hoping he would have brought it up to his mouth and kissed the backside of my hand? He seemed like the type who would do that.

For the love of all things, Kaelynn, this isn't a fairy-tale movie.

But then he winked, and it was so much better than a kiss on the back of the hand. "So you're the one helping Morgan start her new adventure?"

I loved that he called it that. It was going to be an adventure. One that would help so many people.

"Yes, that would be me."

"At least now I know your name."

Laughing, I nodded. "Same to you."

"Any good pick-up lines yet?" he asked with a teasing smile.

"No, thank goodness!"

We stared at each other for a few moments before Nash focused on his sister. "So when are we busting out the cake? You know I only came for Danny's cake-making skills."

Morgan hit his shoulder. "Yeah, right. Are you going to give a speech?"

I waited for him to tell her no, that there was no way he was going to stand in front of all these people and speak. He surprised me, though, with his answer.

"If you want, there isn't anything I wouldn't do for you."

Morgan beamed with happiness as my heart melted on the spot. Then she turned to me, a look in her eyes that said she was about to do something I wasn't going to like.

"How about you dance with poor Kaelynn? No one has asked her yet."

Nash caught my gaze, his eyebrows turned down in disbelief. "What type of pansy-ass friends do you have, Morgan? I mean, who could resist that shirt she's wearing?"

She laughed and shook her head. "Just do me this favor, will you?"

When he smiled, my breath stilled. It actually caught in my chest. He wasn't even smiling at me, for Pete's sake. It was the way his smile said so many things. That he loved his sister and would do anything to make her happy. That he'd dance with a lonely woman at a birthday party so she didn't feel left out. Yeah, he looks like a keeper.

I glanced around the private room we were in. It was on the small side, so I couldn't imagine Nash would really ask me to dance in these tight quarters. The Sedotto itself was huge. The main bar area had a small dance floor set off to the side, and the private room we were in had a stage area that was also being used as a makeshift dance floor and a display for all the food.

When Nash put his hand out for mine, I almost declined. So many things were spinning around in my head. This was my best friend's brother. He had vowed off all women, especially women like his ex. I might not be exactly like his ex, but I was pretty sure the fact I had more money than I knew what to do with would probably play a huge factor in how extremely opposite I was to her. It was best if I declined and went about my business.

But I didn't. Oh no. I had to make everything complicated.

Ignoring every warning bell going off in my head, I found myself placing my hand in his. When his hand rested lightly on my lower back, guiding me through the crowd, my entire body heated. I'd never had a man's touch make me feel this way. For a moment, it threw me off balance and I couldn't focus. On anything.

It's just been a long time, Kaelynn. When was the last time a man actually touched you? A beyond good looking, caring, sweet, body-to-die-for man?

As we made our way onto the small dance floor, the fast song changed to a slower song. I paused and waited for Nash to change his mind. He didn't. He shrugged.

Lord help me.

Had Morgan never showed me a picture of her brother? Maybe she had and I didn't pay attention.

I glanced up at Nash.

No, if I had seen a picture of this man, I would have most definitely remembered.

"Shall we?"

Nodding, I let him pull me closer as Shania Twain's "From This Moment On" played.

We moved together flawlessly across the floor. He didn't hold me too close, yet close enough that my heart pounded, and I found myself aching for him to draw me in a bit closer. I couldn't tell if he felt how ridged and stiff I was. My entire body was wound so tight, and I wasn't sure if it was from the feelings I was having or the fact that this was Nash . . . Morgan's brother. Maybe it was a little bit of both.

Yes, that's what it was.

Leaning down, he spoke into my ear, his hot breath fanning over my skin, causing me to gasp for a breath. "Tell me about yourself, Kaelynn."

My heart stopped, and I took a small step away from him. I needed the bit of distance between us to think straight. Regret instantly filled every inch of my body because I knew I was about to run. It would be easier to walk away than not tell him about me. Oh sure, I could sugarcoat it, but if I told him the truth, he would probably smile and give me some polite excuse as to why he had to leave. My mind and heart was in an instant tug of war. *Tell him about yourself and have him walk way from you, or don't tell him and savor the few moments you could have with him.*

He frowned. "Is everything okay?"

Great. Make yourself look like an idiot, Kaelynn.

"Um, yeah, sorry."

Nash tilted his head and asked, "Did you want to keep dancing or stop?"

Stop. Just stop this now, Kaelynn, and walk away from him. It's the easiest thing to do.

Unfortunately, my body refused to listen to my mind. I stepped back into his embrace.

"I take it you don't like to talk about yourself."

I let out a nervous laugh. "No, well, I mean, I don't mind. I'm from Utah. Born and raised there."

He nodded.

"Family still there?"

"Yep. All of them."

He smiled down at me, and I was pretty sure he felt my legs give out because he held me a bit tighter.

"I have an older brother and a younger sister who both live right outside of Salt Lake City."

"I've always wanted to go to Utah. I hear it's beautiful."

There was no way I could not return his smile. "It is. Very beautiful. I think my favorite time of year is when we get that first snowfall. Everything is so beautiful and untouched. White for as far as the eye can see."

"I've never seen real snow."

My brows lifted in wonderment. "Real snow? As opposed to?"

He laughed and I couldn't help but notice how my body reacted to that lovely sound.

What in the world is happening to me?

"Okay, I've never gone skiing or seen a major snowfall. It's snowed a few times here in Texas, but nothing like what I imagine y'all get."

Nash has the sexiest accent. It wasn't too southern, but the slight draw to it let you know he was from Texas. Visions of Nash whispering in my ear as he made love to me flooded my brain.

Stop this. Kaelynn, focus!

"Up in the mountains they really get a good amount of snow. You'll have to take a trip and see what real snow looks like."

"I'd like that."

There was something more to his reply than a simple, polite gesture. Something I wanted so desperately to read into, but then I remembered Morgan stating her brother had sworn off women . . . forever. He was being polite. That was all. This was all for his sister. That thought was something that physically made my chest ache.

"Morgan said you moved here recently? Is it a permanent move?"

"Yes, I think to both. I can actually work from anywhere since I own the company. I do have office space in Lehi, Utah, but I don't work out of it. Well, I do when I need to, which isn't often. At all. Really ever."

He nodded and had good enough manners not to laugh or roll his eyes. "Where are you living?"

Crapola.

"Right now I'm in a hotel until I can find a place to rent. Morgan said she would help me with finding the right area in town."

"The east side is booming right now. We're actually bidding on a pretty big job over there. Would bring in a lot of money for my father's construction company if we get it."

"He must do well with how things are growing here."

Nash shrugged. "It's okay. My father tends to take on smaller jobs, whereas I'm the one who has to push him to take on bigger projects. I built my best friend's house a few months back. Biggest house Barrett Construction has ever built. I'm pretty proud of it and am hoping it will open up the door for future projects outside of commercial. That's where my dad has always concentrated his business ventures. We just needed to get our name in the hat and it sort of stuck."

Smiling, I stared up at him. I hadn't even noticed the song had changed. We were both still dancing slow even though the song had sped up.

"I guess the song changed!" I said with a giggle.

"Can I buy you a drink? Oh, wait . . . I need to do this right. Cheesy pick-up line, at your service. Ready?"

I couldn't help but smile at his goofiness.

"Wanna know what my shirt is made of? Boyfriend material." We burst out laughing, and I found myself wanting to reply to his offer to have a drink.

Pressing my lips together, I fought to find the right answer. My mind said to say no while my heart screamed yes. *Yes! Yes! Hell yes!*

The moment this man found out my family background, he would walk away. I couldn't shake all those conversations with Morgan where she told me what had happened or what was going on with her brother and his ex-girlfriend. She cheated on Nash with a guy who worked for her father's company. A man with a financial portfolio that matched hers, or was very close to it. Morgan told me how she had hid their relationship, not wanting anyone to know she was dating Nash, someone not up to the same social standards as she was. It was hard to believe he was best friends with her brother. Or at least that was what Morgan had told me.

It was just a drink. What harm would come from a drink? Would anything really happen between us? I doubted it. Still, I wasn't sure I wanted to start this friendship on half-truths. But then, did people really blurt out, *hey, I'm an heiress with a family loaded in money?* No! They didn't. I wasn't lying. I just wasn't telling him everything.

So what is the big deal here, Kaelynn? Stop overthinking it.

"Kaelynn?"

My eyes snapped back up, and I was lost in his gorgeous, honey-colored eyes. "I'd love that."

His dimples made an appearance again, and I knew I had made the right decision. After all, it was only a drink.

Three

NASH

KAELYNN AND I were lost in conversation as Morgan's birthday party went on without us. I'd walked her to the main bar, where we ordered our drinks and continued getting to know one another. There was something about her that pulled me in. She was beautiful, funny and smart, and her heart seemed as wholesome as Morgan's.

"Do you do a lot of mission trips?" I asked before pressing the beer bottle to my lips and taking a drink.

"I try to do at least one a year. It's something my parents taught my siblings and me early on. Always give back in some way. Big or small, it all means something. It also helps to ground me, make me realize that there are others in this world who are less fortunate than we are."

I nodded. "Morgan has done a number of them as well. She always comes back a changed woman . . . and I mean changed for the good."

She took a drink, then asked, "What about you?"

"I've done a few, yes. It feels good to give back. Our church works with a charity to bring fresh water to communities that don't have any. I've gone on two of those mission trips, and Morgan and I went on one down in Central America to help build a church, and we repaired a lot of the houses . . . if you can call them houses. We also made some wonderful friends while there."

Her eyes filled with sadness. For a few moments, she seemed to be lost in a memory.

Clearing my throat, I went on. "Our parents were pretty big on teaching us that even though we didn't live in the fancy, expensive houses like most of the other kids in our school did, we were still blessed beyond measure. And we were, no doubt about it. Money doesn't buy happiness."

She smiled, then looked down at her drink.

Christ, Nash. Could you have said that with any more bitterness in your voice?

I noticed Lily walking our way.

Shit. I shouldn't have suggested we come out to the main bar.

"Nash, who's your friend?"

Glancing over Lily's shoulder, I saw Mark talking to Tucker. When I didn't answer Lily, Kaelynn took it upon herself to make the introductions.

"Kaelynn Dotson. I'm a friend of Morgan's."

Lily looked Kaelynn over before giving her a fake smile. "I see. I'm Lily. Nash, may I speak with you, please? In private?"

I took another drink of beer and stood. Taking a step closer to Lily, I answered her in a voice that wasn't quiet. "Lily, we have nothing to talk about, like I told you not that long ago. Your husband is waiting for you."

Turning to see Mark standing there, Lily pulled in a deep breath before glancing back at me.

She lifted her chin, smiled, then said, "Enjoy your evening then."

When she walked away, I took my seat again. "I'm sorry about that."

"Old girlfriend, I assume?" Kaelynn asked.

"Yes."

She had the courtesy to not ask anything else. For all I knew, Morgan probably already told her the whole story.

We sat in silence for an awkward moment before I decided to come out with it.

"She cheated on me with a guy, actually. He was waiting for her just then. He was more up to her . . . standards."

Kaelynn lifted a brow. "What do you mean?"

Slicing my fingers through my hair, I let out a gruff laugh. "I have a group of friends from college I've remained good friends with. My best friend, Tucker, owns this bar."

"Really?" she said with a grin. "Morgan didn't tell me she knew the owner."

I shrugged. "Lily is his sister. She came into the group a bit later since she's younger. We started dating a few years back, and she wanted to keep me her little secret. She told me it was because of her brother, that she was worried he would be pissed we were dating. I had to admit, I was afraid of that as well, so I went along with it. But she kept insisting we couldn't tell anyone about our relationship. Looking back, I should have realized she was embarrassed by me."

Kaelynn gasped. "What? Why in the world would she be embarrassed?"

"I didn't—don't—have the kind of money she has. I'm the only person in our little group of friends who is considered middle class, working my ass off every day to earn the good ol' dollar. Not that my friends don't work their asses off, because they do. Tucker especially does and has never really taken much from his folks. His father was a wealthy businessman here in Austin, but he passed away last year. Lily was being groomed to take over the business and was forced to find a husband suitable to her dad's liking. Mark was the guy her father picked out for her."

"I'm so sorry to hear that they lost their father."

Nodding, I replied, "Yeah. It was hard on Tucker."

"I can't imagine," was all Kaelynn said. I wasn't sure if she was saying she couldn't imagine losing a parent or couldn't imagine the bullshit Lily pulled.

"All of them are good people, down to earth, and have great hearts. Charlie and Tucker, especially. They are considered to be the power couple simply because Charlie is CEO of a large and profitable consulting firm. Y'all would probably hit it off."

She grinned and replied, "Probably."

"Anyway, when Charlie and Tucker got married, the press naturally wanted to put his rich surname and Charlie's name together and make it a big issue. Call more attention to it than either of them wanted or cared to. Charlie is still CEO of her company, but after the baby is born, she's most likely going to be stepping down, or at least sharing the role to free herself up to enjoy being a mom."

With a small gasp, Kaelynn leaned forward. "Charleston Middleton, formerly Charleston Monroe, of CMI Consulting?"

I nodded. "Yeah, how do you know Charlie?"

She laughed. "Oh, I don't. I've heard of her."

"That's cool."

"Yeah, I'd love to meet her."

Standing, I took her hand and said, "Then come on. I'll introduce you now."

"Really? She's here? That would be awesome."

Placing my hand on her lower back, I tried to ignore the way it made my fingers itch to explore more of her body.

I guided her over to the table where Charlie sat with Terri.

We stopped and they looked up at us. Both of them smiled.

"Terri, Charlie, this is Kaelynn Dotson. She's a friend of Morgan's and is helping her get everything set up for her new business."

Charlie smiled. "You're the business start-up consultant?"

Kaelynn returned the smile. "Among other things. My company helps individuals and companies with start-up projects like nonprofits, charities, charity functions—things that deal mostly with helping our veterans. I'm really just helping Morgan with getting connections to be able to reach out to veterans as well as giving her some advice on getting her business set up and going. Location, marketing, all that fun stuff."

"That's amazing," Charlie said, motioning for us to sit down. "How did you get into that?"

Drawing in a deep breath, Kaelynn answered. "My brother was in the Marines and something happened when he was overseas. He's never talked about it, but he lost a few friends because of it. He was never really the same after. He reached out for help a few times while still in the military, yet was turned away. Then he attempted suicide. I was in my freshman year of college at the time. I knew from that moment on I needed to do something more for these people who had served and are still serving our country and don't have the support they needed. I needed to do more for my brother and for every other member of the military.

So I started small within our community while still in college. I focused on coordinating groups of volunteers who would counsel vets and help them when they didn't feel like they could turn anywhere else. Then I started having small companies reach out to me to start programs for their employees who were vets or to help recruit them for jobs. I planned a few benefits and worked for a nonprofit for a bit. It sort of went gangbuster, all starting from that."

"That's amazing, Kaelynn. Your parents must be so proud of you," I said.

Her smile faded before she gave a small shrug with her shoulder. "They're supportive, to a point. My father wanted me to go into the family business, but that wasn't something I ever saw myself doing."

"Been there, done that," Charlie mumbled.

"Charlie, I admire . . . well . . . you! What you've done for CMI in the short amount of time you took control is amazing. I love to see a woman in the lead make something that was successful even more so."

Charlie looked from Kaelynn to me, then back to Kaelynn. "Okay, I like you a lot. I think I want to keep you."

We all laughed.

"So, Kaelynn, how did you and Morgan meet?" Terri asked.

"Mission trip last year. We sort of bonded while building a small school in Africa and really hit it off. We have a lot in common."

My mind drifted to Mike, and I was positive Terri's and Charlie's had as well.

"I admire that you give your time like that. I work for a nonprofit here in Austin," Terri stated.

"Really? What do you do?" Kaelynn asked.

Terri smiled. "I work for a company that partners with primary care physicians and other physicians. We help with providing care management through all stages of life and illness. Support tools, guidance with decision-making, as well as making sure patients and families are educated and have the support that they will need. I went to school for nursing and loved it, but when I found this job, it felt like where I needed to be."

Kaelynn smiled warmly and said, "That's amazing, Terri."

Then Charlie jumped and gasped. When she held onto her stomach,

I panicked.

"You okay?" I asked, standing. "It's not time. Not yet!"

Charlie rolled her eyes. "Sit down, Nash. I swear, you're worse than Tucker. The baby kicked me, hard."

"When are you due?" Kaelynn asked, looking as though she was attempting to hold back the giggle she wanted to let out.

"Three weeks. Three very long weeks."

Terri laughed. "She's been a pain in our asses the last month. I think we're more ready for her to pop that baby out than she is."

"I seriously doubt that," Charlie said with a sigh. "I love being pregnant, but man, these last few weeks have been tough. I feel like the little monster inside of me is fighting with all my organs."

"I bet. My cousin had a baby recently, and she was two weeks overdue."

Terri and Charlie both let their mouths fall open. "Two weeks?" They said.

Kaelynn nodded.

"I didn't think they would let you go that long anymore!" Charlie said, a level of fear in her voice.

Kaelynn shrugged. "I don't know; all I know is she was a royal bitch those last few days. Everyone pretty much steered clear of her."

"I bet. God help us all if Charlie goes over." Terri chuckled.

"Goes over what?" Tucker asked as he glanced around the table and landed his gaze on Kaelynn, then back over to me. He had a knowing look in his eyes. When he lifted his brows, I shook my head. I knew Tucker would read into this. All I was doing was entertaining my sister's friend. That was it. Never mind the way she made my body feel. My reaction to this woman baffled me and honestly scared me a bit.

My eyes drifted over to Kaelynn, her face wearing a wide smile as she waited for Terri to answer Tucker.

"Her due date," Terri answered.

Tucker visibly shuddered. "Shit, don't say such things, Terri."

Everyone laughed, even Charlie.

I looked at Tucker and began the introductions. "Tucker, this is Kaelynn, a friend of Morgan's."

Reaching his hand to her, Kaelynn shook it and said, "Kaelynn Dotson. It's a pleasure meeting you."

"The pleasure is all ours. Mine. Well, probably all of ours. It's been so long since I think any of us has seen Nash actually talking to a woman, so him inviting you over to meet the best friends . . . seems serious." Tucker waggled his eyes, causing me to groan internally. Jerk.

Kaelynn didn't miss a beat, though. "Well, we were going to just bust out of here, head to his car, and get it on there before heading back to his place, but he insisted I had to meet the friends first. Old-fashioned, I guess."

She rolled her eyes and shrugged. Then glanced at me and sighed dramatically. "He better be worth it; that's all I can say."

Charlie pointed to Kaelynn. "You have just moved into my best friend role. How would you like to be the godmother of my child?"

"Hey!" Terri cried out with a laugh.

Tucker slid in next to Charlie and kissed her on the mouth before giving me a quick look. Then he asked, "Where is Jim?"

"Jim?" Kaelynn asked.

"Jim is my fiancé. He had to step outside to take a call from his mother. Something about his father's foot being stuck between the steps. Lord only knows with those two."

Kaelynn turned her attention on me and raised her brows.

"Don't ask," I whispered, causing her to chuckle.

"So Nash said you own the bar. How do you like running a bar?"

Tucker grinned from ear to ear and faced Kaelynn. "I love it. It's been a great experience, and it's doing a lot better than I ever thought it would."

"That's a good thing, though," Kaelynn added.

"A very good thing. Charlie and I moved out to the country a few months back, so I've learned to not be here every single night. It's been a hard adjustment, but one I'm glad I've done. Especially with the baby coming."

"Have you ever done a military night or anything, geared strictly toward those who have served and are currently serving? I've seen other bars do it and it's a big hit. Some even do monthly game nights, and they play all of these board games. It's kind of hilarious to watch. Especially when you see big bulky guys sit down and play Chutes and Ladders."

Tucker looked at Kaelynn for a long minute. She cleared her throat. "I'm sorry; it was just a suggestion. I should probably get back to Morgan's party."

She started to slide out of the booth when Tucker reached over and placed his hand on her arm.

"No, no, wait. I was letting your words float around in my head and trying to think of all the reasons why I haven't come up with that idea before."

He turned to me. "Maybe even once Morgan gets going full time, she could come by, introduce herself. There might be someone who would benefit from talking to her."

Kaelynn smiled as she looked between Tucker and me.

"I think that's a great idea," Charlie added. "A really great idea. We can have CMI sponsor it, buy all the games and donate them."

Tucker gave Charlie a look that screamed how much he loved her. "That would be amazing, babe. I'll have Maddie, my marketing manager, look into ways to making this work."

"I'll do the same with my team over at the office. This is such a great idea, Kaelynn."

Kaelynn slipped out of the booth and reached into her purse. With a wide grin, she glanced between Charlie and Tucker, then handed Tucker a business card. "Great, I'm glad you like the idea. I'm more than happy to help. No charge, of course. Charlie, good luck with everything. It was great meeting all of you. Sorry I missed Jim."

Charlie smiled. "It was our pleasure. I hope we'll be seeing you around."

Taking in a slight breath, she politely smiled then faced me. "Thank you so much for the lovely evening, Nash. I had fun."

"Same goes for me."

Before I even had a chance to slip out of the booth, she turned and walked away.

"What did you do to her to blow that?" Charlie asked.

I watched Kaelynn until she blended into the crowd before I turned back to the table. "What do you mean? I didn't blow anything."

They all huffed in their own ways. Tucker rolled his eyes. "Dude, you didn't see the way the girl looked at you? I mean, you brought her over here to meet your friends, then let her walk off by herself back to the party."

"She wanted to meet Charlie."

"Me? Why me?"

"She'd heard of you and said it would be really great to be able to meet you, so that's what I did."

Terri folded her arms and glared at me. "Nash Barrett, when did you lose your manners? I mean, you didn't even walk her back to the party."

I looked around the table at the three of them before landing my confused gaze on Tucker and silently urging him to help a fellow out.

"Sorry, bro, I'm with the girls on this one. You kind of were a dick at the end there."

"Oh, for fuck's sake," I mumbled as I slid out of the booth and made my way through the crowd. I knew Kaelynn would already be back in the private room and most likely talking to Morgan.

When I spotted her, though, she wasn't back at the party. She was talking to some guy. And smiling at him. Then laughing at something the dirtbag was saying. I wasn't sure if I should walk up to her or walk by her. I opted for the first option.

"Hey, you took off so fast you didn't give me a chance to walk you back to the party, but I see you're okay."

The guy gave me a once-over. "Yeah, dude, she's fine. You can move along."

I laughed as I looked at him. He couldn't have been more than twenty-two, maybe twenty-three, if I was being generous.

"Move along?" I asked, glancing between Kaelynn and the guy.

"You okay here?" I asked, then took a step back.

"Actually, I'm feeling a headache coming on and was going to see about an Uber."

"I'll take you home, babe," the younger guy said.

Kaelynn gave him a soft smile and said, "Thank you, but I've got some friends here who will most likely be heading out with me. Enjoy your evening."

When she reached for my hand and tugged me along after her, I wasn't sure if I should ignore the way her touch made my entire body shudder or ignore the urge to stick my tongue out at the bastard like I was eight years old.

In the end, I went for ignoring both.

The moment we got into the private room, Kaelynn dropped my hand and raised up on her tippy-toes as she looked for what I could only assume was Morgan.

"Are you really ready to leave?" I asked, leaning in from behind her and talking directly into her ear. She froze and slowly turned to face me. I took a step back when I saw the confusion in her eyes. "I didn't mean to interrupt anything with that guy back there."

Her eyes danced around on my face before she closed them, took in a deep breath, then snapped them back open. Something had changed in those pretty eyes of hers. She stood up a bit taller and let loose. "Listen, Nash, your sister already told me you've sworn off women. It's pretty clear you and I had an attraction to one another, but this won't work."

"Had?" I asked, a smirk lifting at the corner of my mouth.

With a roll of her eyes, she sighed but couldn't help the small smile that played over her face. "Fine. It's pretty clear you and I are attracted to one another. I'm not looking for a casual one-night stand."

My eyes widened in shock and she seemed to realize her statement might have been way off base, which it was.

"Oh God. You're not attracted to me and not the least bit interested in . . ."

Her hands slapped over her mouth and she groaned. The sound made the lower half of my body come to full fucking attention.

"I'm so stupid," she mumbled. At least that was what it sounded like she said. The music was now playing again, and it was beginning to get harder to hear.

"I'm sorry!" she shouted. "Let's just forget any of this conversation took place."

I could have just let her go. Let her think that I wasn't interested in her. But I didn't. Stupidly, I reached for her hand and gently tugged her closer to me.

"Kaelynn, I'm not interested in a one-night stand."

Her cheeks heated and her eyes grew wet. Damn it.

"What I mean is, I like you. I enjoy talking to you and I would love to be . . ."

Everything inside of me screamed to tell her the truth. But something held me back at the last minute. That wall I had built around my heart was refusing to give way, no matter how much I wanted it to for this woman.

"I'd love to be friends."

"Friends?"

It was hard to miss the disappointment in her voice. Hell, the moment the word came out of my mouth, I wished I could take it back.

Before I could respond, she nodded, stepped away from me, and repeated the word again, as if trying to remind herself that that was all we should be . . . that it was ultimately the best thing.

"Friends." Then she forced herself to smile. "Sounds like a plan."

Four

KAELYNN

WITH A LONG sigh, I dropped the folder onto the desk. I couldn't seem to focus at all this morning. A week had passed since Morgan's birthday party at Sedotto and I had thought I would be able to forget about Nash. I was so wrong. So very wrong.

I stood up and walked out onto the private balcony I had at the Hotel Saint Celilla. I had been staying in one of their studio rooms for the last month or so. I really needed to find a more permanent place; hopefully today would be the day.

As if on cue, my phone rang with my mother's ringtone.

Quickly walking back in, I swiped to answer the call.

"Hey, Momma."

"Hello, darling. How are things down in the vast open spaces of Texas?"

I chuckled. "It's Austin; nothing vast and open about it. It's like any other big city."

"Well, it's still Texas. Not Utah."

Rolling my eyes, I dropped on the small sofa and pulled my knees up to my chin.

"Later today I'm going to look at a few condos."

"Oh, Kaelynn, darling why do you insist on staying there?"

"I like it here, Momma. I'm my own person here. It's hard to explain."

She sighed. "I honestly do understand, sweetheart. There was a time in my life I needed to be away and figure out who I was as well."

"I know who I am and I know what I want. Right now, Austin is what I want. I love being here and helping Morgan get her business going. I'm going to be driving to Houston tomorrow to meet with a company who is wanting to set up a scholarship in one of their employee's son's name. He was killed in a helicopter accident during a military exercise a few months back."

"How nice of them to do that. Poor woman, give her our blessings."

I nodded, even though she couldn't see me.

"You want to tell me what's on your mind?" she asked in a hushed voice. I could hear a door click behind her.

"What do you mean?" I replied with a light chuckle.

"Kaelynn Shae Whitaker, I know when something is wrong. I hear it in your voice."

My eyes widened in shock. It was sort of scary my mother knew me so well. It was also weird hearing her use my full name. It caused a pang of guilt to rip through my body. I introduced myself to everyone as Kaelynn Dotson. My mother's maiden name. It wasn't my legal name, but it had been useful when I was back in Utah, where our family name was known by most. The moment you mentioned Whitaker, people started plotting ways to use you. At the time I had met Morgan, I had already been using Dotson as my last name. I had meant to tell her the truth; it just never came up or seemed necessary. Now it felt too late to say anything, and honestly, what did it matter? My fear was Morgan would think I was doing this to help her because money wasn't an issue, not because I truly believed in the work she was setting out to do. Or course, deep in my heart, I knew that was not true.

You've dug your hole, Kaelynn. Figure out how to climb out of it.

"Nothing is wrong. I'm simply ready to get out of this hotel. Well, this studio in the hotel. It was cute and charming at first, but that wore off quick. I need my own space."

"Your sister said you were keeping your place here. I was glad to hear that."

"Of course I am. It's home. I may still move back if things don't . . ." I let my voice trail off.

I could hear my mother's head spinning with that little bit. "Please tell me you haven't fallen for a boy."

Laughing, I replied, "A boy? Mom, you do know I'm twenty-six. I've long since moved on from *boys*."

"Ha ha. You know what I mean. I hope this melancholy I hear in your voice is not caused from a boy. I mean, a *man*."

"It's not. Like I said, I just need to get out of this hotel and into my own space. I've asked Jack to send me a few things once I get settled."

"You mean you won't be coming back home to get your things? Oh, Kaelynn, this is going to break your father's heart."

Needless to say, my parents were not thrilled when I told them I was moving to Austin, Texas. My brother and sister, on the other hand, thought it was a great move. Me being the middle child and all, not much attention was drawn on me. With this move to Texas, though, it threw all of my parent's attention on me. Freeing my brother and sister for a bit from the watchful eyes of our parents.

"I promise I'll be up to visit. With Morgan getting started, I really want to be here for her. Besides, I need to go dress shopping with Millie. Is she getting more excited?"

"That was a clever change of subject. Yes, she is getting excited; we all are. Now, are you coming home for both holidays?" my mother asked in a hopeful voice.

"Christmas, for sure."

"Kaelynn, I know it's hard, but you don't have to run from who you are."

My chin wobbled. "Mom, I'm not running from who I am. It's just, it's nice that no one knows who I am here. For once in my life I'm meeting people who like me for me. Not for my bank account."

"Not all of your friends were that way."

"No, that's because they had big banks account too. The whole thing with Jason threw me."

"Does Morgan know though? You two have seemed to become really close friends."

I chewed on my thumbnail.

"Kaelynn, darling, you haven't told her?"

"Would it make a difference, Mom?"

"Not to her, and that is what you need to realize. You're holding back a part of who you are, and it's going to come out, and not in a pleasant way. It's always best to be truthful."

"I'm not lying."

She tittered. "No, I guess not. But you are hiding something from someone you claim to be your best friend."

That familiar guilt started up again, making my head hurt slightly and my stomach ache.

My phone beeped with a text message. Pulling it back, I didn't recognize the number.

"Mom, I need to go. That might be the real-estate agent trying to get a hold of me. Tell Daddy, Jack, and Millie I love them. Talk soon."

"Be careful! Don't be wandering around at night, and make sure Morgan knows if you're going to look at houses with a boy . . . I mean, a man."

I rolled my eyes but smiled at the same time. "My agent is a female and I told her. I love you, Momma. Talk soon."

"Bye, darling. Think about what I said."

"I will," I whispered.

Once the call ended, I pulled up the text message and stared at it for the longest time. My stomach dropped.

> Unknown: Hey there! It's Charlie. I hope you don't mind I got your number from the business card you gave Tucker. We're all going out to a comedy club tonight and would love for you join us. I'm hoping to laugh this baby right out of the womb.

Charleston Monroe . . . or as she was now known, Charleston Middleton . . . was texting me. Inviting me out with her and her husband. My father would be so happy, and no doubt would be trying to get me to talk business. When I told him my plans for my career, I thought he was going to have a breakdown. Luckily though, Millie stepped in and decided she needed to be the next Whitaker to run the family business. My brother Jack and I were thrilled.

Staring at the text, I couldn't help but wonder if Nash would be there tonight. I wanted to ask but knew that wasn't the right thing to do. He made it clear last week . . . friends only. That was what I wanted as well. *Wasn't it?*

After storing her number into my phone and doing a little hop of glee, I replied.

> Me: Hi, Charleston. Wow . . . how sweet of you and Tucker to invite me. I'd love to come.

Chewing on my lower lip, I hovered my finger above the little blue arrow that would whisk my reply back to her. With a deep breath, I hit it.

Almost immediately I saw the little dots bouncing on my phone. I couldn't deny my excitement. I loved being friends with Morgan, but I had longed to make new friends and feel like I was settling in a bit more here in Austin.

Her reply popped up.

> Charleston: First, call me Charlie. Second, of course! We can pick you up or meet you at the comedy club. If you plan to meet us, I would suggest taking an Uber. Parking is sort of hard to come by.
> Me: I can meet you guys there.
> Charleston: Perfect! Meet us at the Austin Comedy Club at 8 tonight. See you then!

I changed Charlie's name in my phone and headed over to the closet to change. The Realtor would be here any minute. I paused and looked back down at my phone. I wonder if they had invited Morgan? Why had Morgan not been a part of their group? I couldn't help but wonder. I made a mental note to ask her about it.

Three hours later I stood in the lobby of the Austonian. My Realtor wore a huge smile.

"So? What did you think, Ms. Whitaker?"

I sighed. "Well, the ones we saw were all beautiful; pricey, though."

"You're not going to get a better view anywhere in the city."

"Is there something else that isn't so . . . showy?"

"Kaelynn?"

My body froze and I spun around to see Nash standing there.

"Nash?"

He smiled and my stomach dropped to the floor, at least, it felt like it had.

"What are you doing here?" I asked.

"I'm here to meet a client. What are you doing here?" His gaze moved from me to the Realtor.

"Looking at places, but I was just telling my agent here this was a bit . . . much."

I wasn't lying. I had told her that. To her credit, the Realtor nodded along with me.

Nash's smile turned into a full-blown grin. "Yeah, you won't find a bargain deal here, that's for sure."

"Nash, thanks so much for meeting me here."

Glancing over his shoulder, Nash turned and reached his hand out for the older gentleman's hand. "My pleasure. I'm excited to see the project."

"You're doing something here? In this building?" I asked.

With a smile still present on his face, Nash nodded. "Yes, Mr. Dillion was recently at Charlie and Tucker's home for a party and liked my work. Asked me to give him a bid on a buildout for his penthouse. Mr. Dillion, this is Kaelynn Dotson. Kaelynn, John Dillion."

The Realtor snapped her head to stare at me with a confused expression. I knew it was because Nash had used Dotson as my last name.

When I looked at Mr. Dillion, I gave him a polite smile. "It's a pleasure meeting you."

"You as well."

I let out an awkward laugh. This is where my small white lie was going to start blowing up in my face. I could tell myself I wasn't lying to anyone all I wanted, but it wasn't true. I was living a lie. The thought made me feel sick to my stomach.

The need to get out of there became overwhelming. "Well, I won't keep you from work. Great seeing you, Nash."

He nodded, then lifted his hand in an awkward wave. "Was great seeing you, Kaelynn."

Watching him walk away, I let out the breath I was holding in. My agent walked up next to me and softly said, "Ms. Dotson?"

"My mother's maiden name," I replied, pulling my gaze off the elevator and focusing back on her. "Okay, truth is, I need something that doesn't say I can afford a two-and-a-half-million-dollar condo in downtown Austin. I don't want to be the friend who has all the money. I want to blend in."

"No judgment from me. I think I have the perfect place for you. Let's go."

Fifteen minutes later, I was standing in a two-bedroom condo that overlooked Zilker Park. It still had a price tag, but it was far less than all the other condos we had looked at today. I stepped out onto the patio and grinned like a fool. The green park below led out to the Barton Springs Creek. It was a beautiful sight. I could see all the way over to the park itself. It was the top-floor penthouse condo, but it was a far cry from the penthouse I had looked at earlier at the Austonian. That was something my folks would like. I had a private little area up on the roof that would be perfect for snuggling up and reading a good book or maybe writing some. It wasn't over the top, even though they considered it the penthouse.

"It's two bedrooms, two baths. A little over a thousand-square feet and all with the price tag of five hundred thousand. It's been on the market for a number of months, so I'm sure we could get them to come down at little. There is an on-site club house, fitness room, spa, and office space that can be used for meetings and such."

I listened to the agent while I took in the view. "This is it. It's perfect! I'll take it!"

Now it was her turn to smile. "Awesome! Then let's head back down to the office. I'm so happy you found one you liked."

"So am I! So. Am. I."

I'd had just enough time to race back to my place, give my notice to the hotel of when I would be moving out, and get ready for tonight. After calling an Uber, I sent Charlie a text.

Me: I'll be there in about two minutes.

Charlie: Perfect! We're already here. Just come on in and we're sitting in the back corner to the right. See you soon.

"Okay, Austin Comedy Club," the Uber driver said above his loud music. I hadn't minded the music, though. It was nice to have my thoughts drowned out on the way over here. The conversation I had with my mother earlier kept replaying in my mind. I needed to tell Morgan the truth. I knew she would understand once I explained it. Morgan wasn't the type of person to judge me.

So why hadn't I told her the truth already?

I knew the answer. I loved having her as a friend, loved the raw genuineness of our relationship, and I didn't want that to change. Friends in the past always made snide remarks about how I could afford to go on a trip to France, or why did I drive this car when I could easily afford that car.

I sighed. "Poor little rich girl and her problems," I mumbled, hating myself for worrying about this when other people had real problems in this world.

"What was that?" the driver asked, pulling up to the club.

"Nothing. Thanks!" I said, slipping out of the car and making my way inside. Once in the building, I headed to where Charlie said she and Tucker were. I stopped when I saw them. It wasn't just Charlie and Tucker.

"Crap," I whispered as I saw Terri, and who I was guessing was her fiancé, Jim. Then next to Jim was another guy I didn't know. He was good lucking with dark hair and scruff on his face that made him look both relaxed and businesslike. He laughed at something Jim said. Then to the right of that guy was . . . Nash.

"Oh. No. Charlie, why?" I mumbled. I was about to turn around and leave when my eyes caught hers. She smiled big and used both hands to wave me over, making sure everyone at the table saw her in the process. When my gaze drifted back to Nash, he was looking down at his phone and hadn't seen me yet.

"Kaelynn! Come on!"

That made him jerk his head up and look around. My eyes popped over to Charlie, and I focused on her as I approached the table. I could feel his eyes on me, along with a bunch of other people. Charlie's nonstop flailing of her arms and calling my name caused a number of people to look up and watch me.

"Hey, um, hi, everyone. I didn't know, I mean, I thought . . . I guess I . . ."

I finally stopped talking as I let my gaze wander around the table.

The dark-haired guy sitting between Nash and I think Jim, gave me a once-over. Nothing but sinful thoughts swam in his eyes. I smiled politely, but I didn't feel anything toward him. No attraction at all.

"Kaelynn, I didn't know you were coming," Nash said, standing. Nash, on the other hand, was another story. I felt a very strong attraction toward him. Everything inside of me came to life the moment he said my name. I chewed on my lip and gave him a soft smile. My eyes darted to Charlie, who was wearing a shit-eating grin on her face. She clearly had seen the attraction between myself and Nash.

"Did I forget to mention it was the whole gang?"

Narrowing my eyes at her slightly, I replied, "Yes. I believe you did."

Five

NASH

TO SAY I was shocked to see Kaelynn was an understatement. I gazed over at Tucker, who simply raised his shoulders in a sad attempt to say he was clueless. Looking at Charlie, she winked at me before focusing back on Kaelynn. I was going to kill her.

"I invited Morgan, as well, but she stated she wasn't sure she would be able to make it."

"Morgan?" I asked, a bit shocked. We had never included my sister in anything we did as a group. Ever. Not that I didn't want to; it just never came up. Morgan had her friends; I had mine.

Charlie shrugged. "Yeah, I mean, I felt kind of bad we never invite her."

"Morgan? Your little sister? How's she doing these days? I haven't seen her in forever. Still smoking hot?" Blake asked as I turned and gave him a heated gaze. The asshole grinned and winked at me.

Bastard.

I went to pull out Kaelynn's chair when Blake jumped up. "Why don't you sit over here next to me, sweetheart."

The anger I felt was probably similar to what Tucker felt when Blake endlessly flirted with Charlie all those years. Even though Blake had moved to the Northeast after college graduation, he still made his way back to Austin to visit. And he still found a way to flirt with Charlie as much as he could before she and Tucker officially became a couple. Now that Charlie was off the market, it looked like he had set his sights on Kaelynn. There was no way I was going to let that happen.

Using my hand against her back, I guided Kaelynn into the chair I'd pulled out for her next to me.

Glancing back over to Blake, he rose a brow and smirked. When I sat down, he leaned in so only I could hear him.

"Was that your way of calling dibs, dude?"

I shot him a dirty look. "No."

He smiled and replied, "Good to know then."

When I reached for my beer, I shot a look over to Kaelynn. She smiled as Terri introduced her to Jim. I saw Jim extend his hand and they shook. Then Blake spoke.

"Blake Grant, how do you know Charlie?"

Kaelynn reached her hand in front of me to shake Blake's hand. "Oh, well, um, it was actually Nash who introduced me to Charlie."

Blake's brow rose again, and for some reason that really pissed me off.

"How do you know Nash?" Blake asked.

A slight blush hit Kaelynn's cheeks, causing a weird feeling in my chest. I could see the little matchmaker Charlie watching my every move.

"She's friends with Morgan, helping her with her new business," I answered for Kaelynn.

That caught Blake's attention. "Really? What do you do?"

The tap on the microphone brought the audience's attention to the stage, and everyone focused on the host. Everyone but Blake. He was still staring at Kaelynn. When he saw me watching him, he held up his hands.

"What?" he asked, then broke out into laughter before turning his sights forward. I was positive I shot him daggers, and I had no idea why.

That was a lie.

I knew exactly why. He was attracted to Kaelynn. And why wouldn't he be? She was attractive, friendly, had a heart of gold, and was not by any means Blake's type. He'd work at getting her into bed, then would walk away looking for the next one-night stand.

Sighing, I took another drink of my beer. When I felt Kaelynn's body against my arm, I froze. The heat it sent rushing through my body shocked me, yet at the same time, it made my dick make my pants feel tighter.

"If you'd rather I not be here, I can say I need to leave."

The warm feel of her breath against my neck as she leaned over to speak to me had me fighting to find my own air. I turned my head to look at her, causing her to pull back slightly. Our faces were so close together I could practically feel the pull of her mouth to mine.

"What?" I managed to get out.

"I can leave. You seem a bit agitated Charlie invited me. I totally get it, and it's okay."

Swallowing hard, I forced my mind to make my mouth move. "I don't want you to leave, Kaelynn. I'm glad you're here."

When she smiled, it wasn't just my chest feeling funny. It had moved to my stomach now. If I hadn't known any better, I would swear I was on some thriller ride that had been spinning me around and upside down.

I returned the smile and had to fight to divert my wayward thoughts, so I brought my attention back to the comedian the host had introduced.

The rest of the evening was spent pretty much laughing. We had dinner, laughed, talked a bit, and then laughed some more. When the night began to dwindle down, Kaelynn excused herself to use the restroom, and Blake excused himself as well. I watched him as he followed Kaelynn down the hall to the bathrooms.

"So, are you going to sit there and let Blake go flirt with Kaelynn? Or are you going to realize you need to go take a whiz too?"

It was Terri's voice that pulled my attention away from the retreating back of Blake.

"What?"

She rolled her eyes as Jim laughed. "Dude, you know Blake is going to hit on her. I wouldn't be surprised if he tries to talk her into a quickie in the bathroom.

Charlie huffed. "Kaelynn doesn't seem the type to be into a guy like Blake."

"Agreed, but if you're interested in her, letting Blake get the upper hand is not smart," Terri stated.

"I'm not interested in her that way. She's a friend of Morgan's, so she's a friend of mine. Morgan would probably kick my ass anyway . . . Well, I mean if I was interested in her in that way."

All four of my friends stared at me like they knew the words coming out of my mouth were bullshit.

Charlie reached across the table the best she could with her stomach preventing her from getting closer to me. "Nash, it's time to move on. Open yourself up to someone. Not all women are going to treat you like Lily did." Charlie looked at Tucker and said, "Sorry, babe."

He held up his hands and said, "You won't get an argument from me on the behavior of Lily. I'm still pissed at her."

I let out a breath and gave her hand a light squeeze. "I appreciate you being concerned, Charlie, but I'm fine. I'm not looking to get involved with anyone. Besides, she's Morgan's good friend, and who knows how long Kaelynn will even live here? Starting up something with her would be the wrong move."

Charlie looked disappointed in me as she let go of my hand and leaned back in the booth.

"That has got to be the worst excuse I've ever heard. Like seriously the worst."

"I agree," Terri said.

The waitress came and cleared our table, and I couldn't help myself. I glanced over toward the restrooms.

Where in the hell were they? Was Jim right? Had Blake put a move on Kaelynn and they were now steaming up the bathroom mirrors as we speak?

Finally, Kaelynn emerged with Blake next to her. She laughed at something he said. I couldn't help the frown that quickly appeared on my face.

"Don't worry, dude, Blake isn't that fast, and a smart woman would know how full of shit he is," Jim said with a chuckle. Terri hit him on the chest while I shot him a dirty look.

Stopping at the table, Kaelynn smiled as she looked at me and then Charlie.

"I better get going. I've got to drive to Houston tomorrow to meet with a client."

"What? We were going to go get coffee. Since my plan of laughing this baby out tonight didn't happen, I'm thinking coffee might do the trick," Charlie stated with perfect assurance.

Kaelynn laughed. "I wish I could, but I really need to be going."

"Do you need a ride home?" I asked.

"I already offered, dude," Blake stated, his hands in his pockets and a shit-eating grin on his face.

My eyes darted over to Kaelynn. Her cheeks turned slightly red. "Thank you for the offer, though."

Blake placed his hand on her lower back as he said, "Y'all behave tonight."

I stared at him, wishing I could jump up and punch him. I didn't care that in that moment he was one of my best friends.

"Well, looks like maybe Blake did have enough time after all," Terri said as I looked back at the table.

Forcing a smile, I shrugged. "If Blake is what does it for her, then I guess he's going to be getting lucky tonight."

Charlie huffed. "I haven't known Kaelynn long, but she doesn't seem like the type of woman to go off and have a one-night stand with Blake."

It took every ounce of power I had to keep the neutral expression on my face when I reached for my beer and finished it off. "I'm going to head out. Good luck on trying to get the little bugger out of there. Call me when that happens, okay?"

Charlie smiled but there was a bit of sadness in her eyes. "Thanks, will do."

When I stood and went to turn to leave, Charlie called out my name. "Nash?"

"Yeah?" I asked, glancing back at her.

"I'm sorry. I wouldn't have invited her if I had known Blake was going to . . . well . . . be Blake. I thought maybe you were attracted to her."

"I told her not to play matchmaker," Tucker said.

Charlie shot him a dirty look before meeting my gaze again. "I'm really sorry."

With a lighthearted laugh, I shrugged. "It's fine, Charlie. Honestly. Y'all have a good one."

By the time I reached the front of the club, Blake and Kaelynn were gone. The sick feeling I had in my stomach was only getting worse as I looked up the street one way, then the other. Blake had most likely driven and had valet parked his fancy-ass sports car, making for an easy getaway.

"Fuck," I mumbled, jerking my fingers through my dark hair. It was no one's fault but my own. I sat there and let Blake go after Kaelynn. No one to blame by myself for my own stupidity.

"Sir? Did you valet?"

"No, I need to order an Uber."

The young kid nodded. "Right."

As I stood there and waited for my ride to show up, I couldn't stop myself from thinking about Blake with Kaelynn. His hands on her. His mouth on hers. I swore for a moment in the club she seemed like she had wanted to kiss me. Maybe she remembered how I had said I only wanted to be friends.

Friends.

A horn honked, pulling me out of my thoughts. "Nash?" the caller called out.

"Yeah, that's me." Climbing into the car's backseat, I sat there and tried not to think about Blake and Kaelynn. This was probably for the best. Yeah, it was for the best. The way she made me feel couldn't have been a good thing anyway. I thought I was ready to move on, but it was clear I wasn't.

❧

MY PHONE RANG in my pocket for the fourth time in a row. Cursing under my breath, I stepped away and pulled it from my jeans.

Morgan.

My heart sped up a bit as I swiped over it and answered. "Morgan? Are you okay?"

"Yeah, sorry, Nash. Daddy said you were out on site at the Miller project. It's just, I need a huge favor. Like a really, really big favor. You're the only one I can count on for this."

I headed toward my truck and away from all the noise of the

construction site. It was only seven in the morning, but the earlier the crew got started, the better. Even in late November, the temperature in Texas could climb and we had less daylight to work with.

"What's up?"

"Well, Kaelynn was supposed to leave this morning for Houston. Her car will not start, even after being jumped. The tow truck just left with it. She asked me if I could give her a ride, but I have to meet with a client for Dad at eleven, and they aren't able to reschedule. Is there any way you can drive her to Houston?"

I laughed and then stopped when it was met with silence. "Wait, you're serious? You want me to drop everything to drive Kaelynn to Houston? Why can't she just rent a car, Morgan?"

"She left her purse somewhere last night."

With a scoff, I replied, "Just have her call Blake. Maybe it's in his BMW or at his house."

"What are you talking about?" Morgan asked. "She left it in the Uber she thinks."

Wait, what? Blake didn't even have the decency to drive her home? What a douche. Not surprising, though. "Blake couldn't even give her a ride home after they hooked up?"

"Hooked up? What in the hell are you talking about, Nash?"

"Morgan, she left with Blake last night. Why doesn't she ask him for a ride?"

"What is wrong with you? Why are you being such a dick? This isn't like you at all. Listen, I'll find someone else to take her."

Morgan hung up the phone and I pulled it back, staring at it in disbelief. "Holy shit. She hung up on me."

"Who hung up on you?"

My gaze lifted to see Blake standing there. "What are you doing here?"

"Your dad hired me to give him a second opinion on the architectural design of the building."

The feeling of being gut punched had me leaning over. I had already approved the design, and he knew that. "He did what?"

Blake went to take a drink of his coffee, then stopped. "Dude, he told me you knew. Said it was your suggestion."

I shook my head. "Son of a bitch. Why can't he trust me? For once, why the hell can't he trust me?"

This fucking day was getting worse by the minute and it was only 7 a.m.

"Listen, Nash, you know I would never do anything behind your back. I honestly thought you knew. I'll let you and your dad handle this."

Holding up my hand to stop him, I interjected, "No. No, you're here, so let's just have you take a look around. The plans are in the trailer on my desk."

He smiled, then nodded before he started toward the trailer.

"Blake, did Kaelynn leave her purse in your car last night? Morgan said she can't find it."

He spun around and walked backward. A huge smile covering his face. *Fucker.*

"Dude, she took an Uber home from the club last night. I struck out with her."

I stared at him as he turned back to his original path.

A surge of relief mixed with guilt consumed me as I remembered how I had acted on the phone with Morgan earlier. "Great. How am I going to explain this to Morgan?"

Six

KAELYNN

PACING OUTSIDE THE hotel, I glanced at my watch again. "Morgan, where are you?"

The sound of a vehicle coming down the road caused me to stop and look. I tried to shield the sun from my eyes but could hardly make out the vehicle. It appeared to be a truck.

Not Morgan.

I went back to pacing as I pulled out my cell phone to send a text to Morgan.

Me: Where are you?

My phone dinged.

Morgan: Nash should be there any moment.

Stopping in my tracks, I stared at her reply.

"Nash?" I said out loud.

"Hey! Sorry I'm late."

The sound of his voice sent shivers through my entire body. I slowly turned to see a black Ford truck with the passenger-side window down. He smiled, and it felt like the street might have jumped a little under my feet. For a moment I paused and wondered if earthquakes were native to Austin.

"What . . . why . . . I . . ."

Nice, Kaelynn. Really nice. Talk much?

"Come on, if we leave now you can still make it on time as long as we don't hit any bad traffic."

"Nash? What are you doing here?"

"Morgan called in a favor; hope you don't mind."

I stood there for a few moments, simply staring at him. Why did he have to be so good looking? How did he get that perfect, unshaven look on his face and why in the world was he wearing a baseball cap? A dirty one that read Barrett Construction on it. It was sexy as hell.

"Kaelynn?"

His voice pulled me from the dirty places my mind was getting ready to travel to. "Right. Sorry! Sorry! I guess I was just surprised to see you," I said, opening the truck door and climbing in.

A quick glance around showed it to be clean on the inside. My white linen pants were safe.

"It's so clean in here."

I regretted the words the moment they came out. *What in the world is wrong with you, Kaelynn Shae?*

"Um, thank you? Were you expecting it to be dirty?"

With a quick shrug of one shoulder, I dug myself in deeper. "I figured with your job and all, your truck would just be dirty."

The look he gave me made my stomach twist in disgust at myself.

"Right, because of my job."

"Wait, Nash, that's not what I meant. I just thought since it's construction and you're getting in and out and it's a truck. You know . . . all women think guys' trucks are dirty."

He nodded, then put his signal on and pulled out.

Crap. Crap. Crap. Way to sound like a snob, you idiot.

"I didn't mean for it to come out like that. I wasn't meaning it in a bad way."

"No worries, Kaelynn."

He kept his eyes on the road in front of him.

Terrific. He's probably comparing you to his snobby ex right this moment.

"My brother has a truck. I swear, I think mice live in it, and I'm pretty sure I found a pizza box in the front seat that had to be six months old."

Nash glanced at me, a smile on his face.

"I'm a bit of a neat freak, so no worries about a mouse climbing up your pant leg. I can't even stand to leave a cup of coffee in my truck."

"Good!" I replied with a chuckle. Then, chewing on my lip, I added, "I really didn't mean anything by that comment. I hope you know that."

He nodded. "I do. I'm sorry for my reaction. It's just . . . well . . . I'm sorry."

"So what did Morgan have to do to talk you into helping me?"

"Nothing. We had a bit of a misunderstanding at first, but once I got my head out of my ass, I told her I was more than happy to help out."

"Why did you have your head in your ass?" I asked, staring at him. Lord, this man was handsome. My fingers itched to reach over and run my fingers through his hair.

"Well, it's sort of embarrassing to admit, but I thought you went home with Blake last night."

My eyes widened in horror. "What? As in went home and hooked up with him?"

He sighed and his cheeks turned a hint of red. I looked straight out the window.

"I know we don't really know one another, Nash, but I'm not that type of person."

"That was what Morgan said after she bitched me out for even suggesting it. Truth be told, Kaelynn, I wasn't the only one who thought that. Y'all had disappeared in the club, then came back and both left at the same time. Blake also said he was giving you a ride, so everyone's mind went there, ya know."

Embarrassment raced through my veins. The rest of them thought that as well? I flipped back through the conversation and paused in horror. It would have seemed that way, especially with the way Blake had hinted at taking me home.

"I'm so embarrassed. I didn't . . . oh gosh. Your friends must think I'm a . . ." I let the words trail off.

Nash reached over and squeezed my hand. "It's okay; you're a grown woman and can go home with whomever you want, Kaelynn."

I turned my head and looked at him. "Wait. So you didn't want to drive me when you thought I had slept with Blake, but found out I hadn't and you were okay with it?"

He paused for a moment. "Well, I mean, if you had spent the evening with him, I didn't want him to be pissed at me. Like I was moving in on . . . anything."

His reason made sense. For the briefest moment I had wanted him to be jealous at the thought of me being with another man. Wishful thinking on my part.

Slowly pulling in a long breath, I stared out the window and let it come out equally as slow.

"You okay?" Nash asked, concern laced in his voice.

"Yeah. Sorry, it's just that I'm a little worried about my purse. I can't believe I left it in the Uber."

"Did you call the driver?"

"Yeah, he hasn't returned my call yet."

As if on cue, my phone rang.

"Hello? Yes, this is Kaelynn. You did? You do? Oh, that is amazing! If you could drop it off at the front desk of the hotel you dropped me off at, I would appreciate it. I'm headed to Houston right now. There's an envelope there for you as well; be sure to get it. No, *thank you* so much!"

I hit *end* and fist-pumped. Nash laughed and looked at me. His eyes seemed to sparkle when he was happy.

"I take it that was the Uber driver?"

"Yes! He worked a late shift and the passenger who got in last found my purse on the floorboard and handed it to the driver. He had just woken up and gotten my message."

"I'm so glad he found it. Hopefully everything is in there."

"Yeah, I already put a hold on my credit cards that were in there, so fingers crossed they're okay."

"You might want to get new cards anyway. Nothing says someone didn't write down your information to use later on."

My thumb came up to my mouth, and I started to chew on my nail. "Oh, I didn't even think of that."

An instant wave of heat hit me when I felt him touch me. Pulling my thumb from my mouth, Nash squeezed my hand before releasing it.

"That's a terrible habit."

I giggled as I turned to look at him. "Yes, *Dad*, it is."

Nash grinned and even from his side profile the man was insanely good looking. Then he gave me a glance and winked, which sent my libido into overdrive before he dutifully focused on the road ahead of him again.

I couldn't help but wonder what in the hell was wrong with Lily, his ex-girlfriend. From what I'd seen so far and heard from Morgan, Nash was a stand-up guy. He was sweet, kind, cared about his sister and his friends. Morgan had told me last night how he helped plan the last-minute wedding between Charlie and Tucker. Plus, there was a fierceness in his eyes, one that I couldn't really explain, but I got the clear impression that if this man was a friend of yours, there wouldn't be anything he wouldn't do for you.

His cell rang and he hit the button on the steering wheel. "Nash Barrett."

"Nash, it's Terri."

"Hey, you're on speakerphone. What's up?"

"Who's with you?"

Nash peeked over to me and replied, "Kaelynn, I'm driving her to Houston; her car broke down . . . it's a long story."

"Oh! Hey, Kaelynn!"

Smiling, I replied, "Hi, Terri."

"Listen, Nash, I have a huge favor to ask of you."

"What's up?"

"I want to surprise Jim with something during the wedding."

"Okay, what do you need from me?"

"Do you think you or Tucker can help me get Jim's passport information? He thinks he can't get off at work, but I've already arranged it with his boss for Jim to take two weeks off. I want to go to Ireland."

Nash's face exploded in a full-on grin. "Terri, he's been wanting to go to Ireland for as long as I can remember."

"I know! Charlie said she has a friend who has a lovely little cottage that sits on this bluff that overlooks the ocean. I really think Jim is going to be over the moon. I don't know how to keep it a secret, though, if I have to ask him for his passport information to buy the plane tickets. The airline needs it ahead of time."

Nash's face went serious as he thought about it. "I think I know how to get it."

"Oh my gosh, really, Nash? I will owe you so big if you can get that information to me as soon as possible. I think I can buy the tickets now; I just need to get the information put in before the trip. With the wedding not that far way, I don't want to risk anything."

"It's no problem at all, Terri. When do you need it by?"

"As soon as you can?"

"I'll take care of it."

You could hear little yelps of joy coming from through the phone. It was clear Terri had tried to cover the phone as she cried out in joy. "Nash, you are the best. Thank you! I'll call later to find out the plan. I have to run. Love you! Bye, Kaelynn."

"Bye, Terri!" The line went dead and I let out a chuckle. "She was excited."

He nodded and smiled. "Yeah, those two have been dating forever. I'm glad to see them finally making it official."

"What does Jim do for a living?"

"He's a veterinarian. Works mostly with horses. Especially racehorses. He's been known to fly to Kentucky, Europe, all those fun places where people with more money than sense seek his or his dad's advice or help."

"Wow . . . your friends are all pretty successful in their careers."

Nash nodded and replied, "Yeah. They're a great group."

"It's great to see Charlie finally getting to pursue her dreams," he continued. "She gave up a lot, including Tucker, just to make her father happy."

"What do you mean she gave up Tucker?"

"Back in college they had the hots for each other. We all saw it except for the two of them. One weekend, they finally gave in to their attraction. Charlie ended up walking away, though, leaving Tucker pretty heartbroken. Her father put a lot of pressure on her to take over CMI someday, and Charlie put the company before everything else in her life for the longest time."

I stared out the window. "Wow. But they made their way back to each other?" I asked, glancing back over to Nash.

Nash laughed. "Yeah, they did. In a crazy way, like only the two of them would. It's a crazy story. They're happy though, and that makes all of us happy. It was pretty tough the first few years with them hating on each other. Made the rest of the group feel weird, but we adapted. I think deep down we all knew the two of them would end up together. They were meant to be."

Tilting my head, I regarded him for a few moments. He must have felt my stare because he gave me a quick look and asked, "What?"

"Are you a romantic, Mr. Barrett?"

Nash grinned. "I like to think so. I believe we each have someone out there our heart is meant to merge with. Someone our soul is waiting on to make it feel whole."

This didn't sound like the man who had been burned and vowed never to let another woman in.

Turning my head, I stared out the passenger window as the scenery turned from hills to flat, expansive farm land.

"You don't agree with me?" he finally asked, breaking the silence.

"I totally agree with you. I guess I haven't been lucky enough yet to find that person. I asked my mother once how I would know when I found him."

"What did she say?" Nash asked.

Smiling at the memory, I stared down at my hands twisting on my lap. "She told me everything would simply make sense when I found him. Like the entire world around you would suddenly seem clearer." A slight chuckle slipped from my lips as her words came back to me. "Like when you're sitting under a tin roof and the rain is hitting it. After you fall in love that sound is the most beautiful thing you'll ever hear. Even though I think it's beautiful now, according to her, it will be even more. Or how during a storm you will swear you can hear his whispered words among the thunder. That even the leaves in the fall will hold a more brilliant color when you're in love. She said love changes everything."

My teeth dug into my lip, and I wished I could take back the last few moments of this conversation. I had opened up and poured out all that nonsense. Even though I didn't think any of it was nonsense.

"Stupid, I know," I whispered.

"I don't think it's stupid."

Lifting my gaze, our eyes met for a brief moment before Nash focused back on the road.

"Have you ever been in that kind of love?"

Oh. My. Gosh. Why did I ask him that? I already knew the answer. Kaelynn, you are so stupid and a sucker for punishment.

Nash didn't say a word for a good minute. It was long enough to make me look back out the passenger window and curse myself for being so stupid.

"I thought I was in love with Lily. Thought I wanted to spend the rest of my life with her. It took me a long time to figure out that maybe it wasn't just my heart I thought was broke, but more my pride. She left me because I didn't make the type of money she made, and that really was a gut punch. I wanted to believe I couldn't have loved someone so shallow, but deep in my heart I knew all along."

"Oh, Nash, are you sure it had to do with money?"

He laughed, but it sounded empty and cold. "Trust me, it was. She kept our relationship a secret, and I thought it was because she didn't want Tucker to find out. She was embarrassed, plain and simple. The first guy to come along with a bigger wallet turned her head, and she ended up sleeping with him and getting pregnant."

I felt guilty making Nash think I didn't already know the story.

"I could see why that would hurt you, her cheating on you, and then getting pregnant."

He shrugged. "Yeah, at the time I felt pretty bitter and pissed off."

"Time has healed that?"

When he turned and our eyes met, he smiled. "Yes, and other things made me realize it was time to move on."

Lifting a brow, I asked with a smile, "Oh . . . do tell of these other things."

His eyes turned dark and I felt a bit of excitement, or maybe it was anticipation, race through my veins.

We both jumped when Nash's phone rang through the truck.

He hit the button and said, "Hello, yeah, Nash here."

"Nash, it's Rip, we have a problem at the Jefferson site. City inspector is here and he is saying we didn't get the final permit on the plumbing, and we're set to pour the foundation tomorrow."

"We have the permit, it's in my office in the project folder. Just have Morgan go in and get it, scan it over to you, and you can show him. That should be good enough for him to sign off. Tell Morgan to send it to his email."

"Her. Email."

Nash groaned. "Shit. Is it Jessica?"

"Yep. Nothing like an old lover scorned."

My head jerked over to Nash. His cheeks filled with red as he shook his head and cursed.

"I'll take care of it."

Pulling over to the side of the road, Nash grabbed his phone. "Sorry, I need to make a quick pit stop. I know we're on a tight schedule."

Motioning with my hands, I replied, "No. Take care of it."

I watched as Nash got out of the truck and paced in front of his hood. His hand sliced through his hair I swore every few minutes. The frustration on his face was evident. What had the guy meant when he said an old lover scorned? It was wrong of me to do it, but I lowered the visor, then I rolled my window down some. Leaning forward like I was looking at myself, I adjusted myself to try and hear him.

If your mother could see you now, Kaelynn Shae. Listening in on a conversation clearly meant to be kept private.

He stopped at the corner of the passenger side as he looked out over the field. I strained to hear him.

"Jessica, you know all I have to do is send the permit over to your boss, and he's going to see you're dicking us around. It was a one-night stand months ago; we both knew that going in. Why are you so fucking bitter about it?"

I leaned back in my seat and sighed. The thought of Nash and this woman together made my stomach ache, and that bothered me. I wasn't with Nash. I laid no claim to him. Yet . . . . something deep inside of me wanted more with him, and I couldn't deny it.

Flipping the visor up, my gaze caught his.

He was staring at me.

Busted eavesdropping. You've hit a new low, Kaelynn.

He raised a brow, and I gave him a shy smile and stupidly lifted my hand in a wave.

When he smiled at me, I knew he wasn't hearing a word Jessica was saying to him. He was too focused on me, and that made my heartbeat instantly speed up. Butterflies replaced the ache that had previously sat in my lower stomach like a rock. I swallowed hard as the pulse between my legs grew stronger.

Oh no. I want Nash Barrett.

"Kaelynn, what are you doing?" I mumbled.

My tongue ran over my parched lips, and I saw the corner of Nash's mouth twitch up, as if he wanted to smile but stopped himself. Then he narrowed his gaze. I swore the sound of my pounding heart filled the truck. I somehow managed to pull my eyes away from him in an attempt to regain what little bit of self-control I had left.

Taking in a deep breath, I steadied my breathing and caught a glimpse of Nash making his way back into the truck. I raised the window and blew out a steady breath.

The urge to jump across the seat and push myself against him was something new. Where was this side of me coming from? My libido was in control here.

"What is happening to me?" I whispered as I forced myself to breathe normally as Nash opened the door, climbed into his seat, and flashed me those dimples.

"Sorry about that. Ready?"

The only thing I could manage to do was nod. I was ready for something all right. Just what that something was, I hadn't quite figured out yet.

Seven

NASH

STANDING OUTSIDE THE tall building in downtown Houston, I waited for Morgan to answer.

"Barrett Construction, Morgan speaking."

"Did that contract come through on the Miller project?"

"Hello to you too, Nash. My gosh, can't you take a day off?"

"Thanks to you, I'm going to be behind with work."

"I'm sure it is killing you to be stuck in your truck with a beautiful woman for the day."

I sighed. "Did the contract come through?"

"Linda said it did."

"Linda?" I asked, frowning. "Who is Linda?"

"The new office manager Dad hired. I thought you interviewed her."

The anger that rose up in my body made me pull the phone away and let out a few curse words. I closed my eyes and brought the phone back up to my ear. "No, I didn't interview her. I thought we had agreed on hiring Karen."

Morgan chuckled. "Dad said she wasn't what the company needed."

"What in the fuck does that even mean?" I bit back.

"Hey, don't get pissed at me, Nash. You need to have that sit-down with Dad sooner rather than later. Things aren't getting any better, and I hate to say this, but even Mom is starting to ask me if you're feeling a bit bitter."

"Bitter? About what?"

The silence on the other end told me Morgan was no longer alone.

"Just have the conversation. I need to run; everything here is fine. Please just take the rest of the afternoon off. Enjoy the road trip and get to know Kaelynn. She really is such a sweetheart."

Another sigh slipped from between my lips. "Let me know if you need anything."

"Yes, boss."

Boss. That was a joke. My father was clearly making a statement he was still very much in control of Barrett Construction. Never mind the fact I had landed us two huge projects that would put Barrett Construction on the map in Austin. We would make a great profit when it was all said and done. My father didn't care though.

"Fuck it," I said as I scrubbed my hands down my face.

"That doesn't sound good."

I spun around to see Kaelynn standing there. The corner of her mouth lifted in a smile.

"Sorry about that. How did it go?"

"Amazing. You haven't been waiting long, have you?" she asked as she walked closer to me. Just her being near me today was making my mind wander off in directions I knew it shouldn't be going. When I had caught her eavesdropping on my call to Jessica, I had to fight the urge to question her on it. She looked so damn cute with that blush on her cheeks. I also had to fight the urge to get back in my truck and pull her into my lap, Jessica be damned.

"Nah, I went over to the Starbucks and worked on some paperwork for a bit."

"Good. I already feel so bad about you driving me all the way here and wasting a day."

"Kaelynn, it's not a big deal. Especially with you helping Morgan out like you are."

She shrugged. "It's my job, and I love doing it."

"Speaking of," I stated, pointing to the giant building behind her. "How did it go?"

"Great. The company hired a lawyer, and the board of directors was also on hand, so it was pretty simple to explain the process of setting up the scholarship. I think it is amazing that such a large corporation is willing to do something like this for one of their employees. It makes your heart feel good."

"How's the mom doing?"

Her smile faded. "She's doing as well as can be expected. Her son gave the ultimate sacrifice for our country. I think with her employer doing this for her, it is helping with the healing. She pulled me to the side and asked me if I could send her a list of reputable charities for her to support."

We started walking down the street to the public garage I had parked my truck in.

"Do you have a favorite?" I asked.

"There are some amazing ones out there, but my personal favorite is the Gary Sinise Foundation. I interned there for a bit. I've helped a few corporations set up support missions with the foundation. I even met a woman who didn't have millions to leave but wanted to leave it to someone who would help our military. Gary's foundation was my first thought. They help more than just our veterans and military; they also support first responders."

"I've heard of it. He has his own band, right?"

She grinned. "Yeah. He does. The Lieutenant Dan Band."

I let out a soft laugh. "That's right."

The rest of the walk to the truck was in silence. Not an uncomfortable silence, by any means. Kaelynn seemed lost in thought, and I wanted to let her deal with whatever memory she was focused on.

A few hours later, I pulled into the town of Elgin and parked in front of my favorite barbeque place.

"In the mood for some barbeque?" I asked.

"Sure. I'm sorry I've been on my laptop this whole time. I feel terrible; I know you have your own work to do."

Slipping out of the truck, I looked back at her and said, "No worries. Work will always be there."

Her head tilted as she regarded me for a moment. Then she turned and opened her door as I shut mine.

As we stood in line waiting to order, she bumped my arm. "How are you going to get Jim's information?"

"I know the combo to his safe. I'll just sneak a peek."

She laughed. "Okay, what is your reason for sneaking a peek?"

We were next in line, so I leaned down and put my mouth to her ear and whispered, "I have my ways of getting what I want."

Her entire body trembled, and her breath hitched. When the cashier called out next, I stepped up and rattled off my order. I needed to ignore the way my cock ached for Kaelynn. The longer I was around her, the more I found myself wanting her.

"Brisket, side of beans, potato salad, and a drink." Glancing down to Kaelynn, I asked, "You know what you want?"

Her eyes jerked up to meet my gaze. When her mouth opened a bit, I had to hold back the moan threatening to slip out. Then she smiled, and I swore the whole damn building shook.

"I do know what I want, and I also have my ways of getting exactly what I want."

My brow lifted as she kept staring at me. With a smirk, I asked, "Are we talking about food or something else?"

She shrugged, winked, then turned to the very confused girl waiting to take her order.

"I'll have the same thing he is having."

With a nod, the cashier read back our order, handed us two cups for the drinks, and told us to have a great day.

Once I slipped into the booth, Kaelynn only seconds behind me, I took a quick glance around. The restaurant wasn't very crowded. Probably because it was between the lunch and the dinner rush. Regardless, I appreciated the quietness of the restaurant so we could talk freely without having to raise our voices.

"So, tell me about your family," I said, deciding not to address the attraction I was pretty positive we both felt toward one another.

"My family?" she asked, a nervous edge to her voice

I laughed. "Yeah. You know . . . Mom, Dad, siblings. Are y'all close? What do they do back up there in Utah?"

Her eyes looked down at her drink and away from me. She shook her head and drew in a slow, deep breath while trying to act like this wasn't a subject she wanted to discuss.

I couldn't shake the feeling she was hiding something about her family. Maybe she wasn't very close to them or had some sort of falling out. I hadn't gotten that impression when we met. It was clear from her reaction she did *not* want to talk about them.

"Not much to tell. My dad works a lot, my brother is doing really good settling in with life after the military, and my sister is a pain in my ass who thrives on making my father happy."

The nervous chuckle she let out made me draw my brows in some. "Do you not get along with your family?"

"What?" she asked as a shocked expression covered her face. "Yes, um, yes, we all get along great."

"Okay," I said with a chuckle. "That was just the vaguest answer I've ever heard someone give me when I asked about their family. You said they support your career?"

She nodded. "Did your mom and dad not want you to go into the family business?"

I let out a roar of laughter. "Oh yeah. My dad pretty much told me I would be disowned if I didn't follow in his footsteps. When I first mentioned wanting to go into the Marine Corps, I thought he was going to have a heart attack. I wanted to be a pilot. Even took some lessons in high school when I saved up the money to pay for them."

Her eyes lit up. "Wow! The Marines? Your dad didn't want you to join?"

"Nah. He was in and loved serving his country, but he came home and took over the construction business his father had started. It had been struggling and there were times we hardly had food on the table. But my father got it going, made enough money that we lived good, not great, but we had food and money to have decent holidays and family vacations. He put us through college, and in some way, I think he feels like I owe him for that. When I told him what I wanted to do, he told me it would break my mother's heart and she'd do nothing but worry like she had when he was in—and he would never speak to me again."

"Nash, that's terrible."

"It is what it is. I did what he wanted me to do, went to college, got a business degree, and went to work for Barrett Construction. It's not the life I thought I would have, but I met Tucker and Blake my freshman year, then Jim, Terri, and Charlie. We've been best friends ever since. I can't imagine my life without the five of them in it."

Our food was brought out and Kaelynn started firing off question after question. I knew it was her way of keeping me from asking about her family.

"How did Morgan manage to get away from the family business?"

"She's a girl. Dad knows she wouldn't make any kind of a living being the office manager. She's always had a passion for art and helping people since the girl could hold a paintbrush. I guess he figured that was a better way of life than being a Marine."

"Are you happy though? Working for your dad?"

"I am, I guess, for now. I live a simple life and don't really want for much. Some day I'd like to buy some land . . . a few hundred acres in the hill country. The price is going up, though, so I'll probably have to be pretty damn far out. Doesn't make sense to buy and try and build. Not when most of my work is in and around Austin."

"Where do you live now?"

"In a house in south Austin. The lady was desperate to get out and was selling low. I purchased it, and within three years it's pretty much doubled in value. It's in a nice neighborhood. Nothing fancy, houses are a bit older, but everyone takes care of their places. I'll make a nice profit when I sell it."

She smiled. "You're lucky."

"How so?" I asked, taking a bite of food.

"I don't know. You're just so down to earth and so nice. I've never met a guy like you before."

"What are the guys like in Utah?" I asked with a chuckle.

"Not like you. It's about the people you surround yourself with, what's in your heart that makes for true happiness, and it seems like you have that. I can see how much you and your friends care about each other. I've never really had friends like that. Not until Morgan anyway."

Staring at her, I finally let a small smile play on my lips. "I guess I am lucky in that sense then."

Kaelynn chewed on her lip. "Morgan told me you swore off women after what happened with Lily."

That statement had caught me off guard. "Yeah, I suppose I did."

"Why?"

"Why?" I asked.

"Well, I mean, just because one woman does something bad doesn't mean all women will be the same."

"I know that."

"Okay, so why swear off *all* women?"

"Maybe it's just the multimillion-dollar trust-fund type of women I am swearing off."

Kaelynn stared at me. She opened her mouth to say something, then snapped it shut. Something I had said seemed to bother her.

"I'm kidding, Kaelynn. I mean, I'm not really looking at getting into another relationship with someone who is in Lily's financial situation. Not when I can't compete with it."

"Why do you feel like you have to compete with it? Do you not think a woman should be able to make more than you?"

I stared at her, shocked that her tone had turned a bit angry.

"No, I don't think that at all. I guess I used the wrong wording. It was clear to me that Lily left because I would never be able to provide for her the things that she was used to, regardless if she could provide them herself. I tried that path and it burned me. I'm not looking to repeat history."

"Nash. I'm sorry she did what she did to you, but to insinuate or think all women are like Lily . . ."

"No, they're not."

The rest of the meal was small talk. Forced small talk. Once Kaelynn got back into the truck, she got on her computer and worked the rest of the way back to Austin. It was clear whatever I had said earlier didn't sit well with her.

When I pulled up to her hotel, I reached for her arm before she slipped out.

"Kaelynn, I think I came across as a dick earlier. I'm not against women being independent and wealthy. Hell, one of my best friends is one of the wealthiest women in Texas."

"Charlie . . ." she said matter-of-factly.

"Yes, Charlie. It's just, the whole situation with Lily threw me and it's taken me a bit to get myself back to the point where I want to start thinking about a relationship. Opening myself up like that again has been an obstacle I haven't been able to overcome just yet . . . but I know I'll get there."

"I understand."

"No, I don't think you do, because you clearly got pissed off. I get it, you're a successful woman, and judging from the hotel you're staying at, you manage your money well. I think that's great. I want to see my own sister succeed at her career, and I hope she's financially independent. I shouldn't have said what I said, especially to you. I'm trying to let the past go because I really want to move on. I want to let that guard down and trust again."

Her shoulders relaxed and she smiled. "I'm sorry if I was judging you earlier. I think we both misunderstood each other."

I returned her smile. "Are you free tomorrow? Maybe we can grab some dinner?"

Kaelynn's eyes filled with something that looked like panic. "I can't, I'm sorry. Thank you again, Nash. I really appreciate you taking your whole day and driving me to Houston. Thank you for dinner as well. Have a good evening."

My eyes widened in shock as she got out of my truck and headed to the entrance of the hotel. That was it? She was just going to walk away? Had I been reading this all wrong? Maybe Kaelynn didn't feel an attraction toward me. I did tell her I was only interested in friendship, but I had sworn that I felt a few times throughout the day that we had connected. The way she was looking at me, the flirting that we exchanged. What in the fuck happened the past hour?

I watched her walk into the hotel and disappear. She hadn't even glanced back over her shoulder once.

With a deep sigh, I shook my head and pulled out of the parking lot. I was done trying to figure out women. It was time to move on, and it was clear I wouldn't be doing that with Kaelynn Dotson.

Eight

MORGAN SET A box down in the middle of the room and spun around. "I can't believe this is my office. My office."

She smiled at me, and it was infectious.

"Yep, and if we don't get things unpacked, you're going to be seeing your first patient in an office that is filled with boxes."

"Right. Thank you to so much, Kaelynn, for the suggestion of going to the VA hospital up in Killeen."

"That's what I'm here for. It was your idea to reach out to the support groups around town. That was a smart call. I'm happy you have four people booked to see you."

"I know. The first thing I want to do is set up the art room. My office can wait until last since we have the therapy room to get settled."

I motioned for her to lead the way. "You're the boss."

By the time we had everything unpacked and set up how Morgan wanted it, I was starving. My stomach growled and Morgan and I let out a laugh at how loud it was.

"We should probably take a break and get something to eat," Morgan said, wrapping an arm around mine.

"I will agree with you on that. I'm so hungry."

Pulling her phone out of her pocket, Morgan glanced at the screen and frowned.

"What's wrong?"

"Nothing. It's from Karen, the new office manager at Barrett Construction. I texted her earlier to ask if she had any questions or concerns and she said no. Just getting this poor girl hired was a task. My father wanted one person; Nash wanted Karen. It was a fight for Nash."

With a chuckle, I replied, "That's a good thing . . . right? Getting someone hired?"

She shrugged. "I guess. I mean, I knew by looking at her resume she was the perfect fit, and Nash had to fight tooth and nail with my father to hire her. I've spent the last two weeks training her, so I know she can do the job. Of course, all the guys voted for her."

"Why?"

Morgan rolled her eyes and replied, "She's adorable with a body to die for."

I smiled. "Well, I guess as long as she gets the job done, that's all that matters."

Wiping her brow, Morgan nodded. "Yeah. She said she was going to dinner with Nash. That's strange. He never mixes business and pleasure. I need to give him a call really quick."

With a forced smile, I started for the door that led outside. Morgan trailed me. Pulling up my own phone, I read the text messages I had gotten from Nash a week and a half ago where he has asked me out again.

Nash: Hey, Kaelynn, are you free to grab coffee or maybe dinner?

I closed my eyes and tried to ignore the ache in my chest before I looked at my reply.

Me: I'm sorry, I'm super busy with work.

After Nash's comments in his truck about Lily and not wanting to go down that road again, I knew I had to distance myself from him. I'd felt the heat between us that day, saw the look in his eyes that said he wanted me as much as I wanted him. I couldn't do it. For one, there was no way I could lie to Nash. I'd been withholding the truth, and that was bad enough. If he kept asking questions about my family, I was either going to tell him the truth, which would push him away, or lie. The second was not an option. Ever.

Nash had neither replied to my text, nor had he texted me again.

"Oh my gawd! What? Now! How exciting!"

Turning, I saw Morgan smiling as she did a little jump. Then she said, "Charlie is in labor. Everyone is at the hospital now."

"Finally!" I said with a chuckle.

"It's Kaelynn. She's been helping me move the last of my stuff in and get things in order. No, it's okay, Nash. I know how busy things have been, so please don't stress about it. You and Tucker helped me move in all the big stuff the other day; all the little stuff I've got with Kaelynn's help."

I couldn't help but wonder if my name did anything to Nash. Did he care I was with Morgan? Had he thought about me at all since his last text? I wouldn't blame him if he hadn't. The way I had just blown him off, leaving no room for discussion about dinner or coffee. Still, I longed to see him, hear his voice, and know if he was thinking about me as much as I had been thinking about him.

Turning away from Morgan, I silently scolded myself. *For crying out loud, Kaelynn. You're not a love-struck teenager. You're a grown woman who made a decision . . . now stick to it.*

"Let me know when she has the baby. Oh, I'm sure Kaelynn would love to. She has a bit of a girl crush on Charlie."

My mouth fell open, and I glared at Morgan, who laughed.

"Hey, Nash, why were you going out to dinner with Karen?"

I'd have given anything to hear his answer.

"Okay, well, you're keeping it business, right? Oh . . . you do, do you?"

Peeking over to Morgan, I watched her face grow into a full-on grin. "A serious date? With who? Nice. Are you finally moving on?"

I swallowed hard and waited by the passenger-side door of Morgan's car for her to unlock it. She was so caught up in whatever it was Nash was saying to her, she stood there, her keys in her hand.

"Morgan?"

Her eyes jerked up to look at me, and she mouthed she was sorry. Unlocking the doors, we both got in.

"Well, I'm glad you're moving on, Nash. I love you, and tell Charlie I can't wait to see the baby!"

Morgan hit *end* on her phone, set it down, then started her car. We drove for a few moments in silence before I couldn't take it another second.

"Nash is going on a date? With Karen?"

She laughed. "No, not Karen. He said he and my father were both meeting Karen to go over her first two weeks on the job and the expectations from here on out, but then Charlie went into labor, so it would just be my dad meeting Karen. My father can handle it all."

"I bet Charlie and Tucker are excited to find out if the baby is a boy or girl," I stated.

"There is no way I could do it! I'd have to find out the moment I knew I could. I'm hoping it's a girl. Sorry about the girl crush comment. I know how much you look up to Charlie."

With a small shrug, I replied, "It's okay. So, who is Nash going on a date with and when?"

Morgan turned and gave me an incredulous look. "It's someone he met on the coed softball team he plays on. He said she's been flirting for a while and he wasn't feeling it, but he thinks he'll give it a try. Kaelynn, do you like my brother?"

I nearly choked on my own spit as I started coughing. "What? Why? I mean, what makes you ask that?"

"I'm not stupid, and I saw the way the two of you looked at each other at my birthday party. I'm pretty sure you were the first woman he had shown any interest in since Lily."

"He told me he was only interested in being friends."

Morgan laughed. "Okay, and you believed that? I honestly thought the two of you would go out after spending a whole day in a car together. I was surprised that nothing came from that. Nash said he invited you to dinner, but you blew him off."

I twisted my hands together and stared out the window. "I didn't blow him off, I couldn't make it that night. It's probably for the best, anyway."

"Why do you say that?"

How did I tell Morgan the real reason I needed to stay away from Nash? The problem was, I didn't want to stay away from him. I wanted to get to know him better. Spend more days together like we had two weeks ago. It was so easy talking to him.

Ugh. Why is this happening?

"It's hard to explain, Morgan."

She let out a breath and said, "Okay."

"That's it? Just okay? You're not going to push me on this? Ask a million questions?"

Shaking her head and laughing, she answered, "No. I mean, if you've changed your mind about Nash, I get it. I thought the two of you would make a cute couple, and I have to admit, when you said how hot he was at my birthday party, I got a little excited y'all might start dating. But if things didn't work out, then they didn't work out."

We sat in silence for a few moments before I broke it. "When is he going out on his date?"

Morgan smirked at me before she answered. "Tomorrow night."

With a gigantic sigh, I looked out the window and said, "Oh, that's nice."

This time she laughed, but being the good friend she was, she didn't say anything. I knew she could see right through me. She knew I liked Nash, but she would never know why I couldn't pursue things with him. In my heart, I just knew that they would both hate me if they ever found out the truth about me.

Nine

NASH

I STARED OUT the window as we all waited in the waiting room of the hospital for Tucker to come out.

"Penny for your thoughts," Terri whispered as she bumped my arm and stood next to me.

"I hope you have a lot of pennies."

She chuckled. "Jim said you're going out on a date tomorrow night. A girl on your softball team."

I nodded. "Yeah, figured it was time to move on."

The heat of her stare made me glance her way. She had indeed been staring at me. "What? Just come out and say it, Terri. You never were good at holding things back."

With a small shrug, she replied, "I don't know. I kind of thought you might have gone out with Kaelynn. You two seemed to have an attraction there."

"Yeah, I thought so too, but I guess not. I also told her I wasn't interested in anything but friendship, but then thought I had corrected that statement to let her know I was maybe interested in pursuing a relationship, but somehow pissed her off."

"Ugh. Men. Why do y'all do that shit?"

I chuckled. "It comes natural? Hell, I don't know. I did ask her out to dinner, though, but she turned me down. I think she doesn't have the highest opinion of me after a few comments I made about Lily."

Terri rolled her eyes. "Well, if she knew anything about Lily, she would understand."

"It was more of a comment about her money. She took it as me saying women shouldn't make more money than men. Or some shit like that."

"Did you explain yourself to her? Because if she knew you, she'd know that was not how you think."

"I tried, but she was pissed off and pretty much just walked away. It is what it is. There's something about Kaelynn, though. She's hiding something from me, and honestly, I can't deal with that right now. So it's probably for the best she blew me off."

Terri nodded. "I get that."

"Guys?"

Tucker's voice had us spinning around, and Jim and Blake quickly stood. Tucker stood there with the happiest grin I'd ever seen on my best friend's face.

"Well?" Terri cried out. "Tell us, Tucker!"

"It's a girl. Hannah Faith."

Terri rushed to Tucker and hugged him. Before I had a chance to make my way over, I saw her out of the corner of my eye.

Lily.

"I'm sorry I'm late. I couldn't get away from work and then had to find a sitter! Oh my gosh! Tucker . . . did she have the baby yet?"

Terri took a step back and glared at Lily. "You *would* put work before your own niece."

Lily didn't even bother looking at Terri. "She had a girl?"

Tucker smiled and nodded. "Yeah, Hannah Faith."

Lily threw herself at her brother, who wrapped her in a hug.

"I'm so sorry I was late. Honestly, I tried to get away."

Tucker pulled back and smiled. "It's okay." Glancing around to each of us, Blake, Jim, and I all walked up and shook Tucker's hand, congratulating him and Charlie.

"When can we meet her?" Terri asked.

"Maybe give us a bit of time and then y'all can come meet her?"

"I'll have to come back later, if that's okay?" Blake said, shaking Tucker's hand once more.

"Of course it is, come back anytime. Charlie and Hannah will be here until probably tomorrow afternoon. If you want to wait till we're home, you can as well."

"Hell no. I want to meet the first little prodigy of our group before then."

Lily turned and looked at Blake, who acted like he didn't even notice the stare she gave him. I had to admit my chest ached seeing the pain in her eyes.

"Second, Pete is the first."

Lily turned to Terri, a shocked expression on her face at what she'd said. "Thank you, Terri."

Then she looked at me, and I focused back on Tucker. "I'm down for waiting."

"Same here!" Terri said as Jim wrapped his arms around her.

Tucker pointed to them. "Y'all are next."

Jim's face turned white as a ghost. "Dude, let me get through the wedding first."

∼≈∽

TERRI KNOCKED LIGHTLY on the door to Charlie's room before peeking inside.

"Y'all come on in. She's in her happy place now that she ate and has a dry diaper on," Tucker softly said.

As we walked in, I couldn't help but smile as I saw Charlie holding the most beautiful baby I'd ever seen. Hannah was wrapped up in a pink blanket with a pink hat on top of her head, sleeping peacefully.

"Oh. My. Gosh," Terri said, her voice cracking as she fought to hold back the tears.

"Want to hold her?" Charlie asked.

"Yes! Let me wash my hands," Terri said, rushing into the bathroom.

I walked up and stared down at her. "My God, she's perfect. Look at her."

Charlie softly laughed and agreed. "Thank you, Nash. I think she is as well."

Terri and Jim held Hannah first while I sat back and watched the entire scene play out. I couldn't help but notice how insanely happy Tucker was, and I was glad for him. For years he had been in love with Charlie, and Charlie had been in love with him. They were both just too damn stubborn to admit what was right in front of them was their future.

I caught Charlie's gaze and smiled.

"It's your turn, Uncle Nash."

Standing, I made my way over and held my breath as Tucker gently placed Hannah in my arms. She was so tiny and weighed next to nothing. She opened her eyes, and I swore it was like she looked into my soul.

"Hey there, precious girl."

Hannah continued to stare up at me.

"Lord, you better watch out. Tucker, the girl knows a handsome man when she sees one," Charlie jokingly said.

I peeked over at Charlie and winked before focusing back Hannah.

"Man, she's really taking you in, isn't she?" Tucker said, standing next to me. I lifted my finger and traced a light line down her tiny face.

"I've never seen anything so precious." My voice cracked, and that caused Tucker to clear his throat and wipe his eyes.

"I can't believe you made this . . . She has to be all Charlie, because you're too damn ugly to have any part in this," I added as the room erupted into laughter.

Tucker grinned and nodded. "Someday, man, someday."

The ache in chest grew a bit more as I forced myself to nod. My mind drifted to Kaelynn, but I pushed it away as fast as it came.

"We need to take off, but let us know if you need anything," Terri said, kissing Charlie, then hugging Tucker. "Don't forget the wedding shower is next week."

Terri said the reminder to everyone.

"I'm glad Hannah decided not to wait and give you a run for the attention," Charlie said.

Terri giggled. "Oh my gosh, right? Can you imagine if you had gone into labor during the wedding?"

"You have to admit, though, it would have made for a great story for our kids," Tucker added.

Once Jim and Terri left, I started to sway back and forth as I looked down at Hannah.

"Is she getting heavy?" Charlie asked.

Smiling, I shook my head. "Are you kidding? She's light as a feather. Aren't you, sweetheart? Your Uncle Nash is going to teach you so many things that your daddy isn't good at. Like fishing, hunting, shooting."

"Um, what?" Charlie asked, laughing.

"Okay, I'll teach you how to make the best fake tea for your tea parties. I had practice with my sister, Morgan."

"That's more like it, Uncle Nash," Charlie stated.

I wasn't sure how long I stood there holding Hannah. All I knew was I wanted this. A family. Someone to love and take care of. I wanted what Tucker had, and I fought to keep the jealousy at bay.

Feeling a squeeze on my shoulder, I looked up at him. "It will happen. It just wasn't meant to be with Lily."

"I know," I whispered.

"Nash, look at me," Charlie demanded. "One day you're going to meet the person who will make you believe in love again. You'll be the reason for her smile, her tears of happiness, and her comfort in the storm. You'll be the brightest star in her sky and her entire world. Because you deserve all of that and more. And then the two of you will create a family, a legacy, that you can shower your love on too."

Before I could say anything, there was a light knock at the door.

"Come in," Tucker called out.

Glancing back down at Hannah, I smiled. She was out cold, sleeping away safely in my arms.

"Kaelynn? What a pleasant surprise," Charlie said.

My head jerked up to see Kaelynn standing there, a vase of flowers in one hand, and a tutu-wearing moose in the other.

"Is this a bad time?"

Her eyes caught mine and she stopped talking. When they dropped down to Hannah, she pressed her mouth together. I could tell she forced the tears to stay at bay. Then she looked back up to me. Her brows lifted and her smile widened. I swore there was a bit of lust dancing in those hazel beauties.

Kaelynn chuckled as she said, "Wow . . . if the sight of you holding that baby doesn't make a girl's ovaries explode, I don't know what will."

Charlie laughed, and Tucker and I looked at each other, confused.

"She means you look hot standing there holding the baby," Charlie clarified.

Lifting a brow, I gave Kaelynn a smirk. She smiled back and looked at Charlie. "Is this a bad time? Morgan mentioned to me earlier today that you were in labor, and she told me you had Hannah a few hours ago."

"This is the perfect time. Come on in."

Kaelynn walked into the room and set the vase of flowers on the side table, then gave Charlie the stuffed moose.

"When I was little I loved all things moose. I still do. I thought maybe Hannah would like them as well."

Charlie gasped. "It's so soft!"

"I ordered it last week and it got here yesterday. Perfect timing."

"I'll say," Tucker said, walking over and taking Hannah from my arms. "Sorry, Nash, you have to share."

I pouted, which caused both women to laugh.

"Want to hold her?" Tucker asked.

"Goodness, yes! Where can I wash my hands?"

"Here," I said, pointing to the bathroom.

In no time at all, Kaelynn had washed her hands, taken Hannah from Tucker with expert ease, and settled herself into the rocking chair. Watching her with the baby did something weird to my body. I couldn't pull my eyes off her. When I finally snapped out of the daze I was in, I heard Charlie and Kaelynn giggling.

"What's so funny?" I asked.

"Did you hear this tiny little thing just fart?" Kaelynn asked, a beautiful smile over her face.

Tucker bumped me on the arm. "I'm afraid Nash was off in his own little world there for a few moments."

Charlie gave me a warm smile, then looked at Tucker. "I'm starving. Would you please go get me some real food? This hospital stuff isn't cutting it. A taco from Taco Cabana, maybe?"

Leaning down to kiss Charlie, Tucker whispered something against her ear that made her cheeks flush. I couldn't help but look away to give them a moment of privacy. I was positive Tucker was telling Charlie how beautiful she was, or how he couldn't wait to be alone with her. They had a love like that. A love that I wanted for myself one day. "Nash, cowboy up and ride with me, man."

"You got it, Tucker . . . Kaelynn, would you like something?" I asked as I walked up and leaned over some to look at the baby once more. The smell of the newborn and Kaelynn's light soap mixed together and made me dizzy for a moment.

Without looking up at me, Kaelynn smiled as she gazed down at the baby. "No, thank you. I'm perfectly fine."

We weren't even out of the hospital before Tucker dove in.

"So, Kaelynn, huh?"

"What do you mean?" I asked, trying to keep my voice steady. For all the years I had been able to keep the secret of me dating my best friend's sister, I couldn't pull off hiding a damn crush with one of my best friends.

"Don't play around with me, Nash. I see the way you look at Kaelynn. I saw how lost you were watching her with Hannah. And the way she looked at you when she first walked in. I almost needed a bath filled with that soft hospital ice to cool off from all the sexual heat that built up in that room."

I scoffed. "You are way off, dude."

He grabbed me by the arm, pulling me to a stop. "Am I? Nash, I've never seen you look at anyone like that. I saw it at the bar, the comedy club, and just now. You like her. Why don't you just admit it to yourself? More importantly, why don't you just do something about it?"

Signing, I rubbed the back of my neck. "I don't think she feels the same. Plus, I think she's hiding something from me. I can't fall for someone who has secrets . . . not again, Tucker."

With a nod, he turned and headed to the parking garage. "Are you sure she doesn't feel the same way? Maybe she's not hiding a secret, but more like hiding the way she feels about you."

I shrugged off his comment. "Doesn't matter. She sort of made it clear she isn't interested when she blew me off after I asked her out to dinner. Besides, I have a date tomorrow night."

Slipping into the truck, Tucker looked at me with a hard expression. "A date? You're finally going out on a date and wait . . . when did you ask Kaelynn out?"

"Right after our little impromptu road trip to Houston. She turned me down. Twice, actually. I'm not going to beg her. If she's not interested, then I'm moving on."

"Okay, well, who are you going out with then?"

"Lori, a girl on the coed softball team I play on. She's been flirting, and I've been blowing her off. I think it's time I stopped ignoring her. Maybe I do need to get out there and start dating."

"Wow. I mean, I guess I'm glad you're finally getting over Lily. I guess I read it wrong between you and Kaelynn. It's just, damn, the way you two look at each other."

"Yeah, well, I'm not saying she isn't beautiful. She is. And I'm attracted to her; there is no doubt about that. The problem isn't me; it's her. She made it clear to me, so I'm not going to pine over it."

Tucker nodded, then changed the subject and started talking about Hannah's nursery. Before I knew it, I had volunteered to help get the room set up and ready to go for the baby when Charlie and Tucker moved her into her own room. All the talk of fume-free paint and handmade cribs kept my mind off of the image of Kaelynn holding Hannah.

At least it did until we walked back into the hospital room, only to find Charlie passed out sleeping and Kaelynn rocking Hannah back and forth, softly humming to her.

My heart slammed against my chest, and I fought to take a breath for a few moments. Fuck me if that wasn't the sexiest thing I'd ever seen.

When our eyes met while she was still humming, I pulled out my phone and sent a text to cancel my date.

Ten

KAELYNN

NASH AND I stood at the elevator and waited in silence for the doors to open. The second we stepped inside, I broke the silence.

"Hannah is beautiful. Tucker and Charlie look so happy."

"They do. It's been a long time coming with those two."

"Charlie is so sweet to me. I truly appreciate her taking me in as a friend."

He let out a soft chuckle. "Yeah, Charlie is one of the very rare people I know who truly is genuine. She does everything with her heart wide open. She's good to people."

Chewing on my lip, I glanced forward and took a deep breath as the elevator door opened. We walked side by side toward the exit. For a brief moment, I wanted to confess the secret I'd been keeping. Tell Nash the truth about my wealthy family. And I almost did, until he spoke first, breaking the small shred of nerve I had worked up.

"What floor are you parked on? I'll walk you to your car."

"That's sweet of you. I'm on the third floor."

With his dimples on full display, he replied, "As am I."

We walked for a bit in silence before Nash talked. "Poor Charlie. I felt bad seeing her asleep sitting up in bed."

I chuckled. "Charlie was pretty tired after you guys left. She told me she was going to rest her eyes, and before I knew it, she was sound asleep. Hannah was an angel and let her mommy sleep. I was afraid if I put her down she would cry, so I did the right thing and held the angel while she slept."

Nash chuckled.

"She was probably just as happy to be lulled to sleep like that by you. Do you have any nieces or nephews?"

"No, not yet. My brother is dating a girl he's pretty serious about. She's been good for him and supports him so much. My parents love Jill also, so that's a plus. I think he's getting close to popping the big question."

"Wow, that's exciting."

"Yeah, it is." I stopped in front of my car. "Here I am. Got everything fixed on it, so hopefully no more issues with being stranded."

"Good."

Clearing his throat, Nash looked down the garage and then back at me, almost as if he was stalling for something. He let out a soft chuckle before speaking.

"Kaelynn, I know you were pretty upset with me the last time we were together."

I held up my hands to stop him. "No, I wasn't angry at you, Nash. It had more to do with me than it did you. I'm sorry about that. It was a pretty childish thing to do, and I'm embarrassed by the way I acted."

He smiled and my knees felt weak.

"Then, I was wondering if you might want to go—"

My cell phone rang in my hand, causing me to jump and Nash to stop talking. For some unknown reason, I answered it. Maybe because internally I was freaking out. Nash had been about to ask me out.

"Hello?"

Taking a step back, he raked his fingers through his dark hair, causing my insides to heat up. My fire was put out by the sound of another male's voice.

"Hey, Kaelynn."

"Mike, oh, hey. How are you?"

Much to Nash's credit, he tried not to react when I said another man's name, but I saw the way his mouth twitched.

"Just checking in with you to make sure we're still on for dinner tomorrow night. I can't wait."

I chewed nervously on my lip. "We are still on for dinner tomorrow, yes."

Nash's gaze jerked up to meet mine, and I wished I could hit a rewind button and go back in time two minutes. I wouldn't have answered the stupid phone.

Nash shook his head, then lifted his hand and mouthed *see ya around*.

I needed to stop him, and the only way I could that was to cut off Mike. "Listen, would I be able to call you back?"

"Um, yeah, sure? Everything okay?"

"Yes, no, yes! I'll call ya back."

Hitting *end*, I reached for Nash's arm. "Wait. Why are you leaving? We were talking."

His expression looked torn. He wore a smile, but it didn't reach his eyes.

"It doesn't matter now. Hope you have a great evening, Kaelynn."

I wasn't about to let him leave like that. Not when I knew he was about to ask me out again.

"Nash, please, wait. You were asking me to go somewhere. Where?"

His fingers laced though that hair again, and my fingers twitched to do the same.

"I was going to ask you out for dinner tomorrow night, but it's clear you already have a date, so no big deal. I've got to run, so I'll see you around sometime."

Standing there staring at him in disbelief, I watched as Nash shrugged when I didn't reply. He turned and started walking off. Before I could stop myself, the words were out of my mouth.

"I thought you had a date tomorrow."

He turned around, walking backward. A confused expression on his face. Then he called out, "I cancelled it earlier, but like I said, no worries. See ya around, Kaelynn."

There was no doubt in my mind my mouth had dropped to the

ground. What had happened? One minute he was going to ask me out, the next he turned ice cold and walked away.

"You stupid fool. You idiot!" I chastised myself. "Mike . . . dinner. Crap."

Slipping into my car, I hit the steering wheel. "Shit on a brick. Did Nash cancel his dinner date after seeing me today?"

I laughed, then shook my head. That was wishful thinking on my part. Why in the world would I think that just by seeing me it would cause Nash to cancel a date. "Think pretty highly of yourself there, Kaelynn, huh?"

Sitting in my car for another few minutes, I finally started it and headed to my new condo. I made a note to myself to call Mike back and cancel dinner.

⁓≥§≤⁓

"KAELYNN, SERIOUSLY, WHY not have a housewarming party?"

I smiled and stared out over Zilker Park. The weather in Texas in early December was much different than the weather in Utah.

"Morgan, I hardly know anyone here."

"You know me! I have friends. Besides, you're friends with Charlie and Tucker now. And Terri and Jim. And with Nash."

I closed my eyes and let the cool breeze hit me in the face. Looking back out over the landscape, I let out a soft sigh. "I think I'm going to go for a run."

"Party pooper."

"Don't you have work to do?"

"Yes, I've got a patient coming in and I need to give the art room another once around. Hey, I just wanted to thank you again for all your help. I can't believe I'm actually doing the job I always dreamed of."

"And you get to paint! I'm still waiting on that landscape painting."

This time it was Morgan who laughed. "I'll get right on that. I'm coming over for dinner tonight."

"Sounds like a plan. See you later."

Hitting *end*, I sat down and put on my running shoes. I wasn't out the door before my cell phone rang.

My father.

"Daddy? Is everything okay?" I asked, my heart beginning to beat a bit faster.

"Of course it is. Why wouldn't it be?"

I let out a sigh of relief. "For one, you never call me."

"Well, that's not a good thing on my part. I do have a surprise for you, sweet pea."

Smiling, I opened the door to the stairwell and got ready to head down the steps.

"I love surprises! What is it."

"Your mother and I are in town."

I froze.

"And we just bought a small place here, so we can come visit any time we want."

Closing my eyes, I said a silent prayer. Please tell me this is all a joke.

"You bought a place here? In Austin?"

"Yes! We can rent it out if we want while we're not there. I don't know why you didn't buy in this building. We got the penthouse for a steal. We're meeting the architect and the builder here in about an hour. Why don't you come on over and take a tour of the place?"

"Daddy, did you buy in the Austonian?"

"Yes. When your mother mentioned you had looked at it, I pulled it up. It's a good investment. Austin is booming right now. So even if we get it remodeled and fixed up to our liking, it won't be a big deal to sell it when you give up this silly dream of living here."

I balled my fists, took the phone away from my ear, and counted to five.

"Give me a few minutes and I'll leave. I need to change. I was about to go for a run."

"Sounds good, sweetheart. Just let the doorman know you're here for us. We closed this morning, so the place is officially ours."

"Right. Of course you did. I'll be there in a bit."

"Bye, sweet pea."

Two hours later, I was leaving my parents' new condo with them and heading out to grab dinner. I felt someone staring at me and glanced over my shoulder, only to find no one there. The weird feeling in my chest made me look twice.

"What's wrong, darling?" my mother asked.

"Nothing. I thought someone was here."

"Here? What do you mean?" she asked confused.

"It's nothing, Mom. Honestly, I just had a weird feeling someone was watching me. What are you in the mood for?"

My father cleared his throat. "I already made reservations for Perry's Steakhouse, we need to get a move on if we're going to make it."

If only I'd turned around once more, I would have seen Nash standing there.

Eleven

NASH

"DUDE, YOU ARE off in a faraway place. Want to talk about it?"

I hadn't noticed I was sitting on the floor of the nursery, staring at the crib. Blake plopped down next to me and bumped my arm.

"If you need help putting it together, I can probably help. I am an architect."

Laughing, I shook my head. "Yeah, I'm the builder who built the damn thing. I think I've got it figured out. I was just . . . lost in thought."

"About what?" Tucker asked.

Glancing between the two of them, I let out a breath and decided to just go for it. "More like who."

"Kaelynn?" Tucker asked.

"Your sister's hot friend? You do like her! I fucking knew it," Blake chided me, wiggling his brows.

"I'm attracted to her, yes. We've had a few misunderstandings, and I'm not sure if she likes me like I like her."

Tucker leaned against the changing table. "Have you asked her out?"

"Yes. Once in person, once via text, and both times she turned me down, the third time when I attempted to ask her out, she got a call from the guy who had beat me to it."

"Ouch," both Tucker and Blake said at once.

"Okay, so what has you so lost in thought?"

I shrugged. "I don't know, I can't put my finger on it. She's hiding something from me, something about her family. Yesterday I saw her walking out of the Austonian with her parents. She didn't see me, I was around a corner, but I overheard her call them both Mom and Dad."

"What were they doing there?"

"I don't know, but I sort of have a feeling they purchased a place there."

Blake looked to be thinking, then said, "You think she comes from money, obviously a lot of it if her parents are buying a place in the Austonian, and she's afraid to tell you? I mean, with her being Morgan's best friend, maybe she knows the history of you and Lily."

I stared at Blake as everything started to fall into place all at once. The way she avoided talking about her family. How angry she got at me that day we drove back from Houston when I made the comment about Lily and her money. It was all beginning to make sense.

Slowly, I shook my head. "I think that's it. You may be right. I told her all about what went down with Lily, and that's when her demeanor changed completely."

Tucker laughed when Blake's eyes widened in shock. "Holy shit, you mean I got that on my first try? I need to join Morgan and get into therapy and shit. I can really read people."

With a roll of my eyes, I gave him a push, causing him to lose his balance and topple over with a laugh. Standing, I faced Tucker.

"How do I run a background check on someone?"

His smile faded. "What? Are you serious right now, Nash? Why don't you just ask the girl?"

Shaking my head, I replied, "No. If she's lying to me now, what makes you think she wouldn't keep lying to hide the truth? I need to figure this out first, then go from there."

"Yeah, I don't like the sound of this," Tucker said, rubbing the back of his neck.

Blake laughed. "Says the guy who was trying to seduce Charlie first because you found out she was trying to seduce you even though the two of you were still in love with each other and both of you were playing games." Blake frowned. "Wait. Did that shit just make any sense?"

I nodded. "Strangely, yes."

He smiled again. "Damn, I'm on a roll today."

Pointing to Blake, I got an idea. "Your brother Dustin can run the background check."

"Yeah, I'm sure he wouldn't mind doing it. Just get as much information as you can on her and send it to me. I'll have him get on it. He's on vacation for a couple of weeks, though . . . Do you want his associate to handle it?"

"No," I said, shaking my head. "I'd rather Dustin handles it. I'm not in a rush."

Tucker sighed. "Nash, I don't like the look in your eyes. What are you planning on doing?"

I shrugged. "Nothing. I'm going to ask her out again and see what happens. I have at least two weeks to get her to tell me the truth. Maybe I won't even have to run the background check."

"Who are you running a background check on?" Charlie asked. Tucker and Blake both looked white as a ghost. Turning, I saw why.

Kaelynn stood next to Charlie, holding Hannah in her arms. She was dressed in sweats and a black T-shirt with a sweatshirt tied around her waist. Her long brown hair was pulled up into a ponytail, and she wore hardly any makeup at all.

She was breathtaking. I'd never in my life seen a woman so beautiful.

Blake ran his hand in front of my face.

"Someone sees a pretty girl. Is it the baby or the hot chick holding the baby?" Blake asked with a chuckle. Snapping me out of the fantasy I was quickly getting lost in, I slapped his hand away from me.

"Knock it the hell off," I spat.

Kaelynn smiled, and I swore it made my breath stall in my throat. "Hey, Nash. Hi, Tucker, Blake."

"How's it going, Kaelynn? You getting settled into your new condo?" Tucker asked.

With a nod, she replied, "I am. I love being so close to Zilker Park."

It didn't make any sense. If Kaelynn's parents were looking at places in the Austonian, why in the hell was Kaelynn living in a condo that I knew cost her less than three-hundred-and-fifty thousand?

To keep up the charade, maybe?

"Can you see the Zilker tree from your place?" I asked.

A huge smile spread over her face. "Yes! I'm dying to go down there, but Morgan has been so busy, and I don't want to go alone."

Blake bumped me on the arm. I looked his way, and he didn't even try to hide his bobbing head.

"What are you doing?" I asked.

In a hushed voice he replied, "Dude, that is your cue to ask the girl out before I do. She blew me off once, but I have no shame, so I'll totally ask her out again."

That caused my blood to boil. Turning back to Kaelynn, she looked between the two of us, confused.

"I can take you tonight if you want."

Her eyes lit up, which made my stomach feel like I was on a damn roller coaster. That never happened with Lily. Not once.

"Really? Are you being serious? You'll go with me?"

Laughing, I replied, "I'm totally being serious. I used to love going down at Christmas time."

"I think the Trail of Lights is open as well," Charlie added, a smile so wide on her face I would swear she had set this whole thing up.

"So, what brings you by, Kaelynn?" Tucker asked, interrupting both of us.

She glanced at Charlie then to me before her gaze went back to Tucker. "I called to see how Charlie and the baby were, and she told me today was decorating the nursery day. I offered to help, so here I am."

"Here you are," Tucker said, peeking over to me and winking. "You are hereby dubbed the decorating princess. Charlie here is the queen. She drew up a photo of where she wanted each picture, each toy, every little thing in the spare room that I cannot believe a few-weeks-old baby needs."

"Well, she is a woman, so you have to cater to their every whim, right?" Kaelynn threw out with a giggle, and it sent a shiver through my entire body. I turned away and got back to work putting the crib together.

Blake gave me a curious look, but I ignored him.

"Nash, who are you running the background check on?" Charlie asked, taking Hannah from Kaelynn.

"Oh, just someone I need to have checked out who wants a job with Barrett."

Tucker shot me a look, then raised his eyebrow. I narrowed my gaze at him when he shook his head. He was one to judge.

"Oh, good idea then. You can give me the information. I'll have our security department run it," Charlie offered.

"No!"

Both Kaelynn and Charlie jumped. Even little Hannah let out a small cry from the sudden outburst.

"Geesh, fine. Use Blake's brother. My gosh, y'all."

Kaelynn grinned. "Why don't you go put Hannah down for her nap and take one yourself while I supervise these men . . . and I'll try to keep them quiet for you and for Hannah."

"That sounds like an amazing idea." Charlie walked up to Tucker. "You okay? Do you need a break?"

He smiled and both me and Blake groaned. "Dude, seriously, you are not allowed to have sex with your wife while we're all here."

Charlie winked. "I wish. I'm not cleared for fun times yet."

Kaelynn's face turned pink as she looked from Charlie down to the paper Tucker had handed her.

"Go lay down with Hannah; we've got this," Tucker said to Charlie.

"If you need any direction on anything, let me know," Charlie stated.

Holding up what looked like a detailed plan, drawings and all, Kaelynn smiled. "I think you have it all laid out pretty well."

Tucker left with Charlie, and the three of us got back to work. It wasn't until Blake and I had the crib put together, had helped Kaelynn hang six pictures on the wall, and carried in a box of decorations that we noticed Tucker had never come back.

"Has anyone seen Tucker since he left with Charlie?"

Blake and Kaelynn glanced my way, both shaking their heads.

Kaelynn grabbed a baby blanket and draped it over the back of the rocking chair and said, "I'm sure he probably laid down with Charlie and they both fell asleep."

Blake left the room and came back, a huge smile on his face. "All three of them are crashed together sleeping. Poor Tucker is going to have a stiff neck with the way he is sitting up straight and his head is dropped to the side."

The three of us chuckled. Then, with a sigh, I scanned the finished nursery. "I like it."

"Me too," Blake and Kaelynn said at the same time.

Charlie and Tucker had wanted to wait on the nursery until they found out if the baby was a boy or girl. It was painted a soft sage green and the rest of the décor was forest-themed. Sprinkles of pink were scattered around the room, so you knew it was a little girl's room.

"I have one finishing touch to add," Kaelynn said, making her way over to her purse that was on the floor. She pulled out a picture frame and set it on the dresser. Blake and I walked up and smiled when we saw it.

"Kaelynn, this is great. Really great," Blake said, his voice cracking.

"Dude, are you going to cry?"

He shot me a dirty look. "Fuck off, asshole. I'm not going to cry. It just got me right here," he said, hitting his chest with his fist.

The picture was all of us at the comedy club. Charlie and Tucker were in the middle. Terri and Jim were on one side, and Blake and I on the other. We were all pointing to Charlie's belly. Charlie's head was tossed back as she laughed, and Tucker was looking at Charlie. A wide smile and a look of pure love on his face.

"The moment I saw it, I knew I needed to get it framed. You can just see the love on Tucker's face, and with the way you are all pointing to Charlie. It's precious."

"It's perfect," I whispered, looking at the photo and then over to Kaelynn. Her eyes twinkled, and she looked pleased she had made us happy.

She set a card next it and then let out a breath and said, "Well? Should we head on out and let the happy family get settled in?"

Blake nodded. "Yeah, I need to get out of here, I've got a big meeting I need to prepare for for tomorrow."

Reaching for his hand, I shook it and said, "Thanks so much for helping, Blake."

"Yeah, no worries. I probably won't see y'all until we start getting ready for Terri and Jim's wedding next week. I'm knee deep in two projects."

I slapped his back. "No worries. I know Tucker appreciates the help today."

Blake smiled. "There isn't anything I wouldn't do for y'all." Turning, he reached out and gave Kaelynn a quick hug and kiss on the cheek. "Thanks, Kaelynn. See ya around."

Her hand lifted as she replied, "See ya."

I walked Kaelynn out and stopped in front of her car. She leaned against it, and I swore the woman was looking at me like she wanted to crawl inside of me. The feeling was mutual.

"So? Zilker Park tonight?" I asked with a wink.

She giggled. "Okay, is it crazy I'm super excited about this?"

"Nope. Well, unless you're excited about the tree and not about going out with me tonight."

Her cheeks deepened in color while her teeth dug into her lip. She stared down at the ground. Lifting her chin up to meet my gaze, I winked at her. "I like you, Kaelynn, and something inside of me wants to see where this goes."

When her tongue slid across her lips to dampen then, my knees about buckled. "So, does that mean we're leaving the friend zone?" she asked.

Leaning down, I placed my mouth inches above hers and replied, "We are most definitely leaving the friend zone."

Her breathing picked up, and she almost whimpered, "Kiss me, Nash. Please."

My mouth pressed against hers. It was soft and slow, as if we were both taking our time, just feeling each other out. Kaelynn's hands went to my chest where she clung to my T-shirt. She opened to me, allowing me to deepen our connection. We both moaned and her hands slid up my body and around my neck.

The heat between us was hard to ignore. I was becoming lost. Nothing else mattered but this moment. The way her fingers slipped into my hair, or the soft moans she let out as I pulled us farther into the kiss. When we both needed air. I broke free, leaning my forehead against hers. Our chests rose and fell as we both fought to gain control of our breathing.

"I've been wanting to do that since the moment I first bumped into you."

Her only reply was my name, whispered softly from her kiss-swollen lips. "Nash."

Drawing back, I got lost in her eyes. "You're so beautiful."

"I've been wanting you to do that since you first smiled at me. I sort of have a thing for guys with dimples."

Laughing, I cupped her face and kissed her again. This time it was soft and sweet and not nearly as long.

"Do you need to change, or should we head straight to grab a bite to eat and then to the park?"

"I want to spend as much time with you as I can, so my vote is let's go grab food, then go to the park."

My heart still hadn't settled down to a normal rhythm yet. The flush that was still on her cheeks made my knees weak.

"I'll follow your every step," I said.

"How about we go to my place, drop my car off, and then we can just grab something to eat as we walk to the park? There is a plethora of food trailers near my condo."

Motioning with my hand, I replied, "Perfect. Lead the way."

Twelve

KAELYNN

MY LIPS TINGLED from Nash's kiss. Hell, my entire body felt like it was on fire. The moment his lips touched mine, I felt something I'd never felt before. All thoughts of telling Nash the truth slipped from my mind, at least for now. I was going to tell him what I had been withholding. Sooner rather than later. A fear crept into my thoughts.

What if I told him and he hated me? I had been keeping it from him, and now we were moving things to another level. I needed to come clean with him.

Peeking into the rearview mirror, I saw his handsome face. Good Lord, the man was hot. His dark hair was a mess from my fingers sliding in it. His face had a scruffy, unshaven look that should make him seem unkempt, but it didn't. Instead, it screamed sexy and I couldn't help thinking about how it would feel on my every part of my body.

"Ugh. Stop this, Kaelynn!" I scolded myself. Hitting the button on my car, I spoke again. "Call Millie."

It only rang twice before my younger sister answered. "Hey! What's up?"

"Hey. Not much, how are you?"

"I'm amazing. It's snowing here and I'm getting ready to go Christmas shopping for the Make-A-Wish tree at Justin's job."

I lifted my brows. "Things with you and Justin are going good?"

"Never better." She sighed. "Kaelynn, he knows how to treat me. In all ways . . . if you know what I mean."

Giggling, I replied, "I can safely guess."

"Other than that, I've just been working at the office and trying to help Mom plan her New Year's Eve benefit dinner at the country club."

My mother put on a benefit dinner every year, with all the proceeds going to a different charity. She always made each event successful and raised a ton of money for every charity she took under her wing.

"Mom and Dad left late last night. I forgot to ask her what charity she was doing this year."

"Shriners Hospitals for Children."

I smiled. "She loves that one."

"Yeah, she does. What's up? How are things going in Texas? Any hot cowboys you want to take a ride on?"

She laughed as I rolled my eyes. "Well, as a matter of fact."

"Shut up! Oh my gosh, spill the beans."

Glancing into the rearview mirror again, I saw Nash laughing. He was either talking to someone or listening to something on the radio.

"It's Nash, Morgan's older brother."

Millie didn't reply for a few moments. "Your best friend's brother? That could either be a good thing or a really bad thing."

"Morgan's not going to care. As a matter of fact, she would probably be the one handing me a condom and pushing me into the bedroom. I sort of pointed Nash out to her before I knew it was her brother. Then things got . . . weird between us, but now we're going to give it a shot."

"Weird? Like how?"

I drew in a deep breath. "Where to start? Okay, so Nash dated this girl, Lily. She was super wealthy."

"Okay. You stopped talking like I was supposed to know what happened next."

"Right, I forget I never told you. Well, Lily cheated on Nash with this guy she worked with at her father's company. Morgan said she liked this guy for two reasons: he was kinky in bed and he had money."

"Is Nash poor?"

"No! I mean, he's not super wealthy. He works hard for his father's construction business. They do well to live a comfortable life, but I don't think he can just go out and buy a Porsche. Well, hell, I don't know. Maybe he can. It was never something I thought about, much less cared about."

"Got it. So this woman left him because of that? How shallow."

"I know, right? It makes my stomach sick to think of how she treated Nash. He's the nicest guy I've ever met, Millie. He loves his family and friends and would do anything for anyone. He even drove me all the way to Houston because my car was broken down."

"Wow. Okay, clearly this Lily chick was insane. I'm still not understanding the . . . oh no. Shit. Oh, Kaelynn. You didn't."

I pulled my lower lip into my mouth and bit down on it. "I never told Morgan; you know how hard it is when you tell people about it."

"Yes, I know. I've had my fair share of friends and boyfriends only pretend to like me because of the family money. But if you're thinking of starting anything with this guy, he needs to know. Especially with this history. What is the matter with you? You're not in high school. Why are you acting like it?"

"Ugh, God. I know! I know! I really like him and I'm afraid if I tell him now, he's going to walk away. He makes me feel things I've never felt before and he kissed me earlier. Millie . . . it was the most amazing kiss I've ever had in my life. I mean, I'm pretty sure my mind was making all the arrangements for our wedding and how many kids we were gonna have while he was kissing me. I was completely and utterly lost to him."

"That good, huh?" she purred into the phone. I could see her now wiggling her eyebrows and making a crude gesture with either her hands or her tongue.

"Yes. It was that good."

"Imagine what sex will be like."

My face heated.

"That's the problem. I can imagine it. I have imagined it. I want to tell him the truth. I really do. But this is our first date tonight. He's taking me to the park to see the tree, and it's going to be all festive. I mean, what if we date a few times and things don't work out? It won't matter that I didn't tell him I'm the heiress to a billion-dollar fortune."

"One of the heiresses. I'm the other one. Sharesies, remember?"

I sighed. "I'm serious. I think if he finds out, he's going to put me in the friend zone again."

"And the friend zone isn't enough?" Millie asked.

"At first, I thought it was. Each time I've seen him, I fall a little more. So no, the friend zone is not enough."

"Wow." Millie stated. The line was silent for a bit. "When Justin and I first started dating, he had no idea about our family. We dated for a few months before it even really came up. I mean, he asked what my parents did, and I told him my father owned a company in Utah that dealt a lot with real estate. I told him what you did, and what Jack does. He was fine with that. As things got heavier and we started talking about meeting the parents, I knew I had to warn him before I pulled up to our folks' house. I mean, it is a bit overwhelming."

I laughed, but it came out more like a scoff. "To say the least."

My parents' house, well, their main house outside of Salt Lake City, that is, was a rather large house. At just over forty-nine-thousand square feet, it had everything you could wish for, including a two-lane bowling alley.

"He was freaked about it at first, but it never changed his opinion of me."

"That's the problem. I'm afraid once Nash finds out, it will change his. He's been down this road before and it burned him."

"Not every woman with a large pocket book is going to care what his fortune is."

"I know that. He's following me back home, so I've got a ways to go before I get home. I'll think about what I'm going to do. Maybe I'll tell him tonight. Yeah. I need to tell him tonight."

"That's the smartest thing to do. You don't have to go into detail, but let him know the gist of it all."

"Thanks, Millie. I always feel better talking to you."

"Same here. Are you really staying in Austin?"

"I like it here, and if things go well with Nash, I'll have a solid reason to stay."

"Give Justin and me an excuse to come visit. It might be nice to get out of the cold weather. You are coming home for Christmas? Right?"

"Yes. I'll be there for Christmas. I have a ticket to fly up on the twenty-third."

"Awesome! I've got to go. Justin is calling! Good luck, sis. Love you and I'll see you in a couple of weeks."

"Love you too, Millie. Bye."

The line went dead and I let out a deep breath.

Tonight. I'll do it tonight.

Thirteen

KAELYNN

"YOU HAVE TO stand under it and spin."

Staring at Nash, I laughed. "Spin?"

He nodded. "Yeah. While looking up."

"Do you want me to get sick?"

"I'll hold your ponytail out of the way if you do," he stated with a sexy smirk.

Rolling my eyes, I pushed him. "Gosh, thanks. You just made me drink hot chocolate. I ate a s'mores *and* a pretzel. I will surely get sick if you make me spin."

"Don't forget the hot apple cider we had when we first walked up."

"Right. That too."

Nash glanced around, grinned, then grabbed my hand. "Come on. I know a way to let your stomach settle before the great spinning."

Trying to ignore the way his touch made my body ache for more, I allowed him to pull me over to a horse and carriage.

"How about we take a spin around the park?"

"I'd love that!" I replied, letting Nash help me into the carriage.

"The full route, sir?" the driver asked with a joyful smile.

"Yes, my girl here needs to let her goodies settle before we spin around the tree."

With a wide grin, the driver glanced over to me. "You have to spin around the tree. It's a tradition."

"So I've heard," I said with a light laugh. It was hard to focus when Nash's words replayed in my mind.

My girl. He called me "my girl."

"Then I won't offer you any hot chocolate."

Nash held up his hands. "No, just a warm blanket."

The driver pulled the blanket off the seat across from us and opened it. Handing it to Nash, he draped it over us. He lifted his arm and placed it around my shoulders, pulling my body up against his. The heat between us would surely keep us warm.

As we took off, I drew in a deep breath and said, "Christmas. I smell it in the air."

"I bet your Christmas back home is beautiful."

"It is," I agreed, resting my head against his shoulder. "My favorite thing, though, is waking up, going down to the kitchen, and watching my mother make breakfast. It was a huge ordeal. She made everything from homemade waffles to biscuits and gravy, muffins, you name it, the woman made it. My father would always get up with her and help. They said it was their quiet time together before the madness of Christmas started."

Nash chuckled. "Did y'all have Christmas at your house? With family and all? Or you went to someone else's house?"

"Oh yes. Everyone came over in the afternoon. Since my mom cooked breakfast, Christmas dinner was usually a potluck type of thing. Everyone would bring something."

"Sounds nice."

Smiling, I wrapped my arm around his while he lifted the blanket up some. "It is."

"Did you have to wait to open presents until after you ate breakfast?"

"No, we always opened them on Christmas Eve. When we were little, our parents of course spoiled us. As we got older, the presents decreased, which didn't bother us at all. We made a new tradition to only buy each other three gifts."

"Why three?" Nash asked.

"That was how many gifts Christ got."

He kissed the top of my head. "I love that tradition. Are you going home for Christmas this year?"

"I am. I leave on the twenty-third."

"How long are you up there for?"

"Probably a week. If I stay too long, my folks won't want me to leave."

"Have they been to visit you here in Texas?"

I stiffened, and I knew Nash could feel me tense.

"Yes. They were here yesterday. They left late last night."

"Wow, quick trip. What did they come in for?"

Why did he have to ask so many questions? This wasn't the place I wanted to drop my bomb on him.

The truth was the easiest thing to give him.

"They want to buy a place here, with me moving here and all. An investment, if you will, but a place they can come and stay if they want."

"Nice."

I looked up at him and he was looking straight ahead. "What about you? Any family traditions?"

He smiled and I relaxed my body. He wasn't going to ask any more questions.

"Just the normal ones. We always drink hot chocolate and roast marshmallows on Christmas Eve. My mom buys Morgan and me new PJs every year and makes us open them. Then makes us wear them for an annual picture."

I covered my mouth. "No!"

Laughing, he nodded. "Yes. Then we all watch *It's a Wonderful Life*. Christmas morning we wake up and open presents. Nothing grand, just small gifts we exchange. My mom always makes us something knitted."

"That is so sweet! I want to learn to knit."

He looked down at me. "You should learn. There's all sorts of YouTube videos on how to do it."

I nuzzled back against him, loving the way it felt to be near him like this. "Maybe I will."

We spent the rest of the ride in comfortable silence. I wanted to enjoy the time with him. Just relaxing and not worrying about what the future held. I only wanted to worry about what this moment held. The rest would work itself out.

The driver came to a stop, and Nash clapped his hands together and started to rub them together sort of maniacally. "Let's go get our spin on."

Groaning, I folded up the blanket, let Nash help me out of the carriage, and begged the driver to let me stay with him.

"Come on, it's fun."

"Nash, I get dizzy easily."

He stopped us, turned me to face him, and placed his finger under my chin. Lifting my gaze to meet his, he spoke softly. "I won't let anything happen, and I promise you're going to love it. Just go slow."

I nodded. Something about his tone of voice and the way he was looking at me, I knew he meant every word. And for Pete's sake, I was spinning under a tree, not mountain climbing.

Then he leaned down and softly kissed my lips. I had to fight the urge to pull him against me to deepen the kiss. Nash drew back, staring into my eyes.

"I've never felt like this with anyone before, Kaelynn. I'm trying to figure out if I'm just in serious lust over you, or if you're . . ."

I swallowed hard. "Or if I'm what?"

His voice was so low I barely heard the word come out of his mouth. "Different."

Different? Different from how? From who? Lily? Any woman he's been with before? Was it a good kind of different? Or a bad different?

Crapola. I'm thinking about this all too hard.

"Hey, tell me what is going on in that beautiful head of yours."

I smiled. "Different in a good way?"

Nash leaned down and kissed me again, then whispered against my lips, "A very good way."

Feeling like a little girl on Christmas morning, I couldn't help the silly grin on my face. "I feel something, too. Something amazing."

"Well, I don't think I can take all the credit here . . . that feeling could be me, or it could be the excitement and anticipation you have for spinning under the tree."

He spun me around and I faced the tree. Kids and adults alike were all under the tree. Some were running, some just standing and staring up, and some spinning.

I laughed and said, "I bet it's a bit of both."

Nash laced his fingers with mine and walked us over to the center. We maneuvered our way through and got directly in the middle of the tree. He took my hands in his as we faced one another.

"Ready?" he asked, excitement dancing in his honey-colored eyes. The way the light from the tree sparkled in them made my breath catch.

"Ready!" I squealed back, surprised by my sudden excitement to do this.

"Lean your head back and look up."

Doing as he told me to, I gasped at the sight. A swirl of lights captured my attention. "Nash! Oh my gosh, it's beautiful. How many lights are there?"

"I think over three thousand."

I continued to gaze up at the light show. Then I felt him moving, and I gripped his hands harder. We started to spin, and I couldn't help but laugh like a little girl. The lights spun around in the most glorious way. It was stunning.

"I love it!" I exclaimed as I held my eyes fixed up. Then I felt Nash wrap his arms around me as we came to a stop. Looking down at him, I let myself get adjusted from the slight sway of everything. Then I realized he had picked me up and held me so I wouldn't lose my balance.

"Was it worth it?" he asked, his dimples on full display in the bright lights of the tree.

"It was so worth it."

"Good."

Leaning down, I kissed him like my next breath depended on that kiss. Nash held me tighter against his body, and I moaned slightly at the feel of his body against mine. If he asked me to make love with him right now, I would say yes. But I had a feeling Nash Barrett wasn't that type of guy. The fact that he picked me up and held me so I wouldn't stumble and took me on the carriage ride first to let my stomach settle only proved what an amazing man he was. How Lily ever let him go was beyond me.

Not very man was like Nash Barrett. At least, none of the men I had ever met or dated back home were like him.

"Romantic."

"What?" Nash asked, giving me a confused look.

My cheeks heated as I realized I had said that out loud. Shaking my head, I answered him. "Nothing. That was just so much more than I thought it would be."

"Good," he replied, kissing me on my nose as he slowly placed me back on the ground.

"How in the world are you going to top that, Mr. Barrett?" I asked in a teasing voice as we started to walk back toward my condo.

"I would say I would make you breakfast in bed in the morning, but that would mean me staying the night. And I don't think we're ready for that. I sleep naked."

I couldn't help but let out a bellow of laughter. "Wh-what? You sleep naked?"

Nash laughed. "Why do you make that sound like it's a bad thing?"

"What if someone broke into the house and he sees you coming out of your bedroom and you're . . . naked?"

Nash shrugged. "Then I guess he'd be looking to get into a cockfight."

I stopped walking and stared at him, then lost it laughing again. "You are crazy!"

He shrugged, then reached for my hand. "Keeping it real, just keeping it real."

Fourteen

NASH

STANDING OUTSIDE OF Kaelynn's condo, I fought the urge to tell her how much I wanted her. The conflicting feelings running rampant in my head weren't helping any. As much as I wanted her, I could not shake the feeling she was holding something back. There was no way I was going to fall into something with someone I couldn't trust. How in the hell did I ask her?

Hey, Kaelynn, what are you hiding from me, because guess what, I don't trust you? That only screamed that I was the one who had trust issues.

"Thank you for tonight. I had a lot of fun."

I smiled. "I did too. I'm glad you spun."

"You didn't give me much of a choice."

"It was worth it, though, wasn't it?"

Her teeth sank into her lip, causing my eyes to drift down to that pretty little mouth of hers.

"It was," she answered softly.

Bouncing my eyes back up to her gaze, I cleared my throat. "I better go."

Kaelynn nodded, then took a step back, closer to her door.

"Listen, Terri and Jim are getting married this weekend. Did you want to go with me?"

Her eyes lit up. "They wouldn't mind? I mean, I don't really know them all that well."

"You're my date, so that doesn't matter. Plus, I know they would love to have you there. So would Charlie. She really likes you."

"I like her too. And I would love to go. Will I . . . um . . . see you before then?"

Moving in closer, her back hit the door and I leaned in, my lips inches from hers. "I sure hope so."

Her tongue swept over her mouth, causing me to crash my lips to hers. Kaelynn wrapped her arms around my neck. She made the sweetest moan and opened more to me, allowing me to deepen the kiss. When I placed my hand on her lower back and pulled her body against mine, she gasped and tugged a fistful of hair.

I wanted her to feel how hard I was for her. How much I wanted her, because I did. But first I needed my head fucking clear about this and about Kaelynn.

I pulled back, causing Kaelynn to sway from the sudden loss of my body pressed against hers.

"Wow. You really do know how to make a girl swoon."

With a lighthearted chuckle, I ran my fingers through my hair, taking another step back. "Good night, Kaelynn. I'll call you tomorrow?"

She seemed a bit confused for a moment, then smiled. "Night, Nash. Thank you again for a wonderful evening."

I waited for her to get into her place before I turned and headed to the elevator. Hitting the button, I cursed.

"Damn it. What is she hiding, and why is she hiding it?"

⁓⁓⁓

THE CRANE MADE a beeping sound as I watched it back up, holding the roofing material in place as it moved slowly.

"That's good, now you've got clearance," I shouted.

The roofers were in place and ready to start hauling the shingles off the lift and onto the roof. I felt my father come and stand next to me, his gaze lifted to where I was looking.

"Moving along pretty damn fast."

"It's all about staying on schedule."

"I taught you well."

Turning to face my father, I said, "If that's what you want to call it."

He didn't respond and moved on. "How are things going on the Hill Country Gym project?"

Just like my father, keeping it business all the way. "On schedule. As a matter of fact, I was able to get the electrician out early, so the drywall guys can get in there whenever they're free. Rich told me he thought his guys would be finished up today on a project and would be able to head on out there tomorrow."

He faced me, his brows raised in question. "How did you manage to get the electrician out there early?"

"He owed me," I replied, not giving him more. I had referred Bobby to a job over at the Austonian, and it turned out that it got his company three more referrals. When I called in a favor to do this house because the other electrician backed out, he jumped on it. Calling in favors was not something my father did. Ever.

"You called in a favor?" his tone was disappointed.

"It doesn't matter how I got him there early, I did. We're ahead of schedule, Dad. Can you just not be happy about that?"

"Happy? Now what type of favor am I going to owe this guy?"

I let out a frustrated sigh. "None, Dad. *I* got the guy three job referrals. He told *me* he wanted to make it up to me, and I told him I needed an electrician ASAP. He was available and the job got done. You don't owe him a damn thing."

Turning, I walked over to the job trailer, my fists clenched.

"Nash. Nash!" my father called out. I didn't stop and kept walking. When was my father going to cut the fucking strings and let me run this business the way I wanted? He was supposed to be retiring, taking a step back, and all he did was get up in my damn face every chance he got.

I jerked the door to the trailer open and walked in, my father on my heels.

"What in the hell has gotten into you?"

"You!" I shouted. "You have gotten into me, Dad. I've been working for this company since I was fourteen years old. I know how things work. I've increased our profits by forty percent this last year, but that isn't good enough for you. No matter what I do, it's not good enough. I gave up my life for this job."

My father looked like he had been slapped in the face. I wanted to take it back, but the words were already out there.

"You gave up your life? What does that mean?"

It was too late. I'd spoken it, the words were hanging there, so I had to get it out.

"It means I wanted something different, Dad. I wanted a different path, but I could never tell you because you would never listen."

He laughed. "Do you mean the Marines? Or what about architecture? Son, that was a phase you went through. Your friend in college was doing it, and you wanted to follow in his footsteps."

His words nearly knocked me to the ground. "No. You wanted me to follow in your footsteps. How in the hell did you think I met Blake, Dad? In an architecture class. That's what I wanted to do. That was my dream, but you wouldn't allow that. You decided my career was working for your company. Maybe you don't remember it that way, but I sure as hell do."

The door to the trailer opened, and my mother walked in. Concern was etched on her face. "I can hear the two of you from outside."

"Good, did you hear how ungrateful your son is? I paid for his college education, and he's trying to tell me I ruined his life."

I rolled my eyes and blew out a frustrated breath.

"Bob, that is enough."

"Enough? How is that enough? I put him through school, gave him more of a chance to succeed than I ever had. I had to prove to my father I could run this business after serving my time in the military."

With a scoff, I looked at him. "You don't think I've had to prove to you I can take over this business? Is that why you haven't retired? You don't think I can do it?"

My mother rushed over to me. "No, that is not it at all. Your father knows you are more than capable of taking over. Don't you, Bob?"

His face was void of any expression. Turning, he walked out of the trailer and slammed the door shut.

Shaking my head, I mumbled, "Fuck it."

"Do not talk that way, Nash Barrett."

"I gave up my own dreams, Mom, to do this. To take over this damn construction company. This is not what I wanted to do with my life."

Her eyes filled with tears. "I know."

Guilt rushed through my body. Reaching out for her, I pulled my mother into a hug. "I'm sorry, Mom. I didn't mean that. I didn't mean to make you upset. I'm sorry."

"Yes, you did mean it, and it's okay if you wanted a different life."

"I didn't want a different life."

She looked up at me, her brows raised.

"Fine, I wanted a little bit of a different life. I would have still worked for Dad, but I would have liked to do other things as well. Designing buildings was one of them."

"Your sister told me about your degree, Nash. How you kept taking classes. I know you got your architecture degree, and so does your father."

Smirking, I shook my head. "Morgan can't keep her mouth shut, can she?"

"How in the world did you find time to take all those classes?"

I shrugged. "I started doubling up in college."

"Is it true you designed Tucker and Charlie's house?"

"I did. Charlie had some ideas drawn up, and I brought them to life and built it for them. It was one of the reasons it was so easy, because I had my architecture degree. I've designed a few houses, Mom. And I've made some money off it. I had it invested, and I'm looking at buying some land out near Tucker and Charlie to build my own home."

"Near Marble Falls? Will you still drive in for work?"

"Yes, of course. It's not as far out, but the daughter of the former land owner needs to dump the land; she can't afford the taxes. I got a lead on it and am hoping to purchase it before it goes on the market. She just wants out and is pretty cool about giving it to me below market value. She could actually sell it for a bit more. She wants to unload it."

"I see," my mother said softly.

"I'm not leaving Barrett Construction, but if Dad would ever let the reins go, I can make this company even better. I'm building a great group of guys I can trust, and I'm hoping at some point to offer the design element into the business."

Her eyes widened with delight. "Nash! That is a great idea."

Kissing her on the forehead, I said, "I think so too."

"Sweetheart, talk to your father about it. Let him know what you want to do."

"I tried to. He told me my job was to oversee everything, not hire a bunch of people to do my job. He won't listen."

She drew in a deep breath. "Let me talk to him."

I nodded, then gave her another hug. "Good luck, but it won't change anything."

My phone beeped and I pulled it out of my pocket. The moment I saw Kaelynn's name, I smiled.

"Well, I know that look on a man's face. Who is she?"

Lifting my gaze from the phone and over to my mother, I shook my head. "Don't even think it, Mom. We've been on one date."

"My, that one date must have been a tremendous success. Your eyes actually sparkled when you saw who texted you."

My lip snarled. "Sparkled? Seriously?"

"Yes. Sparkled. Nearly lit up the entire room."

I laughed. "Okay, well, I need to get back out there. I love you, Mom."

"Aren't you going to answer her back?" she asked, lifting up on her toes to try and see my phone.

"In a bit. Love you."

She jutted her lip out. "Fine. I love you too! Remember, the rehearsal dinner is Thursday night! Don't forget."

Pausing halfway out the door, she looked over her shoulder. "Are you bringing her to the wedding?"

There was no way out of this one. My parents were invited to Terri and Jim's wedding. Jim was like a brother to me and spent more time at my house in college than he did flying home to Washington. He was like a second son to my folks, so it was a no-brainer when Terri asked my mother for help planning the wedding. Her mom and mine were friends, after all.

"Mom, please don't make this into a big deal."

A huge grin appeared on her face as she held her hands up in defense. "What? I asked a simple question. I'm going to assume that is a yes."

"Yes. She is going with me to the wedding."

I had to give the woman credit; she did a damn good job trying to hide her excitement. She failed once she got outside the trailer and let out a small yelp of excitement.

Glancing back to my phone, I read the text from Kaelynn again.

Kaelynn: Are you free for dinner? My place? Seven?

I felt like a damn kid in high school with how excited I was hearing from her and knowing I was going to see her again.

Me: Sounds wonderful. Do you need me to bring anything?

Kaelynn: Yourself with a big appetite. Oh . . . and maybe something to drink. I don't have any beer.

Me: Beer? So fancy? What are we having?

Kaelynn: Hot dogs. . . .

Laughing, I started back outside, but not before I sent her back a reply.

Me: Make me three . . . I like hot dogs. See you at seven.

Kaelynn: Looking forward to it.

I had a hell of a time trying to keep my mind focused for the rest of the day. My thoughts kept drifting to Kaelynn. Most of them good, a few dirty thoughts, and a few moments when guilt hit me square in the chest about the damn background check. Every time I thought about it, I pushed it away. I needed to know what, if anything, she was keeping from me. I really hoped my gut was wrong about this—even though everything inside of me screamed Kaelynn was keeping a secret.

Fifteen

NASH

BLAKE LEANED AGAINST my kitchen counter, a skeptical look on his face.

"What?" I asked.

"Dude, I'm with Tucker on this one. Just ask her."

"I can't."

"Just because Lily lied to you doesn't mean Kaelynn is going to."

"So now you don't think she's from money and hiding it?"

He shrugged. "I don't know. I mean, she seems really nice. You said you had a great time together last night. Why not just let things progress and see what happens?"

"We did. And tonight I'm going over to her place for dinner."

Blake's brows raised. "Dinner at her place. Okay, that could mean a few things."

I towel-dried my hair then tossed the wet towel onto the sofa. "And those few things are?"

"One, she wants to get laid."

"Dude, seriously? Why do you have to talk like that?"

He rolled his eyes. "Fine, she wants to have sex. Two, she wants to tell you whatever it is she is hiding . . . *if* . . . she is really hiding something."

"And having dinner at home makes you think that why?"

"It's simple," Blake said, folding his arms over his chest. "She doesn't want to see you explode with anger in public. Maybe she figures she can seduce you a little bit, get you all hot and worked up, then drop it on you."

I stared at him, then laughed. "Dude, you've been watching too many movies."

He narrowed his eyes at me, then looked up in thought. "Shit. Maybe I have been. Or the whole Charlie-and-Tucker thing is still in my head."

Holding up my beer, I nodded. "Maybe that's why we came up with this crazy idea she is hiding something."

"We?" Blake stated. "Dude, that was all you. You're the one who said she was hiding something. I simply gave you a few ideas of what she could be hiding. Again, we could both be wrong."

"Shit, I hope so. I really like her."

Blake smiled. "As much as you liked Lily?"

I shrugged. "I was in love with Lily. This is different, though. I feel things I didn't feel with Lily. It's confusing."

"Like what kind of things?"

I wasn't about to tell Blake how my heart hammered in my chest when I thought of Kaelynn. Or how the sight of her left me breathless. Or how my knees felt weak when she laughed or smiled. So I deflected.

"Well, I want her like my next breath."

He frowned. "Bullshit, dude, every guy feels that way about all women they are attracted to. She makes you feel different in here." He slapped me on the chest. "Don't lie. I know you too well."

My silence was all the answer he needed. Blake smiled. "Dude, it's okay to feel that way. It's okay to like her in a different way from Lily. That wasn't the real thing. Kaelynn could very well be."

"Yeah, I know."

"Lily asked you to take her back more than once. You said no. Why?"

I reached into the refrigerator and grabbed a beer. "Well, for one, I would never be able to trust her. I finally realized I don't love her anymore, if I was really ever in love with her. It took me awhile to realize that."

"And when did you actually decide it was time to move on?"

The beer paused at my lips.

Blake nodded then laughed. "Let me guess, after you met Kaelynn."

"I think it was when Lily wanted me back. I knew I didn't want her back. Kaelynn might have reinforced that."

Tipping the bottle, I drank nearly the whole thing in one drink. Walking up to me, Blake placed his hand on my shoulder and gave it a squeeze. "Another one bites the dust. I'm going to be the last man standing in the group."

"Yeah, I can't wait until you meet the person who makes you fall flat on your ass."

Blake laughed even harder. "Not going to happen. I like my freedom—and having my pick of women—too much."

My doorbell rang and I headed to the door.

"I need to get going. Let me know how it goes tonight and if you get laid."

Rolling my eyes yet again, I opened the door to see Morgan standing there. A wide smile on her face.

"Hey! I heard you had a dinner date tonight!" She squealed as she rushed past me and into my place.

She amped up her excitement with a scream and jumped into my arms after I shut the door.

With a chuckle, I set her down and kissed her on the cheek. "I take it that makes you happy?"

"Happy? Oh my gosh. My best friend hooking up with my brother. Hell yes that makes me happy. Lord knows she needs some attention." Morgan patted me on the chest as she walked into the house. "If you know what I mean."

Blake laughed from behind me as I groaned.

"Hey, I'm Morgan, Nash's sister."

Blake held out his hand and gave Morgan a polite smile. "Blake Grant, we've met before. A long time ago when Nash and I were in college."

Morgan stared at Blake until it finally came to her. "Oh . . . Blake who is the architect?"

"That's me."

"Well, it's great seeing you again."

"Yeah, you too. Sorry, but I've got to run. Hot date of my own tonight."

Morgan smiled then gave him a stern look. "Make sure you put a helmet on that soldier, boy. Don't want any little soldiers running around."

Blake's smile faded before he snapped his head to look at me. I shrugged.

"Right. Okay, well, good seeing you again, Morgan."

She wiggled her fingers and called out, "Have fun!"

I shut the door and walked past her, back to the kitchen. "What brings you here?"

"Okay, well, I wanted to stop by and tell you a few things about Kaelynn."

Freezing in my tracks, I slowly turned to face her. Had Kaelynn sent my sister over here to tell me what she had been hiding?

"Did Kaelynn send you over her?"

Morgan jerked her head back. "What? Oh gosh no. She would kick my ass if she knew I was here."

I didn't know whether to be relieved or frustrated. "Fine. What did you want to tell me?"

"Kaelynn is very sweet. I think a little on the innocent side. I haven't really seen her dating anyone serious. The whole time I've known her she hasn't mentioned sleeping with anyone."

My eyes widened. "She's a virgin?"

Morgan looked at me like I had just said the strangest thing. Her brows pulled in tight and she replied, "No. Where in the hell did that come from?"

"I don't know." I said, pointing to her. "You're the one who said she was innocent."

"Yeah, as in she doesn't sleep around with guys. I think she comes from a conservative family. I haven't met them, so I'm not sure what they're like." She paused for a moment then looked up in thought. "You know, she never talks about her family. I mean, she does her brother and sister. She's talked about them a lot. But her mom and dad, not so much."

"Huh, with you too?"

"She hasn't talked about them to you either?"

I shook my head. "Not a whole lot."

Morgan shrugged as if it wasn't a big deal to her. "That doesn't mean anything. She's just a private person."

Nodding, I agreed. "Anything else you needed? I have to be taking off soon."

She smiled. "I'm glad you're getting out there again, Nash. I hope you are finally realizing that Lily wasn't the one."

I grunted.

"She wasn't. You deserve someone who loves you the way you love them. Someone who is honest and caring."

Grabbing my keys and wallet, I faced my sister. "And what if Kaelynn isn't so honest."

Her mouth opened slightly, as if she was too stunned to say anything. Then she closed her eyes and shook her head. "Kaelynn? She's probably one of the most honest people I've ever met. Her heart is pure gold, and there isn't anything she wouldn't do for anyone. Nash, you can't let what one woman did to you pave the way for all other women. Lily cheated on you. She lied to your face and slept with another man and got pregnant. Do we all have secrets? Yes. I'm sure Kaelynn does as well, but she isn't Lily."

I swallowed hard but forced myself to smile. Walking up to Morgan, I kissed her on the cheek. "I know. I do. Thanks, Morgan. I really do need to get going."

"Let's walk out together. Wait, do you have condoms?"

My entire body sagged. "I'm not even going there with you."

"Why not? It's a real question that all responsible adults need to think about in this day and age," Morgan said, walking out the door and toward the elevator.

"I have no intention of sleeping with her tonight; it's our second date."

Morgan wiggled her eyebrows. "Don't underestimate a woman who hasn't had sex in a while. Trust me. I know."

Plugging my ears, I started singing while Morgan laughed and pushed the button for the lobby.

Thirty minutes later I stood outside of Kaelynn's apartment. Knocking on the door, I drew in a deep breath.

"Coming!"

When Kaelynn opened the door, I let my eyes roam over her. She had on a white sweater, jeans, and no socks or shoes. Sweeping my eyes back up her body, I smiled. Her hair was piled on top of her head in a messy bun. Long curls hung down randomly, and she had what looked like flour on the tip of her nose. She was the most adorable thing I'd ever laid eyes on.

Then she smiled even bigger when our eyes met. "You look handsome," she said while motioning for me to come into her place. Her condo wasn't anything huge. It had a decent-sized kitchen with a bar that held four stools. The living room was big enough for a sectional. A square coffee table sat in the middle of the living room. A large TV sat on top of a console, but I saw the box for the equipment to hang it on the wall.

"So, this is my place. If you go in through here, you'll find the bathroom."

I followed her. "It cuts through to the bedroom."

Sitting in the middle of the bedroom was a queen-sized, four-poster, white iron bed. It was all made up with a simple light green comforter and a few decorative pillows. There was no TV and no dresser. Just the bed and a chair next to the window that had a throw blanket the same color as her comforter on it.

"That looks cozy," I stated, pointing to the chair.

"It is the best place to read a book. I love looking out and seeing the park. It has a perfect view of the top of the Zilker tree as well."

"Cute place," I said as we made our way back into the living room. "There is a small bedroom on the other side of the living room. It's my office and has a futon in there if I ever have . . . guests." She shrugged, then laughed. "Not that I really know anyone here."

I took in a deep breath. "Smells delicious. That is not hot dogs."

Kaelynn took the six-pack of beer out of my hands. "No, it's not. It is, however, my mother's secret lasagna recipe."

"How did you know lasagna was my favorite?"

Glancing over her shoulder, she winked. "A little birdy told me. Make yourself at home. I'm not sure what's on TV. I don't watch it very much, but I do have satellite if you want to watch anything."

"Nah, I'm good. Are you going to be hanging it up on the wall?"

Kaelynn walked back in and handed me a beer. "Yeah, I opened up the box and read the first three steps and got lost."

Laughing, I set the beer on a coaster and opened the box.

"Nash, you don't have to do that."

"I want to," I replied. "I like putting things together."

Kaelynn dropped onto the floor next to me. "Need any help?"

"Nope. I got it."

Pulling her knees up and resting her chin on them, she watched me. I liked that we could be together in comfortable silence. That not every second had to be filled with conversation. Lily was the opposite of Kaelynn. She always wanted to talk, no matter what it was about. You couldn't have a moment of peace . . . ever.

"Morgan said you have two degrees. One in business management and one in architecture."

"Yep."

"Do you do very much with your architecture degree?"

"Not yet, but I'm hoping that changes soon. I've designed a few things."

She tilted her head and regarded me. I wanted to reach out and wipe the white off her nose, but I decided she looked too damn cute with it.

"Like what?"

"Tucker and Charlie's house, for one."

She gasped. "You designed their house and built it? It's stunning."

"Yes, I did. It's really what I'm hoping to offer more of, if I can just get my father on board. He thinks I need to be on the job sites every day micromanaging and . . ."

With a laugh, I shook my head and reached for the beer. "I'm sorry. The last thing I want to do is talk about work."

A timer went off and Kaelynn jumped up.

"Excuse me, I have to finish the lasagna up; I'll be right back."

My eyes followed her into the kitchen. The ache in my body for this woman was growing stronger the more I was around her.

Focusing back on the task at hand, I cursed at myself for not putting at least one condom in my wallet.

"Live and learn, Barrett. Live and learn," I whispered with a soft chuckle.

Sixteen

KAELYNN

I PULLED THE lasagna out of the oven and set it on the stove. It smelled heavenly. I cut up the fresh loaf of bread and took the salad I had made out and set it on the bar.

Nash whistled while he worked on putting the TV mount together. I couldn't help but smile. This felt so . . . right. So good. I couldn't explain it, but I knew I wanted more evenings like this. Like last night. I wanted more days with Nash.

I wanted Nash.

"Want me to put some Christmas music on?" I finally asked when I snapped out of my daze.

"Sure!"

"I like Amy Grant. Is that okay?" I said, connecting my phone to the Bose speaker.

"Yeah, sounds good."

The sounds of Christmas music filled the air, and I wasn't surprised when Nash started singing along to the songs.

"Do you need any help?" he asked, walking up to the island.

"If you want to put some salad in the bowls, I'll get the lasagna on the plates."

He washed his hands and got to work putting the salad in the bowls. "Dressing?"

"I've got ranch, Italian, and vinaigrette. I'll take the vinaigrette."

Searching in the refrigerator, Nash replied, "That sounds good to me."

We were soon seated on the sofa, dinner trays in front of us, talking like we hadn't seen each other in days. I loved that about Nash. We could talk for hours, and then not talk at all.

"Do you want another beer?" I asked, standing up to get one.

"Sure, I'll take one more. I drove here, so I'll keep it to just two."

"Well, I do have a guest room and a super-comfy futon to crash on if you wanted more."

Nash didn't respond to my invite and shifted a bit, so I let it go. As much as I wanted this man, I was not jumping into bed with him on our second date. He didn't seem as if he wanted that either.

"Damn, Kaelynn, that was some good food. Italian in the family?"

I smiled. "Yep. On my mother's side. Her mother, my grandmother, was full-on Italian. My grandfather met her in Italy and fell in love. They got married, and she moved back to the US with him."

"Have all of your family's generations lived in Utah?" Nash asked, taking a drink. He watched me intently, as if waiting to see if I would talk about my family. If I was going to come clean, this was the time to do it.

"No. My mother's family is from New York, well, on my grandfather's side. Obviously, grandma's family was from Italy. My grandfather on my dad's side lived in Boston. His father's father, my great-great-grandfather," I said, trying to count. "He was big in the railroad."

Nash nodded his head, seeming interested in the story I was about to tell.

"He did very well for himself in it, and when things were progressing West, he progressed with it. My great-great-grandmother wasn't interested in leaving Boston, though. She stayed behind and raised their two sons and three daughters."

"Did your great-great-grandfather ever return to Boston?"

"No," I answered. "He stayed in Colorado where his mistress was."

Nash raised his brows.

"Yeah. I know. Supposedly, his wife knew about this other woman, and she got to work on her payback. She started making her own investments and taught her sons and daughters the business world that she had learned from dear old great-great-great-grandaddy. The way my father tells the story, his great-great-grandmother was wealthier than her husband. Once he heard about it, he sent for her to meet him in Salt Lake City, where he had moved to after leaving the mistress in Colorado. Promised her a new life and chance to start over."

"Did she do it?"

Nodding, I took a sip of my beer. "Yes, she moved out West. The children all followed except for one daughter who had fallen in love and refused to leave her fiancé."

"So you still have family in the Boston area?"

"No, she got yellow fever soon after her marriage and died, so they didn't have any kids. Then the other sister died when the horse she was riding threw her off. One of the sons died after being attacked by a bear."

"Holy shit. Your family may have had good luck with business, but they sure as hell didn't have very good luck with fate, did they?"

"My great-grandfather was the only living child. He got married and had my grandfather along with a daughter."

"Is your grandfather still alive?"

Glancing down at my lap, I shook my head. "No. He died a few years back. He was a good man. Had a heart of gold and a good head on his shoulders. He was smart and grew the business his father had started to an even greater success. My father runs it now, with my sister at his side."

My eyes lifted and I met Nash's gaze. He was watching me, as if waiting for me to give him more. I lost all my nerve to tell him the truth. I didn't want this moment to end, and I knew the moment I told him, he would be angry I kept it from him.

"What about you? Is your family all from Texas?"

His mouth twitched and he tipped his beer back and drained it. "Yep. At least for the last few generations. Morgan's done the whole family tree thing, but I was never interested in it. I think we're pretty much mutts."

Laughing, I replied, "Aren't we all?"

"Pretty much. Let me finish putting this mount on the wall so we can hang up your TV."

My smile faded some as I watched Nash get back to working on the mount. Standing, I took a deep breath and spoke. "Nash, there's something I need to tell you."

His cell phone rang with the most obnoxious ringtone I'd ever heard at that very moment. *Is that a dog barking?*

"Blake, what's up?"

I covered my mouth to keep from laughing. Blake's ringtone was of a dog barking?

"Um, no, we finished eating and I was just putting together something for Kaelynn. Now? Is it something that can wait until tomorrow, dude? I mean, I'm at Kaelynn's and . . ."

Nash stopped talking, then smiled. It was so big and bright and full of hope. It made my chest pull with a tightness that had me longing to walk up and wrap my arms around him.

"You're kidding me? Tell me you're not fucking around with me."

I headed into the kitchen to start loading the dishes in the dishwasher.

"Give me fifteen to finish this, and then I'll meet you there."

He hung up his phone and looked my way. The look on his face said he was about to leave and he was as upset about that as I was.

"Kaelynn, I'm sorry to run out. Blake informed me Tucker had planned a surprise bachelor party for Jim."

My heart felt like it dropped to my stomach. "I completely understand. Please, don't worry about it."

He finished what he was doing, then hung up my TV. By the time he was done, I had gotten everything in the kitchen loaded up in the dishwasher and put away all of the leftovers and had cut him a piece of Black Forest cake to take with him. Nash stopped and stared down at it in the Tupperware container.

"You made this?" he asked, his eyes piercing mine.

With a small shrug, I replied, "Same little birdy told me it was your favorite dessert."

His entire body language changed as he put the cake down on the island. His eyes turned dark, and he stalked toward me, causing me to back up, only to be stopped by the counter. My breathing picked up and my body trembled with anticipation. Nash cupped my face in his hands and kissed me. It was the most intense kiss I'd ever experienced. I felt every bit of his passion and need for me. I wrapped my arms around his neck and whimpered slightly.

"Kaelynn," he whispered against my lips. "I don't want to leave."

I moaned, feeling his body against mine. I'd never in my life wanted a man like I wanted Nash. My body physically ached to be near him. To feel his skin against mine.

"You can . . . make it up . . . to me . . . tomorrow."

My words were heavy and spoken between kisses. Nash picked me up, and I wrapped my legs around him. He arched himself into me, allowing me to feel how much he wanted me too. I returned the favor by pulling him in closer with my legs, letting him know he was most definitely hitting me in all the right spots.

"Damn it, we need to slow down." he said, nipping at my lips, grinding his hard length between my thighs.

"Don't. Stop!"

I sounded desperate, and I was. He was winding me up so tight that if he walked away now I wasn't sure how I would make it until seeing him again.

"Fucking hell. Baby, what are you doing to me?"

"Nash, oh God. Oh . . ."

He pushed in harder, the friction of his jeans and hard dick was the perfect amount of pressure I needed. My fingers dug into his hair, gripping him and pulling his mouth to mine as my moans mixed with his. I came so hard and fast I swore I saw stars.

Both of us stilled when my body relaxed. I had never in my life let myself do that with a man. How desperate was I that I could orgasm from a man rubbing his hard-on over me. Dry-humping each other like we were teenagers.

I buried my face into his neck. "I'm so embarrassed."

He held me tighter. "Why? That was fucking hot as hell."

Smiling, I kept my face hidden. "That is not me . . . I mean . . . I don't know what you are doing to me."

Nash slowly set me down, his face bent down so that our eyes met.

"Did I not just utter the same words to you only moments ago?"

My lips pressed together before I whispered, "You did."

"I hope you know I wasn't planning on, well, I didn't think anything would happen between us. At least not tonight."

He smiled and my already weak legs wobbled. "Let me rephrase that for you. I wasn't planning on sleeping with you, but I sure as hell like hearing you come."

My entire face heated and I looked away. Nash placed his finger on my chin, drawing my gaze back to his.

"There is nothing wrong with being attracted to each other. I want you, Kaelynn, but I also want to get to know you before we take that step. Just so you know, I'm a pretty creative man, so I'm sure I can come up with ways to make you come without actually being inside of you."

I was positive my jaw had fallen to the ground.

"But what if I want you inside of me?"

The words came out before my brain could catch up. It was true; I wanted him. I wanted Nash's hands all over me. I wanted him to do things to me that no man had ever done before.

I wanted him.

And in order to have him, he needed the truth.

"Nash, I . . ."

His phone started ringing with Blake's ringtone again and we laughed.

"I've got to go. I'm sorry. I'll call you later?"

For a moment, my mind started to panic. Nash had to be worked up, and he was headed to a bachelor party. What if he met someone there? Based on his call with that permitting floozy the other day on our way to Houston, he was obviously okay with one-night stands.

He kissed me on the forehead. "Stop thinking what you're thinking."

"How did you know what I was thinking?"

"It's all over your face, Kaelynn. I have no interest in hooking up with anyone."

I glanced down to see he was still aroused. "But what about . . ."

Nash's mouth was on mine, kissing me until I felt dizzy. "I'm fine. I'll call you later."

Nodding, I replied, "Okay, don't forget your cake."

With a wink, he stepped away from me, causing me to miss his heat.

"I wouldn't dream of it. I plan on eating it before I walk into wherever this bachelor party is being held, and I'll think of you the entire time I'm licking my fingers clean. See ya, Kaelynn."

Pressing my lips together to keep from begging him to stay, I lifted my hand and forced out the words I didn't mean and certainly didn't want to say. "Have fun."

His dimples went on in full display. "I highly doubt anything will top the last few hours."

Warmth radiated over my body like someone had placed a warm blanket on me. I couldn't help but grin like a silly schoolgirl. I stood there and stared at the door after Nash had closed it. My fingertips went to my mouth and my other hand laid across my jumping stomach.

I'd never in my life met a man like Nash Barrett, and the thought of losing him scared me more than I wanted to admit.

Seventeen

NASH

MY MIND RACED as I stood on the balcony of the hotel. The bachelor party was going strong in the hotel room, and I was outside thinking of nothing but how fast I could see Kaelynn again.

The door opened and I turned to see Tucker walking out. He handed me a beer and stopped next to me.

"The party is inside."

With a chuckle, I replied, "Yeah, I know. I needed some air."

"Want to talk about it?"

I pressed the beer to my lips and took a long drink.

"Or not," Tucker added.

"I don't know what I'm doing, Tucker. I'm not the type of guy to play games. I need to just ask her what she's hiding."

He turned and leaned against the railing as he asked, "Then why don't you ask her?"

Shrugging, I looked at him. "Because I'm afraid to hear the truth. I'm afraid to think that I could be setting myself up to be in the same situation as I was before." I shook my head. "I like this girl. This feeling I have with her is completely different than anything I ever felt with Lily.

I thought I loved Lily, but I know now that wasn't love. All the shit I've been through feels like it was just a road I had to travel on to get to her. To Kaelynn. Like she is the gift at the end of a long damn journey."

I laughed and shook my head, continuing on with my word vomit. "Can you actually fall in love with someone so quickly? We've had two dates. Haven't slept together, and I think she's lying to me. What in the living hell?"

Tucker chuckled and put his hand on my shoulder. "The first time Charlie smiled at me, something inside of me went off. It was like my heart caught fire. Even all those years when I dated other women, Charlie was always there in the background. I couldn't commit to anyone because I was in love with her. I was in love with her that first day we met and she tripped over the curb and I caught her. I might not have known it then, but looking back, I sure know it now."

I turned and looked back out over Lake Austin.

"So what do I do? I don't want this game."

"Talk to her; ask her what she's hiding or let it go. See where this takes you. Jump off the cliff and free fall. Just do something, man."

My throat grew thick. "I think she was about to tell me everything tonight."

Tucker squeezed my shoulder. "Take it from me, it's not worth sneaking behind her back to find out the truth. If I learned anything with the mess Charlie and I got into, honesty has to be a two-way street. You can't justify what you're doing because you think she's doing something wrong. Talk to her."

"I will." Turning to face him, I nodded. "I'll talk to her tomorrow."

A look of relief crossed over Tucker's face. "Good. I'm glad. You won't regret it, and I know you're worried, but it's all going to be okay. It's probably something stupid like her father has a weird fetish or something."

My brow lifted. "A fetish? Like what?"

"You know, like having his back rubbed with peacock feathers or some weird shit like that."

We laughed and glanced back to the patio door. "Get your asses in here. We've got some planning to do. Jim just left."

"The bachelor left his own party?" Tucker asked.

Blake rolled his eyes. "Something to do with missing his future bride." Then he pretended to gag. "Now come on, this is the perfect time to plan our little surprise. Time to draw straws."

Tucker groaned.

Walking into the hotel room, I let out a sigh and said, "I better not get fucking picked. I always get shafted with this type of shit."

Everyone laughed as Blake walked around and held out the straws. When I drew mine, the entire room erupted in laughter. I had the shortest straw.

"Dude, this is going to be epic!" Blake said, trying not to laugh his ass off as I glared at him.

∽⁂∼

THE LAST THREE days felt like a blur. I hadn't seen Kaelynn, and it felt like every time I turned around, another problem at work happened.

"Nash, we have a problem."

My eyes closed and I counted to ten. "Rich, if you say those four words to me one more time, we really are going to have a problem."

The supervisor on the high-rise we were building in East Austin stood in front of my desk wearing a bleak smile.

"Sorry, boss, but we really do have problem. The city inspector put out an all-stop just now. Said we didn't have the right permit on file for the work lift with the city."

I stood, grabbed my cell phone and pulled up the office number. "That's bullshit. Is it Harrison?"

He frowned. "Yeah, what's the guy's beef with you?"

Walking past Rich, I pulled open a file cabinet. What Harrison didn't realize was I wasn't my father. I was organized both in the office and at job sites. A copy of every permit was at the ready. Finding what I needed, I pulled the file out and replied, "I slept with his daughter years ago, and he happened to stop by to visit her the morning I was walking out of her bedroom . . . naked."

"Ouch. Did you know it was his daughter?"

"Considering I'd met her at a New Year's Eve party he was throwing the night before, yeah, I knew."

"Damn, rebel back in the day."

I laughed as I put my hard hat on and started toward the city inspector. "Something like that." What I didn't go into was that Harrison and my father were the ones with the beef. I didn't make things better by sleeping with his daughter, though. Something my father has yet to let me forget.

Extending my hand, I flashed the man a wide smile. "Harrison, how is it going?"

"The city doesn't have on file the permit for the work lift; you'll need to shut down until you can get a copy . . ."

I opened the file and handed him the permit. "Here ya go. We don't need to shut anything down."

Harrison looked at the permit, frowned, then glanced back at me.

"Unlike my father, I keep the files organized at each location."

With his lip snarled, he sighed and handed me the file.

"I don't like you, Barrett."

"Really? I hadn't noticed."

This time he shot me a dirty look. "Don't play around with me, Barrett. I can make your life miserable if I really wanted to."

I sighed and glanced out over the worksite. "Listen, Harrison, I get that you're pissed at me and you don't like my father, but do you really want to do this? Last I heard, Laney was engaged and happy."

He glared at me. "Stay away from her."

Holding up my hands, I replied, "I haven't even spoken to her in years."

His anger grew. Fuck. That wasn't the right thing to say.

"Per her request!" I added. "She saw how angry you were, and we both decided it wasn't worth the stress for her if we dated."

Of course, that wasn't what happened. Both Laney and I wanted a one-night stand. Neither of us wanted anything else; that was made clear when we left the party together. Harrison didn't need to know that, though.

He seemed to relax a bit. "Good. I'm glad she came to her senses before it was too late."

"Sir, listen, we're going to be working together in the future I'm sure.

Can we not move past this now? This is the third job site you've tried to shut down on me without success. I don't know what went down with you and my father, but is this really how to be professional, grown men?"

He frowned and looked away. "Make sure you keep everything in order, Barrett."

And with that, the man walked away.

Rich sighed next to me. "I really don't like that guy."

I laughed. "Neither do I, Rich. Neither do I. Now, what other fires need to be put out?"

It didn't take me long to wish I hadn't asked. As we walked the building site, Rich gave me a list of problems. My head spun, and I had a headache coming on. I hadn't slept very well the last few nights. All I could think about was Kaelynn. Her smile. Her kiss. The way she moaned into my mouth and how easy she came for me that night. Totally clothed with just my cock pressed against her.

Fuck.

"What? Am I going too fast?" Rich asked.

"Come again?" I asked.

"You said fuck. Am I going too fast?"

Christ, I hadn't meant to say that out loud. "No, it's just been a long day, and I have a rehearsal dinner to go to tonight."

"Family? Friend?"

"One of my best friends from college. He's getting married tomorrow."

"Nice. Listen, I've got all this under control. I know you need to head to another site, just head on out. If anything pressing comes up, I'll let you know."

I nodded as I rubbed my neck. "Has my father called you?"

Rich frowned.

"I'll take that as a yes."

"He's not used to not running the show. I've worked for him almost as long as you, Nash. I get it. You're doing a good job, and he's going to see that. Just give it time."

"Time," I said letting my eyes roam up the tall building. "Why do I feel like I'm going to need more than that?"

Rich slapped my back. "Go on, I've got this. There's a reason you put me in charge. Now let me do my job."

"Right. I know you're right. I'm going to do what you said and take off."

"Good. I'll let you know if any major problems come up."

"Thanks, Rich. I appreciate it."

After saying goodbye to Rich, I headed back into the trailer, made a few phone calls, checked in with my father, and then headed home to shower and change for the rehearsal.

With my towel wrapped around my waist, I headed into my kitchen and stopped when I saw Blake sitting on my sofa, a hot dog shoved in his mouth, and my TV remote in one hand.

With a grunt, I walked past him. "Remind me why I gave you a key to my place?"

"In case of an emergency. This was an emergency. My brother came back from vacation early, so I gave him Kaelynn's information and he started the background check now. The file is on the island with all the information he had on Kaelynn so far."

I stopped and stared at the file. "Wait, you went ahead and had him start the background check?"

My chest felt like someone was sitting on it; I was having a hard time breathing.

"Yeah, I thought that was what you wanted."

My feet were frozen on the spot as I stared down at the file. I swallowed hard.

"Nash? Nash, he's not going to find out anything bad. If anything, it will be what we suspected. She's from money. And how bad could it be? I mean, Lily was filthy rich. I doubt Kaelynn is anything close to that."

I nodded, still staring at the file. Using my finger, I dragged it toward me and opened it.

There was a picture of Kaelynn. Her full name. Her approximate age and where she was from.

"How did you get her full name?" I asked, looking up at him.

"I remembered hearing her tell Charlie at the comedy club that night. She mentioned her middle name and that she was from outside Salt Lake City. Not sure exactly where, but Dustin will be able to track it down."

"This doesn't feel right. None of it is beginning to matter to me. Not after spending the week with Kaelynn."

Blake shrugged. "It's up to you."

"Yeah, let's just call it off."

"I'll give him a call later and let him know. Meanwhile, if you don't get dressed soon, we're going to be late."

"We? I was picking Kaelynn up, and she was joining us for dinner after the rehearsal. You okay hanging with us?"

"I can be a third wheel. I have no issues with that."

"Of course you don't."

Eighteen

NASH

STANDING AT THE end of the aisle, we watched as Terri and her father practiced walking down the aisle.

"Now, the flower girl will be walking ahead of you, tossing down the petals. Dad, your goal is to keep her walking. You'd be surprised how many brides freeze."

Terri smiled and looked at Jim. "I've waited too long for this moment; he'll be keeping me from running toward Jim."

Everyone laughed.

Standing up at the altar was Jim, me, Blake, and then Tucker.

"You nervous?" I asked Jim.

"Not at all. I can't wait."

I glanced to the back of the church to see Kaelynn. She was walking back and forth across the last aisle with Hannah in her arms. Charlie was matron of honor and was more than happy to let Kaelynn take care of Hannah. It had seemed a bit strange to look over at the other bridesmaids and not see Lily. Terri had told Charlie she had asked Lily and she stated she would be out of town during the wedding. Not sure if that was the truth, but I had to give Terri props for even asking.

Blake poked my back. "Dude, we need to talk. *Now*."

I glanced back at him. "Um, we're all kind of in the middle of some-thing here Blake."

"Yeah, well, this is important," he whispered.

"Can it wait fifteen minutes?"

Blake sighed and then started to text someone on his phone. Terri got to the end of the aisle, and the wedding coordinator started talking again.

"Okay, Dad gives you away. Jim you're going to step here."

She went through the whole process of the wedding. Blake poked me again, this time harder.

"We *need* to talk."

I ignored him.

"Seems simple enough," Jim said as I turned and looked back at Blake.

"What is going on with you two?" Tucker asked in a harsh tone. "Y'all are being rude!"

"Tell that to him!" I stated, pointing to Blake.

"Then we walk down the aisle and each groomsmen and bridesmaid follows. Do you want to practice that?"

"No, we've all been enough weddings to know how it goes. Let's not put them through that torture," Terri said with a laugh.

Blake grabbed my arm when we had been given the all-clear and dragged me away from everyone. Tucker followed.

"What in the hell is wrong with you? I know the plan; we don't have to go over it again," I said, annoyed.

"Nash, this isn't about our little surprise for Jim. It's about Kaelynn."

"Kaelynn?" Tucker asked, looking between the two of us. "Jesus, Nash, tell me you didn't go forward with the background check."

"No. I mean, Blake gave everything to his brother Dustin, but I told him to call it off. You did call him, right?"

Blake rubbed the back of his neck and looked like he was having a hard time trying to tell me something.

"You texted him, Blake. Right?"

"I did. I sent him a text and said you wanted to put a stop on the background check. Before we started the practice run, he texted me back. He said he had already started and can stop, but he found something out that you need to know."

My heart stated to beat faster in my chest, and I looked at Tucker, then back to Blake. Did I want to know? Was it going to matter? I glanced back to Tucker who shrugged then bounced my gaze back to Blake and swallowed hard. Fear started to overtake me. "What did he find out?"

"Dotson is not Kaelynn's last name. At least, he's almost a hundred percent sure it's not. He cannot find a record of any Kaelynn Shae Dotson in Utah. He hadn't started digging deeper, though. He can stop, or he can keep going."

"Well, are we sure she was born in Utah?" Tucker asked.

I nodded as I searched for Kaelynn. She was standing next to Charlie, who had taken Hannah back and was putting her into her stroller. She must have felt me staring at her because she looked up. Our eyes met and she smiled. I made myself smile in return before I replied to Tucker.

"I'm a hundred percent positive she was born there. At least she told me she was."

"Okay, so maybe Dustin missed something. For all we know, Kaelynn could be adopted and that's why she is so scarce about her family."

"That's true; I didn't think about that," Blake said. "So, what do you want me to tell him?"

The warm feeling in my chest as I stared at Kaelynn gave me the answer. "Tell him to stop," Tucker said.

Kaelynn glanced down at her phone and sent off a text, then looked back up to me. The way she looked at me made everything clearer. I was in love with her, and I was going to jump. Feet first and see where in the hell this took me. I could see the flush of her cheeks from across the church.

"Nash. Nash, please, don't do this. Talk to her. Give her the chance to tell you. She might not be hiding anything at all. Nash, are you even listening to me?"

Tucker's voice pulled me from the trance Kaelynn had over me. Turning, I faced Blake and pushed out a deep breath before I said, "Tell him to stop."

With a sigh of relief, Tucker placed his hand on my shoulder. "That's the right thing to do, dude."

Blake stared at me in disbelief. "Man, are you sure?"

I swallowed hard, and I knew Blake saw it in my eyes. I wasn't sure, not a hundred percent. But I needed to give Kaelynn the chance to tell me herself before I found something that would change everything.

"I'm sure."

Turning, I made my way to the back of the church and to Kaelynn. Her head tilted as she regarded me carefully.

"Hey, are you okay?" she asked, lifting up on her toes to kiss me.

"I am now," I replied, pulling her to me and holding her. "Let's get to the rehearsal dinner so we can leave early and spend some time together."

She grinned. "I like the sound of that."

Dinner was at the Barton Creek Country Club, where the reception would be after the wedding. Terri's father was part owner of the club and had reserved an entire room for the small group of us. Terri and Jim had wanted to keep it on the lighter side, so only family and those in the wedding were at the dinner tonight. Kaelynn had come as my guest and sat next to me, talking to Terri's cousin, who was in the Marines. I was trying like hell not to think about what Blake had told me about Kaelynn. My mind went everywhere, though.

Why in the hell would she not use her real last name?

"So, Nash, Jim tells me you own a construction company and you are in architecture. How wonderful. Do you design custom homes as well?"

The woman sitting across from me was Jim's aunt, Dorothy. I forced a smile as I answered her.

"We do. I actually designed and built Tucker's home. His wife, Charlie, helped a lot with the design process, though. I've designed a few more homes, as well. I'm really just getting started on the design side of things."

Dorothy raised a brow. "How exciting. Do you only build homes?"

"No, we're actually working on a new apartment-and-retail complex going in on the east side of downtown Austin. It's our company's largest project right now. We have a few smaller ones going on, as well. A house and another buildout of a salon in south Austin, to name a few."

"How exciting!" she gasped. "My husband likes to build things. Model trains and airplanes. Things of the sorts."

Blake snickered next to me, and I hit him with my knee under the table.

"That's great. My job is a bit different, but exactly the same concept."
She smiled.

The night seemed to drag on. Charlie had whisked Kaelynn away from me every chance she had to introduce her to someone else. When she finally made her way back to me, she wore a sexy grin on her face.

"I'm ready to leave."

"Are you now?" I asked, my brow arched. "And why the rush?"

"I haven't seen you all week. It would be nice to just be alone for a bit."

My body ached for her. I pushed the nagging voice in the back of my head away as I took her hand in mine. "Then let's leave."

"Don't we need to let Terri and Jim know?" she asked.

"Nope."

Before we got to the door, we were stopped.

"Oh. No. You are not taking her away."

Terri stood in front of us, her arms crossed over her chest. "Tonight is my bachelorette party."

"The night before your wedding?" I asked, shocked.

"Yes. I invited everyone to stay here. We're going to be pampered this evening and tomorrow morning. Kaelynn, I really would love for you to stay."

I couldn't help but see the excitement on Kaelynn's face. Then she looked at me, and her smile faded. "Oh, um, gosh thank you so much, and I would have loved that. I don't have anything to wear for tonight and my dress is at my house."

Terri laughed. "Nope. I had Morgan go to your house and get your stuff. She said she knew the dress you were wearing to the wedding, and she got it all for you. She'll be here tonight too. Please, Kaelynn? I would really love for you to stay. Please!"

Glancing back my way, I winked. "You should stay. Have fun, and with Morgan being here, you'll have even more fun."

Kaelynn looked between Terri and me. "Well, it does sound like fun."

"Then you're staying!" Terri cried out!

"I'm staying!" Kaelynn echoed.

"I've already had my father book you a room, so you don't have to worry about that. We'll all be staying on the top floor here at the country club's Omni hotel. We're going to have so much fun."

Charlie walked up to us and wrapped her arm around Kaelynn. "Okay, say goodbye to Nash. It's girls' night!"

"Wait! Wait, let me just have a minute with him," Kaelynn said.

Charlie frowned, but then smiled. "Two minutes is all you get. I had to say goodbye to my precious baby girl, and I need something to drink to keep my mind off the fact I won't see her for a few hours. I need this bachelorette thing to kick the hell off so I can sneak out and go to our room and be with Hannah and Tucker."

Kaelynn giggled while I laughed. She walked up to me. "I'm sorry. It's like fate is trying to keep us away from one another."

Tucking a stray curl behind her ear, I leaned down and kissed her lightly on the lips. "Tomorrow after this wedding, you're mine and I'm taking you away and spending time with you."

"All yours," she said, lifting up on her toes and kissing me. "Text me later?"

"I will."

Taking a step back, Kaelynn reached for my hand and worried her lip. "Nash, there's something I need to talk to you about, though. It's nothing bad. After the wedding tomorrow, I'd like to find somewhere private to talk. It's important to me."

I could hear my own heartbeat in my ears. Tomorrow I would finally know what secret Kaelynn kept from me. The only problem was, I wasn't sure I wanted to know anymore.

Nineteen

KAELYNN

SITTING ON THE large sofa in the Palmer suite of the Omni, I reached for a strawberry and popped it into my mouth. The country club my parents belonged to had a hotel on property as well, but this hotel was amazing. I would have never known Terri came from such a wealthy family. Really, none of Nash's friends were anything like the friends I had growing up. They were all rich snobs who would never think of working for nonprofits, becoming a vet, or spending their holidays helping the less fortunate. Of course, I was blessed with a few friends who were not spoiled brats.

"I want to sneak down and make sure everything is set up for the reception," Terri stated, dropping down on the sofa and grabbing a handful of popcorn.

"No, I'll go check. I'm the maid of honor," Charlie said, standing and pointing to me. She had already gone and spent some time with Hannah before she came back to the party. Charlie reached for my hand and said, "Come on, Kaelynn. Let's go."

My mouth fell open as I stared at what I was wearing. Morgan thought she would be cute and bring my moose PJs and matching moose slippers.

"But I'm in my pajamas and more than slightly buzzed," I said.

Morgan laughed next to me, which made Terri start laughing, then Charlie. The rest of Terri's friends were gathered around the fire pit outside. It was obvious who Terri's dearest friends were.

"I'm in my PJs too," Charlie stated.

"Let's all go down like this!" Terri shouted as she jumped. "My father owns the place. What are they going to say? Leave?"

Another round of giggles echoed in the room.

"Fine, I'll go," I mumbled as I stood.

Terri clapped her hands and ran out to the patio to let the rest of the girls know we were going to the pavilion to make sure everything was set up. I figured at least a few of them would go, but they all declined.

"Snobs," Charlie whispered as I covered my mouth to hide the giggle. "Most of them are daughters of Terri's father's business partners."

Morgan chuckled and said, "That was a mouthful."

Terri came walking back in. She shrugged her shoulders and said, "They're buzzkills. Let's go."

As we headed down the hall, Charlie hooked her arm with mine. "So. How are things going with you and Nash?"

I smiled. "I think good. This past week we've not seen each other much at all. I've never met anyone like him. He has such a kind heart and the way he loves each of you. There isn't anything he wouldn't do for his friends."

"He is a pretty neat guy," Charlie agreed.

"Neat?" I asked, giggling. The wine had certainly gone to my head, and I could feel it the more I moved about.

"Yes, neat. He's always been there for Tucker, even me, when I didn't give him much reason to be."

I glanced over my shoulder to see Terri and Morgan huddled up talking. They were a few steps behind us. Even though Morgan hadn't really hung out with Nash's friends, Jim was like family to Nash's family. I thought it was so sweet for Terri to invite Morgan and me to celebrate with her.

"Charlie, may I ask you something?"

"Of course."

We made it out of the hotel and down a sidewalk that led to the other side of the hotel that housed all of the venues.

"Do you think it would make a difference to Nash if I was rich or poor?"

She stopped walking and looked at me. "What do you mean? He doesn't care about money. Not at all."

I chewed on my lip nervously. "What I mean is, I know Lily grew up very privileged, and she left Nash for a man who was equally privileged. Nash realizes that not all women who come from money are like Lily?"

Charlie laughed. "Of course he does. I mean, he has known Terri and me since college, and we are both from wealthy families."

"Yes, but neither one of you ever made him feel less of himself like Lily did."

With a frown, Charlie stayed silent for a moment. "Lily was, *is,* one of my best friends. I don't agree with what she did to Nash. It took me awhile myself to forgive her for the pain she caused him. But I don't think she was ever really in love with Nash. If she truly had been, she would have never insisted on hiding their relationship. And truth be told, if Nash had been truly in love with her like he thought he had been, he wouldn't have gone along with it. I don't think she meant to make him feel the way he did. Yes, she picked another man, and that man happened to have money and was someone her father wanted her to be with. Now, I'm not making excuses for her, but I think it all played out for a reason. Her father was pressuring her. She wanted someone different because Nash was her first, and she was stupid."

My gut twisted. Nash was Lily's first? That knowledge filled me with a jealousy I didn't know how to make sense of.

"What do you mean she wanted something different?"

Charlie glanced around and leaned in closer. "Kinky. Mark, I guess, is into some pretty crazy sex. Lily was curious, her father was pushing this guy on her, and one night at a party she drank too much and he became something she wanted to try. So, if a woman is truly in love with a man, would another man turn her head?"

"No," I answered.

"No. She simply didn't want to let Nash go. He was a safety net for her, and the reason she still holds out hope of getting back with him."

I stopped walking. "What? She wants to get back with him?"

Fear replaced the jealousy. Would Nash ever consider taking Lily back?

"Don't even go there with your thoughts, Kaelynn. Lily has begged Nash to take her back more than once. He isn't interested. What he is interested in is you, my friend. You should see the way he looks at you. It makes even my tummy drop."

Smiling, I pressed my lips together to keep the girlish squeal inside.

"I will tell you, I never saw Nash look at Lily like he looks at you."

We stopped outside the door to the pavilion. Drawing my brows in tight, I replied, "We have only been on a few dates. I mean, we've spent some time together and we talk for hours on the phone, but I don't think Nash is . . . I don't think he is thinking about things that way."

"Oh, trust me, that boy is head over heels in love with you, Kaelynn."

Tears built in my eyes. Charlie grabbed my hands and squeezed them. "Talk to me, Kaelynn. What's really going on? Am I misreading your feelings for Nash?"

I shook my head. "No, not at all. I didn't think it was possible to fall in love with someone so quickly, but I know I've fallen for him hard. I've also kept something from him. Something that may make him change his mind about me."

Charlie's mouth opened. "Are you with another man?"

"What?" I asked, my eyes widened. "God, no! No, I would never ever do that to Nash. Ever. It's nothing like that."

Relief crossed over Charlie's face. "Whew. Then whatever it is, I'm sure if you just talk to him it will all work out fine."

I nodded. "Yes, you're right."

Terri skipped by us, pulling Morgan behind her as she sang, "I'm getting married tomorrow! I'm getting married tomorrow."

Charlie soon followed after them as I stood there, frozen in place.

Nash. In love with me?

A chill ran through my body, causing it to shiver as I wrapped my arms around myself. The idea of being loved by such an amazing man made my body fill with pure happiness.

The sounds of women gasping had me snapping out of my moment of daydreaming. I glanced over and saw the three of them all standing in the entrance. I could see inside the pavilion now that Terri had turned on all the lights. It was stunning. Nearly everything was white. The only color in the room was the greenery on the tables and the silver chairs.

"It's beautiful," I whispered as I walked up next to the three other women.

Terri broke down and started crying. "It's . . . It's . . . I . . . It's . . ."

"Stunning," Charlie finished her thought as she walked into the room. "Terri, this is so you. Simple, yet elegant."

Morgan walked into the room and spun around in a few circles, then turned to Terri. "Okay, I wanted to get married on a beach, but this is stunning."

I placed my arm around Terri and gave her a hug. "You did beautifully. Terri, this is simply breathtaking. I don't think I've ever seen such a beautiful reception room set up like this before."

She wiped her tears away and made her way over to the tables. She picked up the white snowflake place card and covered her mouth. "Daddy. Oh, my goodness. He wanted to take care of the placeholders and surprise me."

"A snowflake?" I asked.

"Since I was little, I said I wanted to get married in December with snowflakes all around."

Glancing around, I covered my mouth and tried not to cry. "Terri, look!" I whispered, pointing up.

White and blue glass snowflakes hung down from the massive ceiling, catching the flicker of the faux candles that hung from the rafters.

Terri started to cry again, this time dropping down to the floor and burying her face in her hands.

"Thank goodness she came tonight. Do you know how pissed she would have been ruining her makeup?" Charlie said, dropping down next to her best friend.

"Do you like them?" Charlie asked.

"Like them?" Terri repeated, sniffling loudly. "I love them."

"Good! It was my idea!" Charlie said, beaming with pride. I couldn't help but laugh. Morgan also let out a chuckle as everyone sat on the floor surrounding Terri. Even though I hadn't known Charlie and Terri for very long, it felt like we had been friends forever.

"Are you nervous at all?" Morgan asked.

Terri smiled and you could see how much her eyes sparkled. "Not one bit. Jim and I have been together for so long; I knew he was the one I was going to marry almost immediately. I knew it the first time he kissed me."

My own lips tingled at the memory of the first time Nash had kissed me. Morgan smiled. "Do you think he's nervous?"

With a shrug, Terri replied, "I honestly don't know. Tomorrow I'll probably be nervous. Right now, I just want to be his wife and it's all I'm thinking about. Tomorrow it will really sink in that it's happening. It just feels like . . ." her eyes lifted and she let them roam the entire room, floor to ceiling, " . . . a dream."

Morgan and I glanced at one another. There was something in my best friend's eyes. Something that said she wanted this, but was there someone I didn't know about? Surely not. Of course, I hadn't been very open with her about my feelings about Nash. But that was her brother. It was different.

Pulling her knees to her chest, Morgan let her smile widen into a full grin. "I want this too . . . I can't wait to have it someday."

"On a beach?" Charlie asked with a wink.

Morgan shook her head and then looked up and said, "No. I'm going to need a Disney princess-type wedding."

Charlie's face exploded into a full-on grin. "That would be a wedding I would be down for planning."

❧

THE NEXT MORNING Terri had indeed woken up one very nervous bride. Morgan and I had worked on keeping Terri's mind occupied while we got our hair and nails done. Charlie had joined us after Hannah's morning feeding. It didn't take her long to calm Terri down. Watching the two of them together reminded me of Morgan and myself. There was no doubt they were more than best friends. They were sisters.

Morgan stepped out onto the patio and walked up next to me. "Okay, so do you want to talk about it?"

Feeling my stomach twist with anxiety, I faced her.

"Is it that obvious?" I asked.

"No, because I have no idea why your mind is so far away. What are you thinking about, Kaelynn?"

Tears filled my eyes. It was in that moment I realized I should know telling Morgan the truth months ago would not have changed anything about our friendship.

With a shaking breath, I spoke. "Morgan, I haven't been honest with you."

Her smile faded some. "Okay, about what?" I rubbed my lips together frantically. Grabbing my hands, Morgan squeezed them. "Kaelynn, tell me."

My chin quivered. "Well, you see." I sniffed and her face turned from confused to worried. "My family . . . the thing is, my parents are wealthy. Very wealthy."

Her brow furrowed. "Okay?"

"I didn't tell you because I didn't want you to see me for my money and not for me."

Now an expression of hurt washed over her face. "You thought I would only like you because you were rich?"

I shrugged. "It was just easier to not tell you. Then time went on and it felt like it didn't matter."

"So why didn't you say something? Does Nash know?"

Chewing on my lower lip, I felt a tear slip from my eye.

"Kaelynn, no," she whispered. "Exactly how rich is your family?"

Swallowing hard, I looked out over the balcony. "I'm an heiress to a multibillion-dollar fortune. I use my mother's maiden name as my last name, but it is actually Whitaker."

Morgan gasped and her hands flew up to her mouth. "I told you about Lily. I told you what she did to my brother. How could you keep this from him? Me, I don't give two shits if you are rich or poor, and I know Nash doesn't either, but you should have told him before he fell in love with you."

My eyes widened in shock. That was Charlie and now Morgan saying Nash was in love with me.

"I tried to tell him at dinner the other night and he had to rush out. I tried telling him last night and we got interrupted. I told him I needed to talk to him after the wedding today. I'm going to tell him then."

Morgan shook her head and turned away from me. "Morgan, please. I fell so fast for him, and it scared me. If I told him the truth, I was afraid he would walk away."

She spun back around. "Then you don't really know my brother."

"He told me himself he didn't want to be put back in that situation. I would give up every last penny if it meant not losing him."

Morgan stilled, then met my gaze. She smiled. "Do you mean that?"

"Yes! You know me, Morgan."

"I didn't know the real you."

Closing my eyes, I whispered, "I'm so sorry."

She took my hands in hers, causing me to open my eyes and face her. "Tell him today, or I tell him."

I nodded. "I am. I swear I am.

"Kaelynn, I'll always be your friend, but he's my brother and I love him with every ounce of my being. No matter what happens, though, I'm here for you."

Throwing myself into her arms, I started to cry.

"It has to work," I sobbed. "I pray he will forgive me."

Morgan held me closer and whispered, "He will because he loves you."

~§~

"THE WEDDING WAS so beautiful," I said as Nash placed his hand on my lower back and guided us into the reception room.

"It was indeed. There were a few times I had to hold back my own tears."

"I saw that."

Nash looked down at me and winked. My insides heated at once, and I had to force myself not to ask him to take me home and make love to me.

As we walked around the reception I smiled at a few people who said hello to us. Some Nash stopped and introduced me to, some he simply nodded and replied hello back.

I needed to sneak off with Nash at some point and come clean with everything. He deserved to know the whole truth and why I had kept it from him. After coming clean with Morgan, it felt as if a small sense of guilt lifted, but not all. My fear that the truth would push Nash away was stupid. I would apologize to him for behaving like a child and not trusting him. Morgan had been upset with me, but the way she told me she would be by my side made me realize what a complete fool I had been. The fear of people only liking me for my money was something I needed to learn to let go of, it had dictated my social interactions for longer than I could remember. By telling Morgan the truth, it was the first step. I was ready to be with Nash in the most intimate of ways, and I couldn't do that knowing I held a secret between us.

The woman standing before me that I had been talking to was Beth, Terri's aunt. Once Nash had introduced us and he saw Aunt Beth was going to talk my ear off, he excused himself.

"Kaelynn, what a beautiful name. My daughter is expecting her first child in a few months, I'll have to have her add that name to her list."

Taking a sip of my wine, I replied, "It was my great-grandmother's name on my mother's side. I was named after her."

"How sweet to keep that name alive," Beth stated.

I nodded and glanced over to where Nash stood. Blake had walked up to him and had handed him a small envelope. Nash had seemed agitated by whatever it was Blake had given him. He tucked it into his jacket pocket, then looked to be saying something heated to Blake. Raising his hands in self-defense, Blake pointed to the area of Nash's jacket where he had slipped the envelope, then turned and walked to the bar. I frowned as I wondered what in the world that was all about.

"Don't you agree, darling?"

Beth's voice caused me to jump. I had been spying so intently on Nash, I hadn't been paying attention to my conversation with Aunt Beth.

"I'm sorry, what was that?"

"Terri's dress. Don't you agree it was beautiful?"

Smiling, I replied, "Yes, it was very stunning. She looked like a princess."

Beth beamed. "I own the bridal shop where she bought it."

"Really?" I replied as I took another sip of wine.

"Will you be in the need for a wedding dress in the near future?"

"No, I won't. At least, not anytime soon."

Aunt Beth jutted her lower lip. "No one interested in dating you?"

"What? No, that's not it," I said with a chuckle. Her bluntness caught me off guard.

"I have a friend of mine who has a son. He's single and a doctor. I'm sure she wouldn't mind setting you up on a blind date."

"I have a boyfriend," I stated. My eyes scanned for Nash. Where had he gone?

"Oh? Is he here?"

"Yes!" I said too quickly. "Nash Barrett. He was the best man."

Beth's eyes widened in delight. "That is wonderful! He is such a handsome young man, is he not?"

I returned the smile she was giving me. "Very handsome."

"Well, I hope he keeps you happy in bed."

My head jerked back to look at Beth. "Excuse me?"

"I used to be a sex therapist, and trust me when I say, if there is no happiness between the sheets, he's gonna go and cheat."

She nodded as I stared at her in utter disbelief. If my jaw wasn't on the floor I was going to pat myself on the back.

"It's true," Beth stated matter-of-factly.

"Well, we, um, just started dating so . . ."

"Mmm, no sex yet. You're still in the go-no-go zone?"

"Go . . . no . . . go . . . zone?" I asked in confusion.

The DJ tapped the mic and asked for everyone's attention. I silently said a prayer to God that he got me out of that conversation and quickly.

I turned my attention over to the dance floor. Nash brought out a chair and had Terri sit on it as Tucker tied a blindfold onto Jim. With a confused smile, I made my way over to Charlie after I excused myself from Aunt Beth.

"What's going on?" I asked.

Charlie covered her mouth, trying not to laugh.

"Just watch!" she said, laughing some more.

The moment the blindfold was on Jim, Terri jumped out of the chair and Nash sat down. He started to pull up his pant leg as far up his thigh as he could while the DJ put his finger to his mouth to keep everyone from laughing. Nash slipped on a stocking and then the garter belt.

"The rules are, you have to use your teeth to get your bride's garter belt off, while blindfolded. No hands are allowed."

"Oh no," I said, covering my mouth to keep from laughing. Terri stood behind Nash, her hand concealing her own laughter.

"Please tell me someone is filming them professionally because I'm going to need a copy of this," Morgan said, coming to stand next to me and Charlie.

"Oh, there are at least three professional photographers here. One taking pictures, two filming."

Morgan dug out her cell phone and started to video. "This is the best day of my life."

"Okay, remember, Jim, no hands. Teeth only."

Lifting up both thumbs, Jim shouted, "Got it!"

Everyone laughed. Then the DJ stated to play a sexy tune and the crowd lost it in laughter. Nash shook his head and pointed to Tucker and Blake. They were both laughing their asses off.

"How did Nash get to be the lucky one?" I asked Charlie.

She looked at me and said, "He drew the short straw. He always draws the short straw! They tried to get Terri's dad to do it, and it was a hard pass for him."

The crowd went into a full-on laugh as we watched Jim start dancing sexy as he was guided to the chair. He stuck his hands out so Terri put her hands out in front of Nash so Jim wouldn't know.

"No hands!" the DJ called out. I had to hand it to Nash; he kept his laughter in as his best friend dropped down and started to use his mouth to try and find what he thought was Terri's leg. When he nuzzled his face against Nash's leg, I thought Nash was going to fly out of the seat. He closed his eyes and cringed while the rest of us laughed and encouraged Jim on.

He reached his hands out and touched Nash's leg, making everyone cry out in laughter.

"Dude! Do we need to tie your hands?" the DJ called out.

"No! No, I've got this," Jim shouted

My eyes widened as Jim kissed up Nash's leg until he found the garter. Terri had tears streaming down her face she was laughing so hard. She ran her fingers through Jim's hair and Nash glared up at her.

Jim grabbed the garter between his teeth and gave it a shake in his mouth, causing Nash to cover his mouth to keep from laughing. Blake was bent over, gasping for air as Tucker wiped tears off his face.

"This is the best shit ever!" Morgan exclaimed.

Jim pulled the garter belt off and everyone cheered. Then he walked up to Nash, thinking it was Terri, and started to hip thrust in Nash's face.

The guests went crazy with laughter as Nash pushed him away.

Tucker rushed over and untied the blindfold.

Jim looked shocked at the sight of Nash and jumped back, busting into laughter.

"You motherfuckers!" he cried out as Nash pulled the stocking off and let Jim engulf him in a brotherly hug. Then Jim pulled Terri into his arms and kissed her.

Everyone cheered and laughed, but all I could do was watch Nash. He laughed as he sat down on the chair and put his sock and shoe back on. My heart sped up and my lower stomach ached with desire. It was more than just a desire to make love to him, though. I wanted to spend every moment with him. Learn everything that made him happy, sad, angry. I wanted to know him like his friends knew him, but better. I wanted to be the person he went to when he had a bad day or a good day.

I wanted him in my life forever.

This man who loved with his entire being. Who did crazy things for his friends and who took a woman he hardly knew on a road trip to Houston simply because his sister asked him to.

Nash Barrett was unlike any man I had ever known.

And I was head over heels in love with him.

Twenty

NASH

AFTER GETTING MY sock and shoe back on, I stood and let everyone give me a pat on the back for taking one for the team. I had to admit, when Tucker came up with the crazy idea of pranking Jim at his wedding, I was down for the idea. When I drew the short straw I had been pissed, but everything turned out great, and it would be a memory we would all remember and a video that would last a lifetime.

Turning, I looked for Kaelynn. I could feel her eyes on me, crazy as that sounded. When I found her, it was hard not to notice the way she looked at me—like she wanted to rip my clothes off and take me right here in front of everyone. I raised a brow and she licked her lips.

"Shit," I whispered, feeling my cock harden.

I smiled and talked to people as I made my way over to Kaelynn, who stood next to Charlie and Morgan. As I approached them, Morgan hugged me and said, "I'm totally posting this everywhere and tagging you."

Rolling my eyes, I laughed. "I'm sure Blake's already beat you."

Morgan's brows drew in, and she glared over at Blake. "Damn it. If he posted it first, I'm going to be pissed! His sister gets first right of humiliation!"

She took off as fast as she could toward Blake.

"Great job, Nash. I thought for a second he was going to grind on you," Charlie said, trying not to laugh.

"You thought? He did! I was trying like hell to get away from his dick near my junk!"

Charlie lost it laughing. Taking Kaelynn gently by the arm, I guided her away from everyone. She looked a bit dazed.

"Are you okay?" I asked.

"Yes. Just feeling . . . um . . . something."

"Something?" I asked.

Her eyes fell to my mouth then back up to meet my gaze. "Yes. You wouldn't happen to have a room at the hotel here, would you?"

My heart slammed against my chest. "Why?"

Her cheeks turned the most beautiful shade of pink as she peered down at her fingers. "I don't want to wait another second, Nash. I want to feel your body against mine, and we need to talk."

I tried like hell not to let my knees buckle out from under me. "You should probably tell me if you have some weird fetish about me dressing up in women's stockings."

Kaelynn's eyes grew wide with shock. When I winked, she relaxed and started to laugh.

"No fetish. I simply realized I don't want to waste another moment."

I took her hand in mine and led her out of the pavilion. No one seemed to notice, or they didn't care we were leaving.

Fifteen minutes later, Kaelynn and I walked into a hotel room. The moment the door shut, my mouth was on hers. Kaelynn's hands pulled at my jacket as I reached behind to unzip her gown. Tossing my jacket to the floor, I unbuttoned the dress shirt while Kaelynn slipped her shoes off and went for my buckle.

"Nash," she whispered as I pushed the dress off her shoulders and watched it pool around her feet on the floor. "I have to talk to you."

I shook my head. "It doesn't matter. Whatever you're going to say, it doesn't matter."

Her eyes searched my face. "But . . ."

Pressing my lips to hers, I moved my hand over her body. Kaelynn's tense body relaxed.

"I want you, Kaelynn."

She moaned and said, "Please tell me you have a condom."

Smiling, I pulled three out of my wallet and tossed them onto the bed as I kicked off my dress shoes.

Kaelynn's breathing picked up as her eyes roamed over my body. She stood there, dressed in a white lace push-up bra and matching white lace panties and watched me undress for her.

"Are you sure?" I asked, tracing my finger around the lace of her bra. Her body turned pink as goosebumps trickled over her body.

"Yes," she breathed heavily. "I've never wanted any man like I want you."

With a smirk, I replied, "Good."

I dropped to my knees and placed a kiss over her navel. Kaelynn moaned softly. With the lightest of touches, I ran my tongue along her panty line, then slowly pulled them off her. Kaelynn's hands intertwined in my hair and she tugged gently. I couldn't help but smile at how perfect she was. A small patch of brown curls barely hid the treasure I was about to claim as mine. Using my finger, I went from the bottom of her belly button to the top of the curls, then stopped.

"Yes, Nash."

Her voice was deep and full of need. Softly running my thumb over her sensitive bud, I glanced up to see her watching me. Her one hand still in my hair, the other stroking the base of her neck.

"Tell me what you want, Kaelynn."

"Kiss me," she panted.

Smiling, I asked, "Where?"

Her entire body turned red as she tugged my head closer to where she wanted my mouth.

"Say it."

Shaking her head, her teeth sank into her lip. "I can't."

Moving in closer, I licked through the curls, flicking her clit. She gasped.

"Nash. I've never . . ."

I stopped and looked up at her. My heart already pounded in my chest, now it beat so loud I could hardly think. "You've never what?"

Kaelynn swallowed hard. "Oral sex. I've never done this with anyone."

"Are you saying you're a virgin?" I asked, a part of me hoping like hell she would say yes.

She shook her head. "No . . . no . . . I've just never let a man do this before. It never felt right with anyone."

A wide grin spread over my face, almost coming myself at the challenge that I was most assuredly up for. "Good. I'll be your first . . . and your last."

The way her eyes turned dark and hungry had me nearly losing my self-control. Lifting her leg, I placed it over my shoulder and kept my gaze locked on hers as I licked her again. Long and slow.

Kaelynn grasped at the table that was next to her. "Shit," she gasped out.

"I'm just getting started, baby. Pace yourself."

Moving my tongue softly and slowly, I watched as Kaelynn came. When her legs started to give out, I stood and picked her up, carrying her over to the bed.

Her entire body glowed as I grabbed the condom and put it next to her on the bed. I wasn't done exploring her. I needed to know what she liked, all the ways I could make her come simply by touching or licking her.

Cupping one breast, I sucked her hardened, dark nipple, while pinching and pulling the other one between my thumb and finger. Kaelynn arched her body and grabbed my ass, pulling me closer to her. Her legs spread and she moaned when I let my dick rub against her opening.

"I can't . . . think," she mumbled.

I moved my attention to her other nipple as my finger slipped inside of her as deep as I could.

"Yes," she hissed out, jerking her hips to get me to move.

"So pushy," I breathed against her mouth.

Kaelynn pushed her hands into my hair, pulling my mouth harder on hers, exploring the taste of herself as she groaned and hooked her leg over mine.

"I need to feel you, Nash. Don't make me beg."

Her hazel eyes looked glassy, as if she was in a euphoria she didn't want to leave. I wanted to stay lost in them forever. I wanted to keep doing these things to her and making her look and sound the way she did right now.

I smiled and replied to her demand. "What if I want to hear you beg?"

"Then I'll beg. Please make love to me. Please let me feel you inside of me. I can't stand another moment of waiting."

The sound of her voice had me in such a fucking fog of lust and desire, I almost pushed into her without a condom. Reaching for it, I ripped it open and slipped it on. Leaning over her again, I took one of her nipples into my mouth and sucked on it while I pushed two fingers inside of her, getting her ready for me.

"You're so tight," I whispered against her lips. Working my fingers, I felt how much she was ready for me as her wetness coated my fingers.

"Nash, damn it. Please!"

It took all my strength and fortitude not to push hard and fast into her. Instead, I went slow and savored every single fucking inch of her heat. Her face was tight with passion and what looked like a bit of pain. I stopped and stared into her water-filled eyes.

"Are you okay?" I asked.

She nodded and bit down hard on her lip before saying, "It's been over a year and a half since I've been with anyone."

"Relax, baby. It won't hurt as bad if you relax."

Kaelynn's legs dropped open more and she did just that. I slid in so fucking deep I almost came when my balls felt her skin.

"Jesus, I can't move or I'll come. And you don't move either or I'll come."

She giggled and wrapped her arms around me and lifted her hips to get me to move.

"Please," she whispered, her hot breath dancing over my sensitive skin.

"Kaelynn, you feel so good."

Moving slowly in and out of her, our mouths pressed together in a soft kiss.

"Lose control, Nash. Please."

Her words were my undoing. The tender kiss turned passionate as I moved faster, harder. Each moan from her caused me to lose a bit more restraint. Her hands on my ass, pulling me as she met me thrust for thrust wasn't helping my self-control.

"I'm going to come. Oh God. Nash. Nash!"

The way her body gripped around my cock when she came nearly had me falling over the edge with her. But I wasn't done. Not yet.

Rolling us over, I watched as her dark hair started to fall out of its twist and cascade down around her.

"Fuck me, Kaelynn."

She was frozen, not moving as her breathing was fast and heavy.

Then she smiled and did exactly what I asked her to do. I'd never come with a girl on top. Not once, and I had no clue why. But everything with Kaelynn was different. She moved slowly at first. Her hands exploring my chest and stomach. When she leaned over and sucked on my nipple, my entire body jerked. She smiled against my chest, her eyes peeking up to watch me as she fucked me. I was in heaven.

Pure, freaking heaven.

I grabbed her ass and pushed in deep and fast, causing her to gasp.

"Again," she panted.

This woman was going to be the death of me. And three condoms were not going to be enough to get us through this night.

"You're supposed to be fucking me," I reminded her.

"That felt too good. Do it again."

"Bossy . . . I like it."

Kaelynn came again on top, riding me like a fucking pro. I didn't want to come yet, so I rolled us again. When she slid her hand between our bodies and rubbed her clit to come a third time, I lost the battle and spilled into the condom. I leaned my arms on either side of her, kissing her as I kept my weight off her, but I stayed inside. I wasn't ready to pull out of her. Not yet.

Her eyes captured my gaze. She smiled and said, "I want to stay like this forever. You and me, connected like this."

Kissing her mouth softly, I whispered, "So do I."

I pulled out and took the condom off, tossing it into the trash.

"Come take a shower with me, Kaelynn."

With a nod, she crawled off the bed, her legs wobbling a bit as she stood. I reached for her and we both laughed as I kept her from falling back on the bed, her legs obviously a little worse for wear.

Before I walked with her into the bathroom, I grabbed a condom. Kaelynn looked up at me, a gleam in her eye and said, "You can do that again . . . so soon?"

"I sure as fuck am going to try."

Laughing, she took my hand and led me into the bathroom, where we made love in the shower. Slowly. Tenderly. It was a connection I had never experienced before in my life with any woman. It felt real. And nothing else mattered except for the two of us.

By the time we made it back to the bed, we both fell onto it exhausted. A few hours had passed before I felt the bed move. The feel of Kaelynn's hands on my body had my cock instantly up. She pushed me over and crawled on top of me, rubbing her pussy against my hard dick.

"Jesus, you feel so good." I wanted to know what she felt like without a condom, but there was no way I was even going to suggest it. I could be patient. Right now, it was about learning each other. Earning the trust that it would take for that next step.

Leaning over to the side table, Kaelynn ripped open the condom, slid it onto me, and then sank down. We both moaned, and it didn't take me long to come right along with her as she dropped her head back and said my name as we climaxed at the same time.

After cleaning up, Kaelynn tucked her body next to mine. She mumbled something about still needing to talk, then drifted off to sleep. I didn't care about anything but holding her in my arms. I didn't care that we hadn't talked first. I didn't care about the fucking information Blake had given me. I would throw it away tomorrow without even looking at it.

None of it mattered.

The only thing I cared about was that I had the woman I loved in my arms . . . and I never planned on letting her go.

Twenty-One

KAELYNN

THE FEEL OF warmth on my face made me smile. I opened my eyes and immediately shut them when the sunlight nearly blinded me.

Rolling over, I sighed as I felt every single, delicious ache in my body, especially between my thighs. It was an ache I wanted to experience every single day for the rest of my life. My arms dropped, expecting to find a warm body. Instead, I felt a cold bedsheet.

I sat up and glanced around. There was a note on the pillow.

With a silly grin, I picked it up and read it.

Good morning, beautiful!

Went to get coffee and breakfast downstairs. Also stopping at one of the shops to buy you some clothes. I didn't want you leaving in the same gown we checked in with.

Love, Nash

My stomach felt like butterflies were having a party in there as I clutched the paper to my chest.

What man thinks of things like that?

"Nash Barrett," I said, slipping out of bed. My dress was still on the floor where Nash had taken it off last night. Walking over to pick it up, I saw his jacket off to the side. I reached for it and tossed it onto the back of the chair, only to see the envelope Blake had given Nash fall to the floor. Reaching down, I picked it up and went to put it back into the jacket pocket when I saw my name.

Kaelynn Shae Whitaker.

I gasped and felt a rush of cold air hit me right in the face. My eyes stared at the last name.

Whitaker.

How had Blake found out? Is that why Nash looked so angry last night? Blake was telling him the truth about me?

Without thinking, I turned the envelope over and opened it. I unfolded the handwritten note addressed to Nash. The first few lines made me feel sick to my stomach as I covered my mouth to keep from throwing up.

Nash,

Here is the background check you asked for on a Kaelynn Shae Dotson, also known as Kaelynn Shae Whitaker. I'm not sure what all she has told you about herself, but she is an heiress to a multibillion-dollar fortune of very old money. The Whitaker name is well known in the US and is probably the reason she uses her mother's maiden name.

Here is her information from birth and what she has been doing since college. Let me know if you need any more help.

Dustin

Shocked, I sat down in the chair and stared at the floor.

How could he do this? How could he have someone poke into my private life and not say a word to me.

My hands came up and covered my mouth. A sickening thought hit me and caused me to run to the bathroom where I barely made it before I threw up.

I rinsed my mouth out, then splashed my face with water.

"He wouldn't have done that. No. No." I sobbed, shaking my head. "Not with how he treated me last night. How perfect everything was. He wouldn't have used me like that."

Tears started down my cheeks.

Thinking back to how angry Nash was when Blake handed him the envelope. Had he found out the truth about me? Did he sleep with me on his terms so he could leave me because I had kept the truth from him?

My head spun. I needed air. Time to think. I needed to figure out what to do. Nash had hired someone to find out the truth about me. How long had he been planning this? How long had he known?

After getting dressed, I found my purse and called an Uber. I prayed I wouldn't run into Nash on the way out. I headed to the stairs so I wouldn't run the chance of running into Nash on the elevator. If he had really even planned on coming back. For all I knew, he left and had no intentions of coming back to the hotel room.

A part of me knew deep down inside that wasn't true. Nash had made love to me three times last night and had made me come twice as many times. Last night was real.

Wasn't it?

Once I got into the stairwell, I covered my mouth and cried harder.

This was my fault. Had I only been honest with him in the first place, none of this would have happened. He suspected I was hiding something, and he took it upon himself to dig into my life.

I felt numb as I went down each step.

My phone rang, causing me to jump. One quick glance showed me it was Millie.

"H-hello?"

"Kaelynn? What's wrong?" she asked, worry evident in her voice.

"He found out. Nash, he found out who I really was."

"You told him and he didn't take it well?"

Another sob slipped from between my lips. "No," I managed to get out.

Stepping outside of the hotel, I saw a taxi. Not wanting to risk running into anyone while waiting for the Uber I ordered, I slipped inside the cab.

"Austin airport, please," I stated.

"The airport? Why are you going to the airport? Where are you going, Kaelynn?"

"Home," I said, this time letting the sobs free.

"Oh no," Millie whispered. "What happened?"

"He r-ran a b-background check on . . . m-me."

"What?" Millie shouted into the phone. "Are you freaking kidding me? Who does that?"

I shook my head as I as pushed my body into the seat of the taxi.

"Someone who had been . . . b-burned and doesn't t-trust."

"Take a few deep breaths."

Doing as she said, I noticed the cab driver giving me a worried look.

"Okay, one more deep breath in the nose, out the mouth."

"I'm okay. I . . . I'm fine." I hiccupped and the taxi driver looked at me again.

Blowing out a deep breath, I sat up straight and got my shit together. A few more deep breaths and I was able to calm myself down. "I'm getting on the first flight out of Austin."

"Let me see what is the next flight leaving, and I'll book you a ticket. I'll text you what airline."

I wiped my tear-soaked face. "Th-thanks, Millie."

"We can talk about all this once you get here."

"'Kay."

Hitting *end*, I closed my eyes and leaned my head back.

"Miss, you weren't, what I mean is, um, are you okay?"

Not having the energy to move, I lifted my hand and gave the driver a thumbs up. "Yes, thank you. No one hurt me, at least not physically."

The taxi driver remained silent. My phone rang and I glanced down at it, knowing Millie couldn't have bought a ticket that soon.

Nash.

Dropping the phone to my lap, I covered my mouth with both hands and watched it ring. A few minutes later, it dinged to notify me of a voicemail.

"Are you going to listen to what he said?" the taxi driver asked as I popped my head up and stared at him in disbelief.

"What? No! No, I am not going to listen to it."

The man tsked and shook his head. "In my experience, I think you should listen to it before you get on the plane."

I laughed. "Well, with all due respect, I'm not interested in your experience with these things."

He lifted a hand as if surrendering.

"Okay, but I know you will regret this."

Focusing on the scenery outside the window, I wiped a tear away.

"I won't regret it," I whispered. Knowing deep down in my heart I already did.

~§~

THE MOMENT I saw my sister, I dashed to her. Holding open her arms, I nearly knocked her over when I slammed my body against hers and started crying . . . again.

Millie held on to me, whispering that everything was going to be okay.

"Come on, let's get you home."

I shook my head. "I don't want to face Mom and Dad just yet."

"They're not home; they went to New York for some big function Daddy had going on."

Letting out a sigh of relief, I hooked my arm with my sister's.

"Did you check your luggage?" she asked, giving me a once-over in the dress I had worn to Terri and Jim's wedding yesterday.

"No, I went straight to the airport. I don't have anything."

Her brows furrowed. "Okay, let's just get home and then we'll talk."

Millie had no sooner pulled out of the airport, when my head fell back against the seat and I fell asleep. I was exhausted, both physically and mentally. I needed a few minutes of sleep to clear my mind.

The feel of someone shaking my body gently had me popping my eyes open.

"We're home."

With a slight smile, I climbed out of the car.

"Take a hot shower, get some clean clothes on, and meet me in the library."

Without a word, I nodded and walked past my sister and up the stairs. My parents' house was massive, and even if they had been home, I could have probably gone a week and been able to avoid them.

It hadn't taken me long to get to my bedroom, strip out of the dress, and walk to my adjoined bathroom. The feel of the hot water hitting my body felt good. I still ached from all the lovemaking with Nash.

Lovemaking. Was that what we had been doing?

My hand came up to my mouth to stop the sobs. Had it been lovemaking? Or had it been Nash taking something from me because he felt I had been deceiving him? Dropping my body against the back wall, I stared down at the drain, watching as the water made its way down it. How ironic, washing all traces of Nash off my body, both literally and figuratively.

After standing there for God knows how long, I got out, wrapped my hair in a towel and found some sweats to put on before meeting Millie in the library.

The smell of hot cider made my chest ache. I had missed being home. Missed my family. Missed my sister.

Millie sat in one of two oversized chairs in front of the roaring fire. The heat felt good against my cold skin.

I took the mug of cider she handed me.

"So tell me what happened."

The feel of the hot cider going down my throat should have warmed me, but it didn't. My body shook, and I couldn't seem to get it to stop.

"I didn't tell him. I mean, I had planned on telling him after the wedding. Before we slept together. I tried, but he kept kissing me and making my head swirl."

Her mouth fell open. "Wait! You guys slept together?"

I nodded, then took another sip of the cider.

"Wow, how did that happen?"

With a small shrug, I let out a breath. "I'm not sure. I mean, I knew we were both physically attracted to each other, and Nash seemed like he wanted to take things slowly, but then everything changed. I think he found out about the family at the wedding, and maybe it was his way of paying me back for hiding the truth."

She leaned forward. "Okay, listen to what you're saying right now. Does this sound like Nash? He was pissed and enticed you into sleeping with him because he found out you have money like his ex? So by having crazy hot sex with you, he got back at Lily through you. That doesn't sound like the man you've been talking about the last few weeks."

"I don't know who he is, and clearly he didn't trust that he knew who I was either. I don't know what to think anymore. I don't want to think last night didn't mean anything to Nash, but he had to . . ." My voice trailed off as I frowned.

"He had to what?"

Staring at the fire, my eyes widened as the realization hit me like a truck. "No," I whispered. Turning to Millie, I felt the first tear fall. "It was me. It wasn't Nash. It was my idea to leave, to get a hotel room there. He had even asked me if I was sure that was what I wanted. Nash hadn't used me as some sort of revenge last night, it was all me."

Millie shook her head.

"Okay, I'm sort of confused. You thought Nash found out the truth and somehow seduced you into bed. But now that you're thinking clear, it was you who wanted him. Let's back up. When did he find out about you and when did you find out about the background check?"

I shook my head and set the tea down. After explaining everything from the point where I had seen Blake give Nash the envelope to when I read what was in it.

"So you don't know if he read the note from Blake's brother or not?"

"No, but he was angry. I figured Blake had told him what was inside."

"Did he act different toward you?"

"No," I whispered.

"Then the next morning, you found out he ran the background in the hotel room while the man was out trying to get you clothes so you didn't do the walk of shame, and instead of waiting for him to come back and you guys talk about all of this . . . you ran."

The curve of my lip came up, and I snarled at my sister. "The way you tell it, I sound like a crazy bitch."

She nodded. "If the shoe fits."

I buried my hands in my face and let out a scream. It was clear I had messed things up.

"Have you listened to his voicemail?"

"No," I said, my voice muffled from my head still in my hands.

"Let's listen to it, then I think you need to call him. I mean, you running might have just ruined everything, Kaelynn."

"Gee, thanks, Millie," I stated as my hands dropped to my lap. "Way to keep things positive."

"How can anything about this mess be positive? Kaelynn, I told you one of these days this whole pretending you're someone you're not was going to catch up with you. You hid something about yourself from your best friend and the guy you liked. Listen, I get the why . . . because Morgan told you the story of Nash and his ex. I get the fear you had, but I also think it was incredibly stupid of you to hide it. I know we have to be careful with whom we let close to us. No one gets that more than I do, but if you love someone, you have to trust them. If Nash is the type of man you say he is, I don't think he would have pushed you away. He might have been spooked, but he wouldn't have pushed you away."

A tear slipped free and trailed down my cheek. "I know. I really messed things up."

Mille reached for my hand and squeezed it. "Has he called you since that first voicemail?"

"No. I haven't listened to it yet. I'm afraid to."

Holding out her hand, she wiggled her fingers in a motion to give the phone to her, so I did.

"Okay, let's do this together. If he tells you he never wants to hear from you again, you move on."

My eyes filled with tears. "But last night . . ."

She held up her hand. "I don't think he's going to say that, but we need to be prepared for anything."

Glancing down, I watched as I worked my hands together nervously. The moment I heard his voice, my heart felt as if it seized in my chest and I held my breath.

"Kaelynn, please call me back. We need to talk, and I don't want to do it over the phone. I, um, I don't know where you went, and I've searched the entire hotel. Please call me. I'm really worried about you."

Millie's eyes caught mine and she shrugged. "Okay, he didn't sound mad, but more distraught that you weren't there."

"He didn't sound mad at all."

"He sounded sad, Kaelynn." Millie's brows pulled in as she stared back down at the phone. "He hasn't called back though."

Her voice sounded surprised.

"What?" I asked, reaching for my phone. "What do you mean?"

"Look at your missed calls; none are from him. He only called and left that one message. I mean, if he wanted to make things work, I would think he would have kept calling. Did any of his friends call you?"

"No. Not even Morgan. Which is strange, because I'm positive she would have noticed us missing last night from the reception and then would have wanted to talk to me today."

We locked gazes again.

"That's not a good sign, is it?" I asked, my voice cracking. "I messed this up, didn't I? I just lost the only man I think I've ever loved."

Millie was up and next to me in a flash, holding me while I let myself fall into a fit of tears. Again.

Twenty-Two

NASH

THE KNOCK ON my office door had me letting out a low growl. I needed to get this work taken care of and every interruption put me farther behind.

"Go away."

The knock grew louder.

"Go. Away."

The handle turned and Morgan walked in, a scowl on her face. I rolled my eyes and went back to what I was doing.

"I'm still pissed off at you."

"Yeah, well, are you pissed off at your best friend for lying to you?"

Morgan sat in the seat. I could feel the heat of her stare. "I'm a bit disappointed, but in the end, it doesn't change anything. She told me the truth the day of the wedding."

I scoffed. A sickness rolled deep inside my gut. She had tried to tell me as well, but I wouldn't let her.

"How could you run a background check on her and not think she would be pissed?"

"I cancelled the damn thing, Morgan. It didn't matter to me anymore.

Blake never told his brother to call it off. I wasn't even going to read what was in the fucking thing."

She folded her arms across her chest, tilted her head, and narrowed one eye. She had perfected the stare our mother gave to us when we had done something wrong.

"Do you love her?"

"Yes."

Her mouth fell open. "Wait. What?"

"Don't act so surprised."

"I am surprised."

I sighed. "What do you want from me, Morgan? What would be the right answer you want to hear? I fell in love with Kaelynn the day I drove her to Houston. Hell, probably the moment I ran into her in the hallway of Sedotto. I knew then she was hiding something from me. I wish I had just listened to Tucker and talked to her, but I didn't. Now she's gone."

"I haven't called her yet."

This time it was me who frowned. "Why not?"

She shrugged. "This is between the two of you, and I don't want to be involved. I did text her, though, to make sure she was all right. She said she was, and I told her what I just told you—this was between y'all. I did call her sister Millie, though, last night. She told me Kaelynn was home in Utah."

"I already know she's home."

Her brow lifted. "The private investigator Dustin hired found her name on an airline manifest the day she left on a direct flight in first-class back to Utah."

"So now you're having her followed?"

"No. I searched fucking everywhere for her that day when she disappeared on me. I needed to know where she was; he found out for me."

"What are you going to do?"

"I'm leaving this afternoon at two to fly up to Salt Lake City."

A smile appeared on her face. "Shut up! You're flying up there to go get her?"

"I'm flying up there to explain everything to her. Why I started the stupid background check. Then I'm coming home."

The smile faded as quickly as it came. "You're not asking her to come back to Austin with you?"

I sighed and pushed my hand through my hair. "I should have done what I said I was going to do and not gotten involved with anyone. I said I would never open my heart again and look what happened when I did."

"So, that doesn't mean anything. You both made a mistake. We all can't be perfect. She's going to mess up and so will you."

"Trust has to be the main focus of any relationship I have with a woman. Was the secret Kaelynn was hiding something terrible? No. I can actually understand why she didn't tell me."

"Then why are you willing to walk away from a woman you love, Nash?"

"Because she didn't trust me enough to tell me the truth. She didn't trust me to look past that and not think I could compare her to Lily. I know she was going to tell me. I truly believe in my heart she was, but look at the first thing she did when we were faced with a problem. She ran. She left me, Morgan, without so much as letting me know where she was going. You don't do that if you love someone."

"Nash," Morgan whispered. "Don't give up on this. Don't give up on Kaelynn. Don't give up on love."

Glancing down at the desk, I shook my head. "I really need to finish this up before I have to go."

I could feel the weight of Morgan's gaze on me. I glanced up in time to see the look of disappointment on her face.

"I never thought in my life I would ever say this to you, Nash Barrett." She stood and pointed to me. "You are a stupid asshole. I thought you were different from other guys. I thought maybe you were one of the good ones who listened to your heart and not your stupid head. I thought if you found love, you would fight for it with everything you had. You have a second chance to make this right. I didn't get that chance with Mike, and I would give anything to have that second chance." She wiped away a tear and shrugged. "I guess I was wrong. You're no different from the rest of them."

My mouth opened to say something, but words left me. I watched as my sister turned on her heels, stormed to the door, and slammed it shut.

Rubbing the back of my neck, I exhaled before picking up the file on my desk and trying to focus on work.

∽≈∾

COMING DOWN THE escalator in the Salt Lake City airport, I rolled my neck to get some of the tension out as I listened to Tucker and Charlie preach to me about how Kaelynn was perfect for me.

"Listen, guys, I appreciate all the advice. I'm only here to explain to her about the background check, and that's all."

"And you couldn't do that over the phone?" Charlie asked. I could hear Hannah cooing in the background.

"No. The first thing I need to do is get checked into a hotel, then figure out the best way to let Kaelynn know I'm in town."

"How about I just take you to her?"

The voice stopped me in my tracks. Turning to the left, I saw a young woman with the same dark hair and hazel eyes as Kaelynn.

"Excuse me? Are you speaking to me?" I asked.

"Ah, I see you've met Millie Whitaker. You're not the only one who has connections, Nash. I told Morgan to call and let Millie know you were coming. You need someone to help you with this. A woman," Charlie said with a bit of satisfaction in her voice.

Millie stood there smiling as I pulled the phone out and glared at it.

"Stop glaring at the phone. Now go get back the woman you love, Nash!" Charlie exclaimed.

"Dude, listen to your heart. Please!" Tucker added.

"I hate both of you right now. I'm hanging up."

Hitting *end*, I tilted my head and stared down at the younger version of Kaelynn.

"She doesn't know you're here. Morgan called me and told me you were coming."

"Who are you?" I asked.

Laughing, Millie answered. "Millie Whitaker. Younger and much smarter sister of Kaelynn Whitaker, aka, Kaelynn Dotson. It's our mom's maiden name."

"I know," I replied as she frowned for a moment.

"You won't need to stay at a hotel; you can stay at our house."

"Um, I don't think that's a good idea."

"Trust me. It's big enough that you could actually avoid Kaelynn for at least a week if you wanted to. Now, let's get your stuff and head on out. There's a storm coming. You landed just in time. They're talking about shutting down the airport in the next hour or so."

"Shutting down the airport? For how long?"

The girl shrugged, then gave me a wink. "A day, maybe a week. You never know with the weather up here. Come on, we have to get home before it starts really coming down."

With a smirk, I shook my head and followed her out of the airport and through the parking garage. We stopped at a Lexus SUV where she opened the back so I could place my bag in.

"Just one small bag?" she asked.

"Wasn't planning on staying long."

This time she laughed. "Sorry to say, Nash Barrett, you're going to be staying at least a few days. Do we need to stop anywhere?"

I drew my brows in tight and asked, "Stop anywhere?"

"Yeah, you know, like, Target? Do you need more underwear, a pair of sweatpants, a jacket? It's cold here, and you clearly didn't bring a winter coat."

"I came from Texas; we don't have winter coats."

She stared at me, waiting for me to answer her. "Do you have a washer and dryer at your house? I can do my own laundry. I have three days' worth of clothes; that's plenty. I have a return flight booked in two days."

Her hand went to her hip. "Okay, maybe you might want to think about getting some flowers."

"For?" I asked, noting she had ignored me.

She rolled her eyes and waved her hands at me. "Are all men just . . . just . . ."

Smiling, I waited to hear her keep going.

"Never mind. Clearly you're not here to ask her for forgiveness and to come back to Texas with you."

Millie pushed a button, and the back of her SUV started to lower. She stormed to the driver's side and slammed the door shut after getting in.

I closed my eyes and let out a breath, then whispered, "Why are all women so complicated?"

The drive from the airport to the Whitaker house wasn't short. Millie drove toward the mountains, and I kept looking to the left where the sky was turning darker.

"Looks like that is a pretty bad storm coming."

"Yep."

"I've never seen snow," I said, laughing as I looked out at the snow-covered ground.

"You see it now."

Facing her, I smirked. "You really don't like me, do you?"

"What gave you that impression?"

I looked back out the front window. "Let's see. I'm pretty sure I've heard you mumble 'dick' at least four times during the drive so far. You refuse to carry on a conversation with me, and I'm pretty sure, if given the chance, you'd like to do bodily harm to me."

We both turned and looked at each other. The look of evil in her eye made me shudder.

"You know, I'm rich enough to hire someone to do the bodily harm to you and no one would ever know it was me. Hell, I'm rich enough to dispose of body parts all over the world without so much as an inkling that I had anything to do with it. So yeah, you should be worried."

I laughed, then stopped when her brow raised and she stared out the windshield again.

"Right. So we should just go back to me talking and you responding with one-word replies."

"Yep."

Nodding, I sighed.

"Okay, fine. Here it is. You want to know why I don't like you?"

I turned and looked at her, her hands gripped the steering wheel tighter now, and it had nothing to do with the snow coming down.

"You spied on my sister."

"I didn't . . ."

"I'm not done, *Mr. Barrett.*"

I couldn't help the slight lift of my mouth. This girl was a pistol. "I'm sorry, please go on, Ms. Whitaker."

"Thank you. Like I was saying, you spied on my sister, then you only called her once. Once! For all you knew, she was dead somewhere. You didn't even bother to check up on her."

At that moment, she gasped and shot me a quick look before putting her eyes back on the road. "Oh shit. You knew she was here. But how?"

"Does it really matter?"

"You're having her followed!"

I laughed. "I am not."

"You've got a tracking device on her phone!"

Frowning, I asked, "You're a fan of mystery movies, aren't you?"

"Hallmark Movies & Mysteries Channel, yes. It's the bomb."

Chuckling, I said, "I am not tracking her or following her, but I did find out she flew out of Austin and to Salt Lake City the other day."

"Your spy?"

"Something like that."

"Huh."

"Back to one-word responses again?"

The corners of Millie's smile lifted. "If I wasn't so pissed at you, I would really like you."

"I've been hearing that a lot lately."

Millie sighed and pulled up to a massive black iron gate. Looking up, their last name was scrolled across the top.

"Home?"

"Yep. Nash, I just want you to know one thing. My sister loves you. I've never seen her this upset or lost about any other guy. I don't want to see her hurt."

"I don't want to hurt her; I'm just trying to do the right thing here. She deserves to know why that background check was done. Neither of us handled things the right way."

"No, you didn't. That much is true."

She pushed a button, and the large iron gate opened.

"I really care about Kaelynn, for what it's worth."

"I know you do."

"How do you know that?" I asked.

Millie pulled through the gate and stopped her SUV to look at me. "If you didn't, you wouldn't be here."

Twenty-Three

NASH

IT FELT LIKE Millie drove forever before I finally saw the house come into view. "House" wasn't really the right word.

Mansion.

"Holy shit."

"Yeah, it's a little . . . over the top."

I turned to look at Millie. "Over the top? How big is that house?"

She shrugged. "Oh, almost fifty-thousand square feet. Maybe a little over that if you count the garage and storage areas."

My eyes widened as she pulled into the roundabout in front of the house. A giant water feature was in front of the house but had been drained for the winter.

"I don't know if I should be more impressed with the house or the mountains."

Millie laughed, then pulled around and into a covered drive. The six garages sat on the left, with the house on the right and a covered carport connecting them.

"Well, if we're going to do this, you're getting the grand tour."

"What about Kaelynn?"

"She isn't home."

"Where is she?" I asked, nervous Millie might have brought me out to the middle of nowhere to murder me and then hide my body in the mountains.

"Neighbors. She went over a bit ago to help her with setting up for a party. Our estate sits on over a hundred-and-fifty acres, I'll hear her when she comes in. The front gate security beeps on my phone to alert me someone is coming in."

"Of course it does."

She laughed and pushed a button, opening the back tailgate again. I got out of the car, breathed in the cold air, and headed to the back of the car.

"Okay. So the inside is a bit grander than the outside. Just don't judge, okay? I know it's an obnoxious house and all, but it's my folks' place and where we all grew up."

"Why do you think I'm going to judge your family?"

"Well, I'm not sure how much that background check you did on my sister told you."

"I didn't read it."

She stopped walking and forced me to do the same. "What do you mean you didn't read it?"

Lifting my shoulder up in a halfhearted shrug, I replied, "I told Blake, my friend, to not have it done. I had a feeling Kaelynn was going to tell me whatever secret it was she was hiding, and Blake went ahead with it anyway. He gave me the envelope, but I wasn't going to look at it. Your sister happened to come across it before I could throw it out."

A slow smile spread over her face, and she tilted her head as she regarded me. "Okay, I like you a little more now and don't really want to grab you by the balls and twist them until you cry 'uncle.'"

I crossed my legs and winced. Millie laughed, then started walking again. The front door opened as we walked up the steps.

"Ms. Whitaker, welcome home."

"Thanks, Janet! This is Nash Barrett . . . a *friend* of Kaelynn's. Will you be sure to put him in the guest room down the hall from Kaelynn's bedroom?"

"So much for being able to hide," I mumbled loud enough for Millie to smirk then give me a wink.

We walked into the house and I was stunned by what I saw. I had been in some rather impressive beautiful homes. Charlie's parents' house on Lake Travis in Austin was beyond stunning. But this house . . . this thing was stately. The marble floors were polished to perfection. On either side of the giant room there was a winding staircase that led up to the second floor. A huge chandelier hung from the ceiling. But the most impressive thing was across the room. The entire back wall was a picture window with the snow-covered mountains as the backdrop.

"That's beautiful," I whispered.

"I know," Millie agreed. "Come, let me give you a quick tour so you can get your bearings. We have a theater room, a bowling alley, a trophy room where my father displays all of his trophies."

"He likes to hunt?"

She laughed. "Likes to hunt? He lives for it. Do you hunt?"

"Live for it."

"Well, then you'll like that room, and you'll earn a brownie point from my dad." She motioned for me to follow her as she kept talking. "Let's see, an indoor and outdoor playground. A dry sauna, a wet sauna, an indoor pool. A basketball court, indoor archery and shooting range, a meeting room, and if you brought your swimsuit, I believe the lazy river is on."

"You're joking, right?"

"Nope. Our parents wanted to make sure we wanted for nothing. My brother was into archery, so Dad had that built. He liked basketball, so Dad had it built. He wanted to make sure we could use everything year-round."

"I want to say the word spoiled, but . . ."

Millie grinned as she walked up to an elevator and hit a button. "Fastest way down to the fun stuff."

"Holy shit. I'm thinking I should have read the background report."

This time Millie laughed and nodded. "You probably should have. Our family is wealthy, Nash. I don't know this ex of yours, and I'm not trying to be a snob, but I'm pretty damn sure we've got her family beat by a few million. My great-great-great—maybe one more great in there—grandfather put all of his money into railroads and industry like steel and iron. Then you had his wife, who had a smart head on her shoulders, not to mention she was pissed off at her cheating husband who put a lot of money into land in and around Boston, New York, and the DC area. Let's just say between the two of them, they made a fortune and taught their kids to keep growing that. My father is no different. The man doesn't have to work, but he works every single day except weekends. My parents have set up a lot of scholarships, donated a lot of money, and have helped with things that their kids have a fondness for. I like animals, so my father has donated a lot to charities I'm passionate about. Same for Kaelynn and my brother. What we have a passion for, our parents get involved in it. They have more money than they know what to do with, so they do good. You may think I'm blowing smoke up your ass, and to be honest, I don't give a rat's ass. I know the hearts of my family, and that is all that matters."

I gently took Millie by the arm and stopped her. "You don't have to explain anything to me about your family's money. Or what your parents do with it. It's none of my business."

"I know, but it's important you know that just because we have more money, it doesn't mean we don't do good for people. I don't want you to think Kaelynn is like Li—"

Her voice trailed off.

"Lily?"

Trying to hide her face so I didn't see the embarrassed blush on her cheeks, she nodded.

I sighed. "I'm not comparing Kaelynn to Lily. I need you to know that."

"I'm sorry, this whole thing is just . . . I've never seen my sister fall for a guy like she has for you. She hasn't been herself the last few days, and I know you guys haven't even really dated that long, but I also know you slept together."

This time it was my cheeks that burned.

"Nash, I hope you won't walk away from something that is clearly special. You might be telling yourself you owed it to Kaelynn to talk to her in person and explain, but I think you got on that plane today because you needed to see her."

Before I could answer, Millie's phone buzzed and she glanced down at it. "Kaelynn's here."

Lifting my shoulders, I dragged in a deep breath. "Guess the tour is on hold."

"Guess so. By the way, that snow is coming down. I venture to say you'll·have plenty of time to explore this place."

Laughing, I motioned for her to lead the way.

Millie had taken us a different way, and I was already confused where I was in the house. Was I on the north side or the south side? Jesus, I needed a printed map with landmarks on it to make my way out of this maze.

"What side of the house is this?" I asked, walking down a narrow set of steps that led right into a hallway that housed a butler's pantry.

"The north side. The kitchen is on the north side. There are four levels of the house. The basement houses all the fun stuff—the bowling alley, the theater, shooting ranges, the billiards room, and the pool. First floor has the kitchen, formal dining, and living room, the family room, the library, my father's office, which has a meeting room adjacent to it, and the famous trophy room. Second floor has most of the bedrooms and a few other rooms like my mom's craft room. If you ever need to find Kaelynn while you're here, check the library. It's her favorite place."

"Who are you talking to?"

The sound of her voice left me breathless. I had been standing around the corner, so when Kaelynn came in from the garages, she must not have seen me.

"What?" Millie asked, startled that Kaelynn had made it up to the house so quickly.

"How did you get here so fast? My phone just went off that you came through the gate."

"I've been home the entire time, I didn't come in through the gate," Kaelynn said. "Who are you talking to?"

Millie motioned for me to stay back. "Um, shit. That must be Jack then."

"Does he know I'm home?" Kaelynn asked, a bit of surprise in her voice.

"No, but he's about to find out that both of you are here and . . ."

Millie looked at me and then used her head to signal for me to step out. The second Kaelynn saw me she smiled. Then it disappeared as quickly as it appeared.

"Oh shit," Millie and I both mumbled at the same time.

"What are you doing here, Nash? How did you know I was here . . . oh, wait. *That's* a stupid question."

"Kaelynn," I started before she cut me off.

"Did you have me followed here?"

"No! Of course not."

Millie stepped between us. "Okay, stop. Jack doesn't know what happened between you two. He's very protective of his sisters, and if he finds out Nash caused you to run from Austin, he'll shoot him."

My gaze jerked from Kaelynn over to Millie. "What? Shoot me? You're kidding, right?"

Both girls answered me. "No."

My eyes widened in horror. "Well, can I just go hide?"

Kaelynn shot me a dirty look. "My hero."

"Your sister just said he would shoot me! How do you want me to respond to that?"

"No, you're going to have to pretend everything is okay. Kaelynn brought you home to show you where she lived."

"Why can't we just tell him the truth?" I asked. "I'm really not in the mood to play pretend anymore."

Kaelynn looked at me with hurt in her eyes. I felt like a dick, but I was done playing games.

Placing her hands on her hips, Kaelynn lifted her shoulders and stood taller. "Fine by me. Tell him the truth then. I'm sure he'll be very interested in hearing that you ran a background check on his sister, slept with her, and then kept it from her."

"Okay, I'll be sure to note how you gave me a fake last name, never told me about your family except for the things you wanted me to know, oh, and when the going got tough, you ran."

"Is that what you think I did? Ran? Nash, I was in a state of shock. You had my whole life history in an envelope stuffed in your jacket pocket."

"Yes, and I never had any intention of reading it. I told Blake I didn't want the damn background check done. Even when I found out Dotson wasn't your real last name. I had a feeling you were about to tell me. I wanted you to trust me enough to tell me on your own, Kaelynn. Not fucking lie to me. I had enough of that with Lily."

Kaelynn's eyes turned watery, and she looked down at the floor. "I was afraid you'd only want to be friends if you knew the truth."

"You never even gave me a chance to figure that out on my own, which I wouldn't have pushed you away. I . . . I care about you."

Shaking her head, she looked up at me. "Nash, you even said in the car you didn't want a woman who came from money. Take a look around here, will you? I come from *money*. My whole life I've been trying to figure out who is really my friend and who is really out to gain something from me. It was easier to be someone I wasn't to guard myself."

"You should have told me," I stated.

Millie stepped between us again. "Okay, well, I'm pretty sure if Jack hears any of that, he'll want to kick Nash's ass regardless."

"Why would I want to do that?"

We all jumped and turned to see, who I was guessing was the girls' brother, Jack. Kaelynn squealed in delight and ran to him. He caught her in his arms before she knocked him over. I couldn't fight the smile that spread over my face as he spun her around and kissed her on the cheek.

"Hey, it's so good seeing you. I'm so glad you're home."

After putting Kaelynn back down, Jack looked my way. Extending my hand, I said, "Nash Barrett, I've heard a lot about you."

Jack smiled, but I knew he wasn't sure about me. "And I've heard nothing about you except for the little bit of arguing the two of you just had."

"I'm sorry about that," I stated, giving him a firm handshake.

He returned the handshake and asked, "Do you mean it? Do you truly care about her?"

My eyes went to Kaelynn. "Yes."

"Then figure that shit out. For now, let's eat. I'm starving."

Millie clapped and did a little hop as she and Jack headed down the hall. Kaelynn stared at me for a few moments before turning and walking away. I followed her and we all ended up in a dining room that I was pretty sure should have been in a castle somewhere.

Holy shit.

A large white marble table sat in the middle of the massive room that I swore would echo if I decided to yodel. Ten decorative chairs sat around the table. Kaelynn glanced over her shoulder and looked at me as I stood planted in the entrance of the dining room, taking it all in.

"How about we eat in the kitchen?" Kaelynn suggested.

"Sounds good to me," Millie said, grabbing a couple of boxes of pizza as Jack grabbed the rest of them.

It didn't take long to get to the kitchen. For the rest of the house being so grand, I was surprised that the kitchen wasn't fancier. I liked it though. It was white with wood floors and granite counters. A large island sat in the middle with another large island at the end that housed four stools. Jack pulled one around to the other side, while Millie did the same. I pulled the stool out for Kaelynn and pushed it in for her before sitting down.

"This house is incredible. I can't imagine growing up in a place like this," I stated as Jack started opening up pizza boxes.

"You like to shoot?" Jack asked before shoving a piece of pizza in his mouth.

Millie and Kaelynn both jerked their heads up to look at Jack, then me. Millie started shaking her head and motioning for me to say no.

"Um . . ."

Jack glanced up, a wolflike smile on his face.

"I'm not sure what my answer should be here."

Laughing, Jack looked at Millie, then Kaelynn, before focusing back on me. "Did they tell you I would shoot you?"

"Yes, they did."

"Nah. But did you purposely do something to hurt my sister?"

"Jack," Kaelynn started to say before her brother gave her a look to silence her.

"No. But we do have a few things we need to talk about."

He stared at me intently. Then he tilted his head and regarded me even harder. Then he pointed his pizza at me and spoke. "I'm good at reading people and I like you. I get a good vibe from you, dude. So, do you like to shoot or not?"

"Yes. I do."

Another bite of pizza was stuffed into his mouth as he nodded his head, chewed some, then swallowed. "Good. Let's do some shooting after this."

"Jack, he just got here, and I'm pretty sure he came to talk to Kaelynn, not shoot at paper guys with you."

"Archery?" Jack asked me, ignoring Millie.

"I've bow hunted a number of times."

A wide grin grew over his face. "Cool. Then we're on for tomorrow. I'll bring Jill with me so you can meet her. Millie, you bring Justin, and we'll do game night or something."

"That sounds like fun!" Millie said.

Kaelynn tossed her napkin onto the bar. "No, guys, no. We're not going to have game night."

"Why not?" the three of us asked. Kaelynn stared at me. "What if we . . . I mean . . . we haven't even talked yet."

I took a bite of pizza. "Are you planning on ignoring me until then?"

"Well, no."

"Great, then I'm sure we can have game night with your brother and sister and all act like adults, no matter what happens between us."

She stared at me and I wasn't sure if she wanted to kiss me or slap the hell out of me. I'm thinking a mixture of both emotions, so I winked and her lip snarled.

Oh, she for sure wants to slap the hell out of me.

Twenty-Four

KAELYNN

MILLIE BOUNCED OUT of the house and over to her SUV. Before she had a chance to get in, I grabbed her arm.

"You knew he was coming?"

She grinned. "I picked him up at the airport."

"Why didn't you tell me? Give me a warning or something? How did you even know he was coming?"

My sister shrugged and looked at her watch. "Morgan told me. I've got to run, sis. It's already late, and Justin is expecting me."

"Millie, you can't leave me here alone with him."

"Janet will be here."

I rolled my eyes and sighed. "You know what I mean. Seeing him, it unnerves me. I want to be angry with him, but my body keeps tell me to rub up against him like our cat used to do."

"Oh, kinky, sis. I like this version of you."

"You know what I mean. Not rub, be near. Feel him. Crap, I don't know what I mean. When is Mom and Dad coming home?"

"In a week. Christmas Eve."

"What!"

I turned and started to pace, wringing my hands.

"Calm down. He's here to talk. Don't push him away; let him say what he needs to say and you say what you need to say. Act like adults."

"I do act like an adult. It's just, Nash makes me feel all . . ."

"Squishy inside? Like your tummy is dropping and your heart is floating helplessly around in your chest? You can't find words when he smiles at you? Breathing can be a struggle when he's to close and the thought of him touching you makes your body feel like it is on fire?"

Frowning, I said, "Yes. That's exactly how I feel. How did you know?"

She opened the door and jumped into the Lexus. "It's called being in love, Kaelynn. Now go find your Prince Charming and figure this shit out."

After the door shut, Millie gave me a thumbs up then drove off without so much as a backward glance.

Turning on my heels, I walked back into the house and set off to find Nash. He had wondered off after Jack left thirty minutes ago. Lord only knew where he could be. I searched the kitchen and then headed to the living room. Janet, the house keeper, pointed down the hall to the library.

"If you're looking for Mr. Barrett, I showed him to the library. He's got himself a cup of warm tea, would you like some, Kaelynn?"

"I would adore some, if you don't mind."

She smiled warmly. "Of course, dear. Give me a few minutes and I'll bring it."

Nodding, I headed to the library. My heart beat so fast I swore it was about to burst right out of my chest. When I walked into the library, I stopped when I saw him.

Nash stood in front of the fire looking at a picture of me at my college graduation. A part of me wanted to turn and walk away. I didn't want to deal with this right now.

Turning slowly, I started to walk out of the library.

"Kaelynn."

His voice was soft. Like the night he made love to me and whispered my name in my ear.

Turning, I forced a smile. "I wasn't sure if you wanted to talk now or not."

His brows pulled in, as if he was thinking about something so heavy rather than being upset.

"Now is probably the best time since that's why I came."

"Right. Of course," I replied, walking farther into the room and sitting on a chair in front of the fire. Nash sat opposite of me.

We stared at each other for the longest time before he finally broke the silence. "Why did you run?"

I cleared my throat, wiped a piece of imaginary lint from my jeans, and focused back on him.

"I was in shock, I guess. A million things ran through my mind about why you would be doing a background check on me. All of my life people have used me for one thing or another . . . in that moment, with you and after what we'd shared, I felt used."

"Used?"

Nodding, I went on. "I saw Blake give you that envelope. You looked angry when you took it. I know I shouldn't have snooped in your things, but when I saw my name on the envelope and then read it, a crazy thought entered my mind. I thought you were angry because Blake told you the truth about me and that you only slept with me as a payback of some sort."

Nash's eyes grew wide as he dropped back in the chair. The way he looked at me, like I had just stabbed a knife into his heart, made me feel sick to my stomach.

"Did it feel like I was putting on a show for you the night we spent together?" he quietly asked.

I shook my head. "No. And I realized after I got home that it was me who asked you to make love to me that night. It was me who wanted to leave the reception and go to the room. It was everything swirling around in my head at that moment, Nash. I know I betrayed you by not telling you everything about me, and I knew deep down all of this was my fault. Maybe I was trying to place the blame on you, rather than accept the fact that it was me who was the cause of all of this."

"This wasn't your fault, Kaelynn."

My chin trembled and I forced myself not to cry. "I was going to tell you after the wedding. Before the wedding. The night you came over for dinner. So many times I wanted to tell you." My voice cracked, and I paused to regain my composure. "I was so afraid. I know now how stupid it was, and I know I should have trusted you. Everything was happening so fast between us. I mean, after that trip to Houston, I couldn't stop thinking about you. You consumed my thoughts both day and night."

He smiled. "It was the same for me."

"Looking back, I see what a stupid mistake I made, and I would do anything to go back and do it right. That whole 'hindsight is twenty-twenty' phrase comes to mind."

Nash leaned forward and set the mug on the table, then rested his arms on his knees. "Let me ask you something. If you hadn't known about Lily and the history there, would you have told me sooner?"

I chewed on my lip. "I might have. That day we spent in the car and you asked about my family. Yes, I probably would have mentioned it. Maybe not gone into full detail, because like I said, it was always so hard trying to figure out who liked me for me and who liked me for my family's money."

"Kaelynn, I get that. I saw it happen with Charlie all the time. And Terri. I wish you would have given me the chance."

Wiping away a tear that slipped out, I replied, "So do I."

We sat for a few moments in silence when I thought of something. "That day we were at Charlie and Tucker's. That was the day you decided to do the background check, wasn't it?"

He looked toward the fire. "Yes. It was actually Blake who came up with the idea that you might be hiding you came from money. I mean, let's be honest, I didn't keep it a secret how Lily left me because I didn't have the type of money she did."

"Or how you would never date another woman with money like that."

Nash scoffed. "Yeah."

"I'm still the same Kaelynn, though, regardless of what my bank account says."

"I know that."

"Trust works both ways, Nash."

Staring at the fire, he looked lost in thought before he faced me and softly replied, "But I didn't withhold something from you."

"You ran a background check on me, so perspective and all," I said, my voice giving way to my emotions.

"I wasn't being deceitful from the very beginning, Kaelynn."

My lips pressed together to keep in the sob that threatened to break free. It was in that moment I knew Nash would never be able to trust me. It was something he valued, and I had taken it away from him, just like Lily had. Maybe not in the same way, but I had still not given it to him.

I stood and stared down at him. He was now staring into the fire. I said the only thing I knew to say. The only thing I could say that might absolve me of the weight of my emotions.

"I'm sorry."

Turning, I walked out of the library. My hand went to my mouth the moment I was around the corner in an attempt to not burst into tears. I ran as fast as I could to get as far away as I could. Janet gave me a concerned look as I approached her. Slowing, I wiped the tears away and forced a wobbly smile.

"I'll be in my room, Janet. I don't wish to be disturbed."

"Yes, I understand. Your tea?" she asked as I shook my head, then dashed toward the stairs. I couldn't talk; I was crying too hard as I left her question unanswered.

⤚⋟⋞⤙

THE WHITE-COVERED MOUNTAINS looked beautiful as I sat gazing out from the window seat, a book open at my side. The snow had begun to fall heavily late last night and hadn't let up since.

Sliding my knees up, I rested my chin on them and took in the beauty. I hadn't been able to sleep at all last night. Thoughts of Nash and how sad he looked yesterday evening replayed in my mind. I was angry at myself, but equally as angry that he hadn't trusted me either.

Sighing, I picked up my phone and sent a text to Millie and Jack.

Me: Not much in the mood for a game night tonight. Sorry.

Something from outside caught my eye, causing me to sit up and lean closer to the window to look out.

"Nash," I whispered. He was walking out in the snow, taking it all in. I couldn't help but smile. I had remembered him making the comment he had never seen a lot of snow.

"Well, you're getting your fair share now," I spoke to the window. Silence was the only response.

My phone beeped in my hand.

> *Millie: Have you not been watching the weather? Even if you wanted to still do it, Jack and I can't get up to you. The snow is coming down like crazy. I hope Janet stocked up on enough food you guys are stuck up there for a few days.*
>
> *Jack: Sorry, sis, looks like you and the boyfriend or whatever he is to you are stuck there alone. There is plenty of frozen pizza in the freezer.*

I stared at my phone in disbelief. They were just going to leave me stranded up here? Leave Nash stranded?

> *Millie: All flights out of the airport are cancelled. Nash won't be making that flight tomorrow after all.*

With a sigh, I replied to them both.

> *Me: Let's hope the pizza is still there.*

Millie sent me a text separate from Jack's.

> *Millie: How did it go last night?*
>
> *Me: Not good. I think we're over. He can't forgive me for not telling him the truth.*
>
> *Millie: What about him going behind your back and running that report?*
>
> *Me: He said he wasn't being deceitful and hiding the truth about himself all along. He's right.*
>
> *Millie: I'm so sorry, Kaelynn. I know how much you liked him.*

Nash picked up a handful of snow, balled it up into a snowball, and gave it a toss. Janet must have given him one of Jack's old coats with gloves and a hat. He looked adorable outside among the snow.

A tear made a track down my face as I looked from Nash back to my phone.

> *Me: Yeah . . . I really did.*

The light knock on my bedroom door made me jump. "Come in," I called out.

"Good morning, Kaelynn. I have breakfast if you'd like to come down and eat. Mr. Barrett is out . . . well . . . exploring in the snow."

I chuckled. "You mean playing in it."

"It was rather cute to see how excited he got at all the snow coming down. He's on his way back in. Shall I set two plates out?"

"Janet, you don't have to cook or wait on us. Please. Why don't you take the rest of the day off, the rest of the week, and just relax and enjoy the snowstorm."

Her eyes widened in shock. "The week off? I don't think I could do that."

Laughing, I swung my legs around and stood. "Do you have enough food at your place?"

She nodded.

Janet lived in a small guest house just north of the main house.

"And there is plenty of food here?" I asked.

"Yes, I ran to the store after Mr. Barrett arrived. I knew the weather was turning, so I wanted to make sure we had enough in the main house for at least a week."

"A week? How long is this storm supposed to last?"

"Well, at least two to three days of steady snow. The pass will for sure be closed for at least a day or two, depending on how much snow there is."

I wrung my hands as I thought about being here with Nash for a week. Lifting my worried gaze, I asked Janet, "Did Nash happen to mention when his flight back to Texas was?"

Janet's brows drew down. "He did mention yesterday he would be leaving early tomorrow morning. He didn't tell you?"

My stomach dropped. "No, no, he didn't mention it."

She nodded and smiled. "Well, he won't be making it. Are you sure you don't want me to stay and help cook for you two?"

"No, it's honestly fine. I promise not to mess up the house."

Taking a few steps into the room, Janet stopped a few feet from me. "Forgive me if I'm about to speak on something I shouldn't, but I've known you since you were a little girl, Kaelynn. I've also seen that look on your face many years ago on a younger version of me. Don't give up on each other. Whatever it is that happened, don't give up. That young man down there is clearly in love with you."

I scoffed. "He's angry with me, not in love, and he has a right to be, and from the sound of it, he's now stuck with me for days. At least the house is big enough that we can avoid each other if we have to."

"He flew all the way to Utah just to tell you he was angry with you?" she asked, one brow quirked up in question. "No, he flew here because he loves you. If it's meant to be, it will be. It's Christmastime after all!"

"Thank you, Janet," I said, walking up to her and giving her a hug. "And thank you for thinking ahead on the food. I was afraid we would be living off of Jack's frozen pizzas."

She rolled her eyes. "Oh, there is plenty of that as well if you get to feeling like you want heartburn. I made a lasagna, and it's in the refrigerator. There is also some potato soup in small containers in the freezer."

The mention of lasagna made me think of our second date. The night Nash made me come by rubbing up against him. Jesus, that seemed like so long ago.

"Thank you," I said, barely above a whisper.

Janet squeezed my hands, then turned and walked out of my bedroom. Glancing back out the window, I saw that Nash was gone. With a deep breath in, I squared my shoulders and headed down to the kitchen for breakfast.

Nash sat at the island, a large plate of pancakes sitting in front of him while Janet poured him orange juice.

"Where is Kaelynn?" he asked.

I slipped back around the corner and froze.

"She should be joining you. I let her know I made breakfast."

"Is she okay?"

The concern in his voice made me place my hand over my chest. It felt like my heart was fluttering at the same time it was breaking.

"You will have to ask her."

"Right, of course," Nash stated.

"I'll be taking the next few days off," she said. "I hope that is okay?"

"Tell me you're not going to try and leave with this snow coming down?" Nash asked.

"Oh no. I live in the small guest house next to the main house. I've worked for the Whitaker family for over twenty-five years. When they built this house, Mr. Whitaker wanted me to have a place for privacy. Kaelynn told me to take a few days off. She is such a sweet young lady."

"Kaelynn is amazing. I've never met anyone like her."

Janet chuckled. "One of a kind. People like that you don't let slip away."

I closed my eyes. Good Lord. Even Janet was butting in now. I took in a deep gulp of air and readied myself. Stepping into the kitchen, I tried to seem chipper.

"Good morning. It smells delicious, Janet."

She beamed with pride. "I made your favorite. Pumpkin-walnut pancakes and peppered bacon."

My stomach decided to growl at that moment, causing all of us to laugh. Peeking over to Nash, I tried not to let my eyes roam over him. He looked so handsome with the snow-kissed cheeks tinged with the redness of warmth returning to his skin.

"Hey," I said, slipping onto the stool at the end of the bar.

Nash's eyes brightened, and I couldn't help the way my body tingled when I was near him.

"Good morning."

"So, I guess you've heard the airport is closed. I'm sorry."

His head tilted and he smirked. "Ready to get rid of me?"

"What? No? I figured you were ready to leave."

"Not yet."

The way he looked at me made my insides warm.

"Maybe today we can try and talk again?" Nash asked before putting a huge portion of pancakes in his mouth.

"Yes. Sure. Of course." I swallowed hard and focused on the food Janet put in front of me. "Thank you, Janet. Please, go enjoy a few days off. I'll be fine. Nash is here, so it's not like I'm alone."

Janet tried not to grin like a fool, but she clapped her hands. "My sister is in town and has been crafting over there without me. It will be fun for us both to be able to make a few things for family."

"What?" I asked, my mouth dropping open. "Why didn't you say you had family in town? I mean, I know you weren't planning on me being here. I'm so sorry, Janet!"

Waving me off, she replied, "It's okay. She's here through Christmas."

"Go! Go enjoy your time together." This time it was me waving her off. I stood and hugged her as she kissed me on the cheek.

"You two enjoy yourselves," Janet said, hurrying out of the kitchen.

Nash laughed. "She seems like a really nice person."

"Janet is amazing. She's been working for my parents for as long as I can remember. She's more family than anything. My mother would be lost without Janet."

Our gaze locked for a brief moment before I broke it and went back to eating.

"So, I went outside just a bit ago. Got to do what every person wants to do when it is snowing."

"What's that?"

He chuckled. "I leaned my head back and held out my tongue to catch the snow."

"Oh."

I tried hard not to laugh, but I lost the battle. Nash laughed along with me until we fell into another silence.

After finishing breakfast, we both cleaned up and put the dishes in the dishwasher, neither of us speaking. Then he took my hand and started to lead me out of the kitchen.

"Where are we going?" I asked.

"To my favorite room so far in your house. The library."

"That's my favorite room as well."

"I know; a little birdy told me that." I smiled at him, remembering our conversation from my place.

We walked into the room, and I was surprised to see a fire going. Nash walked over and added a few logs to it.

"I started it before I went outside and then threw a couple logs on when I came in."

"We usually have a tree in here by now. I guess with my parents being out of town, they didn't get a chance to put one up before they left."

Nash walked up and stood next to me. "A real one?"

I glanced up at him. "Nope. We have artificial trees."

"Trees? As in plural?"

"Yep!" I said, popping the *p*. "Look at this house! You can't just have one tree!"

Nash chuckled. "I guess that's true."

"The tree that goes in here though is special because it's the family tree. We always spent Christmas morning in here."

"Why?"

I shrugged. "I think it was because it felt smaller, cozier. We felt close to each other. In the main living area, with the picture window, my mother puts up a beautiful ten-foot tree that is decorated with all silver. It's stunning against the mountains. But it feels so. . . ."

"Cold?" Nash asked, sitting down on the sofa.

"Yes. Exactly," I stated, sitting next to him and turning to face him. "The other trees are themed trees. The one on my father's trophy room is woodland themed."

"I really need to see that room."

Smiling, I replied, "Okay. I'll give you the grand tour today."

He lifted a brow. "Can we bowl?"

"Sure. If you want."

Nash leaned forward, a serious look on his face. "I have a very important question to ask."

I swallowed hard. "O-okay."

"Did I hear Millie right? Is there a billiards room? I can also kick your ass at pool."

It took a moment for his words to register what he said.

"That so?" I asked. "Is that a challenge?"

He nodded. His smile faded some and he moved his gaze to the fireplace. Just like he had last night. This time, he didn't leave it there, he focused back in on me.

"I'm sorry about last night, Kaelynn."

"You don't have anything to be sorry about."

"Yes, I do. You got upset and I let you leave. That was a dick move."

I shook my head and went to speak, but he locked his gaze on mine, causing me to go still as he continued to speak.

"I'm in love with you, Kaelynn, and I really don't know what to do with that."

My eyes widened in shock, and I must have opened and closed my mouth at least four times. When I was finally able to speak, it was a simple, "What did you say?"

Nash blew out a breath and focused on his hands for a moment before returning his attention back to me.

"I knew from the beginning you were hiding something. There were a million different times I could have asked you. There were a few times I think you were about to tell me and we were interrupted. That night you made me dinner. You were going to tell me then, weren't you?"

Feeling my jaw shake, I knew words would not come, so I agreed with a head nod.

"For months after Lily and I broke up, I vowed I was done with ever getting serious with a woman again. I wouldn't risk my heart being broken like that. Then I ran into you."

My heart started to beat a little bit faster with each word he said. Nothing else in the world mattered to me in that moment than what Nash Barrett was about to say.

"And just like that, I was ready to move on. I had realized I had never really been in love with Lily. At least not the type of love that meant forever. At the time, I guess I thought it did, but the moment you looked up at me with those eyes of yours, I couldn't remember anything about Lily. Or any other women before. You made me want to take the step, and I wanted to take it with you. And that scared me."

Nash reached over and wiped a tear off my cheek.

"You scared the hell out of me, Kaelynn. I felt heartbroken after Lily, but the thought of falling for you and letting you in and something happening . . . I knew it would destroy me. I have never believed in love at first sight, or falling in love with someone almost instantly until you literally walked into my life."

My hand covered my soft sobbing.

"The whole background check was stupid, and that was why I was angry at Blake at the wedding. I had called it off because it didn't matter to me anymore. I was ready to take the risk with you and trust that what we had together was strong enough to make it through anything. I was pissed off that you ran. I told myself I was going to fly up here and explain why I started down that stupid path with Blake and his brother and then I would walk away. Because that morning when I walked into the hotel room and you were gone, I felt a piece of my heart leave with you and . . ."

His voice trailed off and he closed his eyes for a few moments before opening them and looking at me.

"I don't think I could live in this world without you. I know we haven't known each other very long, and most people would say it's lust, not love. That night we spent together, I've never felt that way with any other woman, and to see you gone, knowing you would just leave without talking to me. It scared the fuck out of me, and I put up that wall again before it was too late. Before I admitted to myself that I was head over heels in love with you."

"Nash," I said, letting my tears fall freely. "I'm so sorry I ran. I'm so sorry I kept the truth from you."

He shook his head. "You don't have to be sorry. You got scared too, Kaelynn. It took me sitting in this room last night, hearing you crying as you ran off, for it to finally freaking set into my thick skull. You did what you did because I think you're in love with me too."

"Yes. So very much in love."

Nash smiled, and it was all I could do to keep from crawling over and straddling him. I wanted his lips on mine. I needed his lips on mine.

I needed him.

"So, now what?" I asked.

Nash leaned forward and used his thumbs to wipe my face clean of tears again.

"We take advantage of being stuck together in a giant playground of a house."

I couldn't help but giggle.

"We admit that we were both wrong, and that in the future, we talk to each other. About anything that scares us, or makes us angry, or whatever the case may be. We trust one another."

"Yes," I whispered as Nash took me by the arms and pulled me onto him. Having me do what only moments ago I had wanted to do. I settled my throbbing core over him and felt him harden. A delicious want grew in my body, but I knew we needed to make sure we had everything taken care of first.

"I'm sorry, Kaelynn. I'm sorry I didn't just ask you from the beginning."

"I'm sorry I didn't trust you with the truth."

Nash looked around the room, then smirked. "It is pretty damn intimidating."

"It's my parents' place, not mine."

He drew his brows in and thought for a moment, then asked, "That day I ran into you at the Austonian, were you looking for a place to live, or was it a place for your folks?"

"Me, but I knew I didn't want anything that crazy expensive or over the top like that. It's not me. I like my place near Zilker Park. Mom and Dad bought a penthouse there, though," I said with a frown.

"I figured. I saw you there with them."

"I knew it! I knew you were there. I had the strangest feeling you had been there."

He laughed and then cupped my face. "No more secrets for either of us."

"No more secrets."

"I love you, Kaelynn Shae Whitaker."

My insides melted as I leaned closer to his mouth. "I love you, Nash . . . What is your middle name, by the way?"

He laughed, and I loved the way it made my heart feel like it skipped a beat.

"I guess I still have one secret."

My brow lifted.

"Nash isn't my real name."

Dropping my mouth open, I gasped. "What!"

"It's James Nathaniel Barrett. Nash is my nickname. My sister, for some reason, couldn't say James and insisted on calling me Nash. So it sort of stuck."

I pressed into him, causing him to moan. "Well, if we're being honest here, I think Nash is sexier than James. Sounds so bad boyish."

He winked. "Me too. I'm pretty sure I wouldn't have gotten laid with a name like James."

Smacking him on the chest, I said, "I love you, James Nathaniel Barrett. Now please kiss me already."

"I'll do you one better. I'll kiss you, then make love to you."

Lacing my arms around his neck, I let him pull my mouth to his. The kiss was slow and sweet at first. Then it heated. Our tongues moving as if they needed to find the perfect rhythm. To find our way back to each other.

"Kaelynn," Nash panted, his hands going up under my sweater. "Fuck, I don't have a condom."

My hands worked at getting his jeans unbuttoned. I needed to feel him inside of me.

Pressing my mouth to his, I slipped my hand in until I found him, hard and ready.

"Oh God. Nash."

He cupped my ass, pulling me against him. I couldn't help but think of the first time I came, fully dressed, writhing against him like I needed my next breath.

"I want you so much, baby."

His words felt like a warm blanket over my shivering, cold body.

"Then take me. Right here. Now. Please."

Our mouth smashed together in a hungry kiss. I squeezed my hand around his cock, moaning into his mouth.

"No. Condom," he panted.

I tugged at his shirt, trying to get it off while he did the same with mine. Our mouths parted only long enough to get the shirts over our heads.

Going back to his pants, Nash grabbed my wrist. "Stop. We need to talk about this."

Lifting my eyes to meet his, I gasped for air. "Okay. I'm on the pill. I've only been with two men before you and have always used a condom."

"I've been with . . ."

I pressed my fingers against his mouth. "Don't tell me a number, Nash. I don't care. Have you always used a condom? Even with Lily?"

"Always. She never wanted to get on birth control."

"Do you want this?" I asked.

His eyes nearly rolled to the back of his head as he laughed. "You're asking me if I want to make love to you without something between us?"

"Yes."

Lifting his hand to the side of my face, I leaned into his touch. He stared at me with such love and passion in his eyes it made my eyes fill with tears.

"I want that more than anything, if it's what you want. Otherwise, there are other things we can do until we can get some. Remember, I'm *really* creative."

Shaking my head and trying not to giggle at his words, I crawled off him and started to take my jeans and panties off. Reaching up behind me, I unclasped my bra and let it fall to the ground. My eyes drifted down to see Nash had a hold of his dick and stroked himself as he looked at me with want-filled eyes. It was one of the hottest things I'd ever seen.

My teeth dug into my lip and I took a few steps back. Nash stood and kicked his shoes off, then removed his jeans. I loved that he had been going commando.

"You're so beautiful, Kaelynn. I'm so in love with you."

Reaching for a blanket on the back of a chair, I laid it out in front of the fire and slowly let my body down until I was lying on it. Nash moved over me, his eyes blazing as hot as the fire felt.

"Kaelynn," he whispered, pressing his lips to mine. "You're mine. Forever."

Twenty-Five

NASH

I COULDN'T BELIEVE it. My head wouldn't allow me to believe that I was about to make love to Kaelynn. In front of the fire, with the snow falling outside a beautiful large window, and nothing would be separating us. No barriers and no secrets.

My hand roamed down the side of her body, causing her to shake in response to my touch. She spread her legs open for me as I gently pressed my thumb against her swollen bundle of nerves. Moving my mouth above hers, I whispered, "Kaelynn." Then kissed her. "You're mine. Forever."

She hissed out a yes as my finger slipped inside of her. I groaned while she lifted her hips in response.

"You're so wet."

"I want you, desperately," she spoke against my mouth. The feel of her hot breath moving over my skin made my insides grow with need.

"Baby, I want you so much. I need you."

"Yes. Please. Nash, please don't make me wait."

Slowly, I kissed down her neck to her breasts. Kissing one nipple, I worked my fingers inside of her while she dug her nails into my back. The little moans and pleas coming from her lips nearly had me coming on the spot. Moving to the other nipple, I sucked and bit lightly as I felt Kaelynn's body begin to tremble.

"Nash, I'm so close. I'm so . . ."

Pressing my thumb against her clit, Kaelynn came undone in an instant. Her hips pumped against my hand and she cried out her release. My mouth covered hers as she clung to me, arms wrapped around my body, the sound of my name coming from between our kisses.

"Now. Please, Nash. Now."

Using my knee to spread her open more to me, I pushed into her. The feel of being inside her, nothing to separate us, was almost more than I could stand.

"Kaelynn . . ." I panted.

Her arms and legs wrapped around my body as we found the perfect pace. It was slow, yet full of passion. I pushed in deep, causing her to gasp, then pull me closer to her, as if she needed me even deeper.

"I love you, Nash. Please don't stop. Don't ever stop."

Our eyes met and I wanted to ask her if she meant don't stop making love to her or don't stop loving her. Right in this moment, with the firelight setting our skin ablaze, we were both in a place that we were always meant to be, and I'd never stop loving her.

"Never," I whispered before kissing her again. Burying my face into her neck, I made love to her until neither of us could hold back any longer. I came so hard I swore I saw stars.

"Don't leave. Please," she whispered as I laid above her, still inside of her. I pulled out of her and rolled to her side. Drawing her against me, I kissed her back and listened as her breathing got slower and deeper. Kaelynn had fallen asleep in my arms after we had shared the most intensely beautiful moment of my entire life.

Closing my eyes, I drifted to sleep next to her.

∼≫∽

"NASH. NASH, WAKE up."

Moaning, I pulled Kaelynn back against my body. "Go back to sleep."

I heard the faint sound of a giggle. "Nash. We have to get up. Someone is here."

Jerking up into a sitting position, I looked around. "What do you mean someone is here?"

"I mean, someone just came through the gate. I think it's my parents."

Kaelynn and I sat naked on the blanket in front of the fireplace.

"Shit!" I shouted as I jumped up and started looking for my clothes while Kaelynn did the same.

"How do you know someone was at the gate?"

"There is a bell that charms when someone accesses the gate with the code. It's an alert system my father had put in, and we all have it on our phones. I turned the app on when I got home."

Kaelynn tried to get back into her jeans as she did a little jumping motion.

"Your bra," I said as I tossed it over to her. Kaelynn was dressed and heading out of the library while I rushed to put my boots back on. I grabbed the blanket off the floor and stared at it. It needed to be washed.

Shit. Where in the hell is the laundry room again in this house?

"Kaelynn?" I shouted as I made my way to the front foyer. "Kaelynn?"

"It's not my folks; it looks like it's Jack."

My heart jumped a beat as I watched someone coming down the drive on a snowmobile.

"Holy shit, how much has it snowed since earlier? And can I just say that I'm glad your dad put that little security system in?"

She laughed and reached up to kiss me. "Me too. I'm pretty sure Jack wouldn't take too lightly to you having sex with me on his favorite blanket."

I held the blanket up. "This blanket? That needs to be washed, now."

Kaelynn took the blanket and headed toward the kitchen side of the house. Instead of turning left to go to the kitchen, we went right.

"Here's the laundry room."

She tossed the blanket into the washer, followed by detergent, and then turned it on.

"There. No evidence of our naughty behavior. We did, however, christen the library."

With a wiggle of my brows, I pulled her body to mine. "I'm thinking we need to break in every room in this house. I see hours and hours of fun ahead of us. Fifty-thousand square feet of hours, if memory serves me correctly."

Kaelynn lifted up on her toes and kissed me softly, giggling as she lowered herself back to the floor. "Me too."

"I see the two of you made up."

Jack's voice had us both stepping away from each other.

"Please, don't act like you're perfect angels. I'm sure neither of you are virgins." Jack stared at me and lifted a brow. "You especially. With that pretty-boy face, I'm sure you've been around the block once or twice."

The pretty blonde standing next to Jack slapped him in the stomach.

"Shut up, Jack." She walked up to Kaelynn and hugged her, then turned her attention on me. "It's nice to meet you, Nash. I'm Jill."

I shook her hand and replied, "It's nice meeting you, Jill. Where exactly did you and Jack meet? Up on the hill? And was the pail of water frozen when you got to it?"

Jack let out a roar of fake laughter then shot me a dirty look. "Ha, like we've never heard that before, dickhead."

"Jack!" Kaelynn and Jill said at the same time.

Laughing, I reached for Jack's hand. "I'm just screwing with y'all. So, a snowmobile, huh?"

Kaelynn groaned. "No, Nash, no."

Jack nodded and said, "Tell me you have snow pants."

"Nope."

"No worries, follow me and I'll get you set up. You ever been on a snowmobile?" Jack asked as I followed him up the stairs.

"Never. This morning was the first time I've ever really seen snow."

Jack stopped and turned to look at me. "You're fucking with me, right?"

"No. I've lived in Texas my entire life."

A wide grin moved over his face. "Dude, we are going to have so much fun."

And boy, did we have fun. By the time we got back from playing on the snowmobile, my face felt like was about to fall off.

Jack pulled up and parked in front of the house and we climbed off.

"Next time I'll have Jill ride one over and we can really have some fun."

Stomping the snow off of my boots before walking into the house, I couldn't help but chuckle. "This is like a damn playground up here."

Jack took off his jacket, scarf, and hat and tossed them over one of the sofas. I looked around for a coat rack when Jack grabbed my stuff and threw it by his.

"We're not uptight in this family."

He glanced around. "Wonder where the girls are."

Laughter could be heard from down the hall. "It sounds like they're in the library."

Jack started down the hall. "I'm not surprised. You'll find out that Kaelynn has two places in this house that are her favorite. The library and the theater room.

We used to find her in the theater reading in one of the recliners. She liked it because it was dark and quiet."

They weren't in the library, so we headed on to the family room. Attached to that room was the billiards room. Walking in, I looked at the large flat-screen TV that had a video from Jim and Terri's wedding pulled up.

"Play it again!" Jill cried out, wiping tears from her face.

"You didn't," I said, glaring at Kaelynn.

She lost it laughing and said, "I did! Charlie sent me this!"

Hitting *play* on her phone, the video on the TV started up.

"Tell me you didn't!" Jack said, jumping over the sofa and landing next to Jill.

There wasn't anything I could do but watch and laugh. It really was funny as hell watching Jim think he was taking the garter belt off Terri when it was really me.

After watching the damn video three more times, Jack couldn't take it anymore. He was on the ground laughing hysterically.

"Dude, he was all up in that! You were . . . dude, you looked desperate to get away!" Jack cried out, making us all laugh again.

"Who came up with that idea anyway?" Kaelynn asked, wiping a tear away.

"Tucker. Then Blake jumped on board. We drew straws to see who would get to be the lucky . . . *bride*. I drew the short straw. Now that I think about it, I always draw the short straw."

They started laughing again.

When everyone settled down, Jack stood. "We need to leave. I only came to bring you guys a few supplies."

"Supplies? Janet said we had plenty of food."

"Food, yeah, but just in case the power goes out, I brought some candles and batteries for the flashlights. I'll take some over to Janet and her sister as well. I need to make sure they have enough firewood to keep a fire going for heat, in case they lose power."

"I can help you with that, if you need me to."

"That would be great. We might want to cut some down smaller, just in case. It's supposed to be a pretty bad storm coming behind the one that already came through. There is a strong chance the power will be knocked out for a few hours."

"It's that bad, huh?" Kaelynn asked. "I haven't even turned on the TV since I've been here."

"Yeah, it's a big one," Jill stated with a worried look on her face. "We should probably get to doing what we came for and get back ourselves."

Now Kaelynn looked worried and walked over to grab the remote.

"Nash, you ready? It will go faster with your help."

"Yeah, let's do it."

Twenty-Six

KAELYNN

THE SOUND OF the wind outside caused me to wrap my arms around my body. The snow hadn't stopped falling and I couldn't see but a few feet outside. Jack and Nash had spent an hour chopping up more wood for Janet and for us. Then we placed candles in the kitchen, bathroom, and library in case the power went out.

"What a welcome home," I mumbled to no one in particular.

I turned on my heels and made my way through the house back to the library. Nash and I had turned it into our own little sanctuary. When I walked in, I slowed to a soft pace and sat down on the coffee table. Nash was sound asleep on the sofa, a book draped over his chest. Chewing on my lip, I let my gaze roam over him. My heart seemed to speed up in my chest as I took in every inch of him. He was so handsome and looked completely at peace as he napped away. Tingles erupted over my skin, and I itched to run my fingers through his dark hair. The stubble on his face was a tease. I wanted to feel it everywhere on my body, especially between my legs. Nash had been the only man to make me come with his mouth, and I could not ignore the growing pulse between my thighs when I thought of it. It was true when I said I ached for this man.

"Nash," I whispered. Dropping to my knees onto the floor, I leaned in closer. "Nash."

Stirring, he rolled over some, the book sliding off his chest and falling to the floor. He didn't wake.

I moved closer and kissed his face. He didn't move.

"Heavy sleeper, huh?"

With my finger, I traced along his jawline, then down his chest to his jeans. I carefully unbuttoned them and lowered his zipper. My sex clenched at the sight of him as my tongue ran over my lips. I moved my body farther down and worked at his jeans until I freed him. Nash moved slightly but remained sleeping peacefully.

Taking him in my hand, I glided my hand over his shaft, watching it grow hard. Nash moaned but didn't wake up. Once he was hard, I took a deep breath and took him into my mouth. His hips jerked, and he whispered my name, which only fueled me to take him deeper.

I moved slow at first, learning the rhythm I needed to use both my hand and my mouth. Nash's hips began to jerk, then lift as he attempted to get deeper into my mouth. I worked down farther, using my hand to squeeze his cock a bit tighter. Then his hands were in my hair as he began to move in my mouth. Lifting my eyes, I smiled when I saw him watching me. A look of pure pleasure on his face.

"Fuck. Yes," he hissed, moving his hips faster.

I moaned and that seemed to cause him to nearly fall over the edge. Nash pulled my mouth off him.

"Get on me, now," he demanded.

Loving the fact I had changed into a dress, I did as he asked. Slipping my panties to the side, I slowly guided him into my body. Coating him with my wetness until he went in easily.

"God help me," Nash whispered.

"What do you want me to do?" I asked.

"Make me come."

I moved up and down slowly at first until the feel of him inside me, building up to my orgasm, became too much. Faster, harder, bodies hitting each other as we were both fully clothed. It was one of the hottest moments of my life. I had never been so turned on knowing I was responsible for this moment.

"Kaelynn, touch yourself, baby. I'm going to come soon."

My hand went under my dress where I found my ultra-sensitive clit. A few strokes and I called out Nash's name as he grabbed me and let himself go. The feel of him coming inside me was something I would never forget.

Once we had both stopped moving, I collapsed onto his chest, breathing heavily.

I looked at him and told him exactly what I felt in that moment. "You coming inside me is the most delicious thing I've ever experienced."

Nash wrapped his arms around me as I felt him still moving a bit inside me. "I feel the same way, baby. You feel like you were made for me."

Still looking at him, I kissed him on the chin, then across his jaw and up to his mouth. "I was made for you, and you were made for me. Let's do this every day."

"Make love?" he asked.

"Yes, that, but especially let's do this spontaneously hot sex. Something about each of us being fully clothed was so hot."

He laughed and I felt his dick jump inside me. He started to wiggle and I felt him getting hard again.

"There is no way you can do that again."

Sitting up, Nash pulled his T-shirt over his head and tossed it to the floor.

"Wanna make a bet?"

Scrambling to both get undressed, Nash rolled us over and he took me to heaven two more times.

I no longer cared about the snowstorm or what happened outside. The only thing I cared about was being with Nash, alone, free to do whatever we wanted.

❦

THE NEXT MORNING Nash and I stood on the back porch and stared out at the massive snowdrift that was up over the banister.

Letting out a long breath, Nash said, "Okay, now I'm starting to worry. It's still snowing."

"I know. Did you check on Janet and her sister this morning?"

"Yeah. They still have plenty of food and were elbow deep in ribbon, beads, and everything Christmas crafts."

I giggled. "It looks like this is the last wave of snow, according to the weather."

The wind began to pick up, and we turned and ran into the house.

"What are we going to do today?" Nash asked.

We were on day four of the snowstorm. Nash and I made good use of our time stuck in the house. We had made love in the library four times before we moved up to my bedroom, where Nash had not been very patient. The moment we got into the room, he tore my dress off and took me against the door, then fucked me fast and hard on the bed, at my request. It had been devilishly amazing. Of course, I would never be able to play pool again without thinking of lying on a pool table while Nash made me come twice with his mouth.

The house should have smelled like nothing but sex. We were having a lot of it. Everywhere. I wasn't sure I was going to be able to look my parents in the eyes when they returned home. I felt like I was back in high school.

Arms came up and wrapped around my body. I settled against his chest and let out a contented sigh.

"Do you know what I want to do now?" I asked.

"I'm not fucking you in your dad's trophy room. One, all the animals watching us will give me performance anxiety, and two, I'm pretty sure your dad would know the moment he walked into the room."

Laughing, I turned and wrapped my arms around his neck. "I want to go out and play in the snow."

His brow lifted. "Okay, but it might be hard for me to keep it up in that sort of cold weather."

Smacking him on the back, we laughed.

"I'm kidding, I know what you meant. I've been waiting for you to say you wanted to go out in this."

"Why didn't you say you wanted to venture out, Nash?" I asked, taking his hand in mine as we made our way up to my room. Nash had moved his small bag into my room, as well as some clothes he took from

Jack's room.

"We've been having a hell of a good time inside. I'm a patient man. Besides, I'd much rather be balls deep inside of you than be balls deep in the snowdrifts." I almost choked when he said that.

"What about oral sex on a pool table? Does that rank up there too?" I asked with a wink.

He smiled and licked his lips. "That was fun."

"Yes, it was."

"Come on, let's go outside and play, then I'll warm you up by getting naked with you."

Fifteen minutes later, Nash and I were outside and he was getting started on a snowman. We worked as a team building it, only to have Nash get bored and start a snowball fight with me. The poor snowman became a shield as snowballs flew back and forth.

I landed one right in Nash's face, causing him to stumble and fall back, landing right on the snowman. He stood, brushed off the snow, and then looked at me like he was ready to take me down.

"No! Nash, you moved and I couldn't help where it landed."

There was snow stuck in his mustache and beard that Nash had grown over the last few days. I loved the way it tickled my mouth when he kissed me. Or how it made my entire body erupt with goosebumps when I moved it across my skin.

"You better run, Kaelynn, or you're getting snow down your shirt."

"My shirt!" I cried out with laughter. "You wouldn't! Nash, please no!" I wasn't ashamed to beg because I knew I was going to lose this battle.

Nash scooped up a handful of snow and started running toward me. Screaming, I spun around and ran as fast as I could to the house. I heard Nash curse and glanced over my shoulder to see he had slipped and fallen. I turned and ran backward, laughing as I pointed.

"Ha! Texas boy can't handle the Utah winter!"

Turning, I thought I hadn't run as far as I did, but I ran smack into the giant picture window, knocking myself flat on my ass.

"Kaelynn!" Nash cried out as he ran over and dropped down next to me. I lay flat in a pile of snow, my forehead pounding and my nose aching. When he dropped down next to me, snow flew up into my face, making me cough.

"Baby, are you okay?" he asked.

I blinked a few times and then tilted my head. "You don't have to worry about that snow. I'm pretty sure it's not only under my jacket and shirt, but down my pants somehow too."

Nash stared for another few seconds before he busted out laughing. Then I started laughing.

"Holy shit! You turned and ran right into that glass! I mean, you hit *hard*, baby!"

I laughed so hard I started to feel tears slipping down my nearly frozen cheeks.

"Bring me in before I freeze out here!" I cried out.

Helping me up, Nash started laughing again. I gave him a good push and made my way through the deep snow to the back door that led to the mudroom.

Nash and I stripped down to our undies, then made our way up to my bathroom to take a hot shower. I was exhausted, and even though I thought sex in the shower would probably be a ton of fun, I couldn't bring myself to make the first move. Nash appeared to be exhausted too.

We dried off in silence and made our way to the bed, where we crawled in. Drawing me against his body, Nash leaned over and kissed me.

"Nap time," Nash whispered.

Hours later I woke up to a pitch dark, freezing house. Glancing over, I could barely make out Nash. He had the cover pulled over him. God, he was so darn cute.

Slipping out of the bed, I shivered. "Crapola. Please don't tell me the power is off."

I searched for the side table and lamp and clicked it on. Nothing happened.

"Nash, baby, wake up."

"No! I'm warm and sleeping."

"The power is off."

Groaning came from under the covers before he pushed them off and sat up.

"Okay, this winter shit is for the birds. I'm totally over the pretty snow and mountains. I want Texas."

"Well, you've got Utah in December. Let's get dressed and head to the library."

"Does Jack have any sweats, do you think?"

I pointed to the few items of clothes I got from raiding my brother's room. "I thought ahead and brought you some."

Nash yawned and got out of the bed. "Shit! Shit! Shit! What is the temperature in here? How in the hell long has the power been off?"

Lighting a candle, I replied, "How long have we been asleep is the better question. I feel like I was asleep for hours."

Nash chuckled. "Me too. Felt good having you beside me; slept better than I have in years, it seems. You know you're going to have to move in with me when we get back to Texas."

"Me move in with you? Why aren't you moving in with me?"

He stopped putting on the sweats and gave my question some serious thought. "I guess I could move in with you. You're not that far from the highway. I could jump on it and get anywhere I needed to go."

My stomach dipped and jumped at the thought of Nash moving in with me.

"Wait, are you serious? You'd really move in with me?"

"If you wanted me to. I was totally being serious. Your place is way nicer than mine, smaller but nicer. Besides, my favorite food truck is right outside your place."

I tilted my head to look at him. "Which one?"

"Hey Cupcake."

Laughing, I tossed a pillow at him.

"So that is the only reason you're agreeable to moving in with me?"

He shrugged. "Maybe."

Grabbing the candle, Nash took my hand as we walked out of the bedroom and made our way downstairs.

The temperature in the house wasn't too bad. It was sixty but felt colder in the expanse of the high ceilings. After making a plate full of cheese, fruit, and veggies, we made our way to the library. Shutting the door, I put down the food and helped Nash build a fire and make a bed in front of it. I knew he wasn't the least bit tired, and neither was I after that long nap we had. He prepared the fire for other activities, all of which made my insides dance with anticipation. If you thought about it, it was a great idea—conserving body heat and all.

"Do you think Janet and her sister are okay?" I asked, pulling out my phone.

"Send them a text; see if they need anything."

"It's four in the morning!" I said with a gasp.

"Wow. We really did sleep for hours."

I sighed as I sat down. "All the sex is making us tired."

He followed my lead, wiggling his brows at me. "That's my kind of tired."

Nash and I snuggled on the sofa, each of us grabbing a book to read. It didn't take long before I felt my head drop to his shoulder and I drifted back off to sleep.

I woke some time later on the sofa, only to find Nash wasn't there. He wasn't in the library either. Stretching, I stood and headed out to find him. Looking everywhere, I started to get worried.

"Nash?" I cried out, my voice echoing off the walls in the house. "Nash!"

My phone beeped in my back pocket, causing me to pull it out quickly. It was Nash.

> Nash: *Janet needed more firewood brought in. I'll be right back. Janet also told me where the Christmas tree was. Want to set it up?*

I couldn't contain my smile if I wanted to. I loved that Nash was making the best out of being stranded.

> Me: *YES!*

I headed to the kitchen to start some breakfast. The power was still off and the house was freezing. I turned and dashed up the back stairs and grabbed a white sweater from my closet before returning downstairs.

Using a lighter, I turned on the gas stove and lit the flame, then started to mix up some pancake mix. I wasn't sure how the food was in the refrigerator, so I passed on that. Then it was on to figuring out how to make coffee with no electricity. I dialed Millie's phone number.

"Hey, how is everything going there? Jack said you guys didn't have any power out that way."

"No, it went off yesterday, sometime in the night. Do you have power?"

"It was off for a few hours, but it's back on now."

"Ugh. Nash is bringing in more firewood for Janet."

"Oh good, I was worried about her. So, Jack said you and Nash made nice."

My cheeks blushed. "We've been making nice all over the house the last few days."

Millie giggled. "Mom and Dad would freak if they knew you were having sex in their house. Tell me you did it in that damn trophy room!"

I laughed this time. "No. Nash was a hard pass on that one."

"Damn. I can't get Justin to do it either. Pussies. So? Is making up fun to do."

Leaning against the kitchen counter, I sighed. "The most fun I've ever had in my life. It feels like we're in our own little world with no one to interrupt us. We've talked for hours, made love for hours, learned so much about each other. I honestly think fate played a hand with this storm. It's been so . . ."

"So what? Don't stop with the deets now."

"Amazing. Beautiful. Romantic. I'm not sure what word would describe it best. I've never met a guy who puts me first with everything, Millie. Even in bed he needs to make sure I'm happy first."

She laughed. "You're *happy*? You mean he makes sure you come first."

My face heated again. "Yes. Sometimes more than once."

"You lucky bitch."

I chewed on my lip. "I am lucky. And I can't believe I almost lost him."

"Well, you didn't, so don't dwell on that. Think about the future. What will happen when you guys get back to Austin?"

"Nash mentioned moving in with me."

"Wow! That's a big step. Are you sure you're ready for that?"

"I'm more than ready. Millie, he's the one. The guy I want to spend the rest of my life with. The one I want to wake up to every single morning, and the one I want to fall asleep next to each night. I've never in my life felt this way. It's like I can't get enough of him. When we are together, I wish I could climb inside of him and say there." I sighed and smile. "He holds me every single time after we've been together. Doesn't matter if it was slow and romantic or fast and passionate. He doesn't let go of me. Like he doesn't want the moment to end. I don't think he realizes he does it. Then, before he pulls out of me, he whispers against my ear, 'I love you, baby.'"

Millie and I let out a dramatic sigh. "Gah, I wish Justin was romantic like that. I mean, he's amazing in bed, don't get me wrong. But once he comes, he rolls over and passes out usually."

I chewed on my thumb nail, thinking back to a few hours ago when I was in Nash's arms as he made love to me. Turning, I flipped the pancakes.

"How have you not run out of condoms?" She laughed. When I didn't reply, she got silent. "Kaelynn, you didn't."

"What? I'm on the pill."

"You have been having unprotected sex, and it sounds like you're having a lot of it."

"Maybe, but like I said, I'm on the pill."

"I don't know whether to be jealous or angry. What if you get pregnant?"

I scoffed. "Um, that won't happen, sweet sister, because like I said, I'm on . . ."

My voice trailed off and I pushed off the counter. Heat raced from my feet up to the top of my head as panic started to set in.

"What? What's wrong? Kaelynn?"

Covering my hand with my mouth, I closed my eyes. A sickness that started deep in my stomach moved up to the back of my throat.

"Kaelynn! What is wrong? I hear how fast and heavy you're breathing. What is happening?"

"I . . . I haven't been taking my pill. The last three days, I've been so wrapped up in being with Nash, I've hardly gone to my room, and they're on the bathroom counter. Oh my gosh, oh no. Millie. He's going to think. . . ."

"No, he won't. Just tell him."

The sound of the back door opened and closed. "I have to go."

"Kaelynn, you're going to tell him, right?"

I hit *end* and put my phone down on the counter next to me. Nash walked in wearing a red-and-black plaid shirt. He still hadn't shaved and he looked so damn sexy with his beard and mustache. Very mountain manish, and it was hot.

The second he saw me, he smiled the most breathtaking smile. I couldn't see his dimples, and that made me sad. Of course, nerves replaced my sadness. He was going to be so angry with me.

"Good morning! Smells good in here."

Forcing a smile, I glanced around the kitchen. "I'm not sure how to make coffee."

Nash frowned, then said, "How about tea? We can boil water."

"Sounds great."

He turned to head to the pantry, stepping inside. "Your folks surely have tea."

I busied myself with taking off the pancakes and putting more batter onto the pan.

"How is the food in the refrigerator?" he asked.

"I'm not sure," I stated with a small shrug. "How long does it keep the cold in there?"

"A good few hours, but if we don't need anything out of it, we should keep it shut."

"Agreed," I said, trying to smile. "Oh wait, butter for the pancakes!"

"I'm good without it if you are."

"Sure, syrup works good for me. How is Janet and her sister?"

Nash chuckled. "Surrounded by stockings and ornaments and everything Christmas. Those two have been crafting fools. I got their fire going good, and Janet was heating water over the fire for oatmeal."

"Oh, that's smart."

Arms came up and wrapped around my body, causing me to shiver with both a sensation of being hot and cold at the same time.

I closed my eyes and took in a deep breath. I needed to tell him. *Now.*

Spinning around in his arms, I looked up into his light brown eyes.

"Nash, I have to tell you something."

The lights came rushing back on and the sounds of appliances coming back to life filled the kitchen.

"Oh, thank God! The power's back on," he stated.

"That's amazing news. Now we won't freeze!" I said with a nervous chuckle. Nash drew his brow in and took my hands, but not before reaching over and turning off the oven. He led us over to the stools and sat down, motioning for me to do the same.

"Talk to me, sweetheart."

I swallowed hard. "Okay, well, the past few days have been so magical, and I have been so lost in this little world we've made here with just the two of us."

"So have I."

"Nash, there is no excuse to forgetting this, and it only occurred to me when I was talking to Millie and she started to lecture me about unprotected sex."

His frown deepened, as if what I said made sense.

"I haven't taken my birth control pill the last few days."

He stared at me in silence.

"Nash, please say something."

Blinking to clear his thoughts, he leaned back in the chair. "So how does this work? Do you start taking it again?"

"Well, I would have thought my period would start, but it hasn't."

"Okay."

"I guess I could start taking it again, or wait and see if I start."

He nodded. "Okay."

"I can call my doctor today; see what the nurse says."

"Okay."

I sighed. "Stop saying *okay*. Nash, I didn't do this on purpose."

He stood and pulled me off the stool. Cupping my face in his hands, he kissed me. It was so sweet and gentle that my knees felt weak.

"There was never a moment I thought you did this on purpose. Kaelynn, I've been so caught up in us, I haven't even reached out to my folks or Morgan. I got a nasty voicemail from Morgan this morning bitching me out for making my folks and her worry. They heard about the snowstorm."

Grinning, I added, "We sure have been lost in each other, haven't we?"

"Yes," he agreed with a chuckle. "It's been the best few days of my entire life."

"So, you're not angry? Are you worried? Because I'm worried sick now."

He shrugged.

"That's it? A shrug? Nash, we haven't even been dating but a few weeks. You can't be that nonchalant about this."

"Why not? Do I want to spend time with you getting to know you before we bring a little one into this world? Of course, I do. I'm not exactly ready to be a father, but if something like that happens, then we will deal with it. I'm not going to waste a moment worrying about it, and I don't want you to either. No matter what happens, we'll make it work."

Staring up at him, I opened my mouth to speak, then snapped it shut. This man was unbelievable. I was freaking out inside, and he was calm as all get out.

"Come on, I'm starving. Let's go finish breakfast."

I tugged on his arm. "Wait. You mean to tell me you're not scared?"

"I'm scared fuckless, but there isn't anything that will come out of worrying. We'll figure this out if or when we need to." He kissed me on the forehead and got back up, making his way over to the pancakes. "Let's start making new ones; these are cold."

I stood, feeling a bit numb but strangely calm. We would figure it out. Together.

After breakfast, Nash and I walked over to Janet's to make sure her power came back on okay. Then we sat on the back porch, a fire going in the outdoor fire, enjoying the beautiful view.

"There is no doubt in my mind I could live up here."

Turning to face him, I lifted my brows. "Really? Full time, or are you talking once in a while?"

Nash thought about his answer for a few moments. "I love Texas, and all my family and friends are there, but I could totally see us buying some land and building a house up here. Maybe to come up and stay a few weeks in the summer and winter. Might be kind of fun."

The quickening of my heartbeat and the tingles in every nerve ending had me stilling in his arms.

"Too soon?" he questioned with a slight chuckle.

In a breathy voice, I replied, "I don't think so."

Nash winked then went on. "Everyone else in the world would probably say we are moving at lightning speed, but this feels so right. We feel so right."

"I agree," I added.

"We probably should see how me moving in first works out, and if you have a bun in the oven."

My eyes widened in shock at his flippant tone, and it took me a moment to laugh at his not-so-funny joke. "That's not funny, Nash Barrett." But I couldn't contain my own laughter.

His arm moved around my shoulders, bringing me closer to him. The warmth of his body and the beautiful scenery made me feel so content. Like everything I needed in the world was right there.

When the front gate alarm went off on my phone, we sat up and looked at each other.

"Who could that be?" Nash asked.

"I'm not sure."

Standing, we made our way back into the house and through the foyer to the front of the house.

I stepped outside to get a better look and Nash followed me. "Sounds like snowmobiles coming again."

"Yes, it might be Jack."

"Hope everything is okay with them. You said he doesn't live far from here?"

"No, a few miles down the road. He lives on the same land my parents own. He has about a twenty-acre parcel he built a house on."

"Nice."

Smiling, I faced him. "In case I haven't told you, I'm glad you followed me up here."

Nash placed his hands on my hips and pulled me closer to him. Leaning his forehead to mine, he smiled and I fell in love with him a little more. My hand went to the side of his face where his beard was.

"When are you going to shave this?"

"I sort of like the whole 'mountain man' thing I've got going on."

I giggled. "I did at first, but I miss seeing your dimples."

"Oh yeah? That's good to know."

My gaze searched his face. I never would have believed I could love a man like how I loved this one. The feelings I had for him were so strong I was often moved to tears just looking at him.

"I love you, Kaelynn Shae Whitaker," he professed with so much emotion I felt a tear slip and make a path down my cold face. Lifting his hand, he brushed it away.

"And I love you, James Nathaniel Barrett. So very much."

The moment our lips pressed together, it started to snow again. We laughed and Nash wrapped his arms around me, lifting me up and spinning me as we got lost in the beautiful moment.

The sounds of the snowmobile brought us out of our little bubble of heaven. Nash set me down next to him and then pulled me closer to his body, rubbing his hand up and down my arm.

"It's Jack and Jill," I said, rolling my eyes when Nash started singing the nursery rhyme.

Climbing off the two snowmobiles, Jill came rushing over to us.

"It's freezing out here; get inside! The two of you don't have coats on!"

Once we were in the house and the fire in the library had warmed Jack and Jill, I headed into the kitchen for something to snack on.

"Is your power back on?" I asked, walking back into the library.

"It came on earlier this morning," Jill replied, taking the two trays I had made up with cheese, crackers, fruit, and veggies. "We figured yours had as well."

"Yep, it came on earlier. We went and checked on Janet. They're doing good."

Jack grabbed the bag he had carried in and tossed a box to Nash. "Here you go, asshole. I'm going to pretend my kid sister didn't call me earlier with a 911 condom emergency. My sisters are only allowed once in their lifetime to ask me for condoms; this was Kaelynn's. Never again."

My hands went to my mouth to hide both my laughter and embarrassment. Nash laughed and held up the box. "We'll put them to good use. Is this all you brought?"

Jack growled and went to stand up when Jill pulled him back down. "Stop that. You promised you would behave."

My brother grunted and looked away from Nash who tossed me a sexy smirk.

Clearing his throat and trying not to act pissed off, Jack spoke. "Looks like they're starting to clear the roads. Did you hear on the news they're thinking the airport will be open to some flights this evening maybe?"

Peeking over at Nash, I replied, "We haven't really had the TV on at all. We've just been enjoying each other."

Jack rolled his eyes. "Ugh, seriously, Kaelynn. I don't need to hear this."

I held up my hands. "What! I didn't say we have been having sex all over the house. I said we haven't had much time to watch TV."

It was Nash's turn to clear his throat. "Um, babe, you might want to stop while you're ahead."

Jack glared at me, then turned his attention on Nash. "You better not hurt her. I will hunt you down and rip your fucking head off if you do."

Nash nodded and a wide grin spread over his face as he stared at me for a few moments, then focused back in on Jack. "I love your sister, Jack. Very much, and I honestly would rip my own fucking head off if I ever did anything to hurt her."

Jill swooned, and Jack shot her a confused expression.

"That was so romantic," Jill mused as Jack rubbed the back of his neck in confusion.

"How was that romantic, Jill?"

She shrugged. "Don't worry, sweetie, you have your moments too."

I wasn't sure if I should laugh at the expression my brother shot his girlfriend. He looked at me and I raised a brow, almost urging him to do it.

Standing, he grabbed her hand and pulled her off the sofa and out of the library. Nash stood. "What's going on?"

Clapping my hands softly, I did a little hop of excitement. "I think you just silently challenged my brother to show you up in the romance department!"

"Ah, I didn't know we were competing. Hell, I would have upped my game."

With a smack on the chest, I grabbed Nash and we followed my brother and Jill out of the library.

"What's happening?" Nash asked in a hushed voice.

"I think he's about to propose."

Nash grinned like a silly boy about to get a new toy. "Really?"

"Yep. Come on!"

The picture window in the living room looked like a scene from a painting. The mountains in the background were covered with a beautiful blanket of a snow. Light flurries were floating down, adding the perfect romantic touch.

Laughing, Jill pulled Jack to a stop. "What in the world are you doing?"

Nash and I stood back, far enough to give them privacy but close enough to hear and see.

Reaching into his pocket, my brother pulled out a ring box, causing Jill to gasp. Tears sprang from her eyes and trailed down her face.

"Baby, you have been here for me at my lowest time. You brought me back from a hell I was living in, and you have made me so happy. There will never be the right words to express to you how much I'm in love with you and how that love grows every moment of the day. I want to spend the rest of my life with you, Jill. And thank you for saving my life. Will you do me the honor of becoming my wife?"

Tears streamed down my own face as Nash wrapped his arms around me and nuzzled his face into my neck.

"I'm pretty sure he won that round."

Laughing, I wiped at my tears and glanced back just enough to kiss Nash. "I do believe you're right."

Jill had dropped to the floor in front of Jack and wrapped herself around him. They kissed, whispered words to each other, and kissed some more. When they both stood and Jack slipped the ring on Jill's finger, I rushed over to them, screaming like a silly schoolgirl. Jill did the same. While Nash walked up calmly and shook Jack's hand. They exchanged a few words, but I couldn't hear them. Jill was too busy crying and mumbling how surprised she was and how this was the best day of her life.

"I think this calls for some celebration!" I shouted.

"I'll go get Dad's best bottle of champagne!" Jack cried out as he ran toward the steps that led down to the wine cellar.

"Damn, the wine cellar; we haven't been there yet," Nash said to me.

I faced Nash and grinned. "You are a bad, bad boy."

"Okay, all the way from France," Jack said, popping open the bottle and pouring everyone a glass.

"To Jack and Jill," I said, trying not to giggle. I would never get used to that, no matter how hard I tried.

"Here's to climbing up that hill!" Nash added.

Jack and Jill groaned, and my brother punched Nash on the shoulder. "Again with the funny jokes."

"I'm so happy for you guys!" I said as we clinked our glasses and drank.

Nash wrapped his arm around my waist, and I couldn't help but dream of the moment when it was us celebrating our engagement.

"I know the perfect way to up this celebration," I said, smiling at everyone.

"What's that?" Jack asked.

"Let's put up the tree in the library!"

Nash and I didn't know it then, but it was the last evening we would spend in my parents' house. The next day the roads were cleared and the airport was open. After booking an afternoon flight back to Austin, Nash and I spent the morning with my brother and sister, as well as with Justin and Jill. It was the perfect ending to the most amazing week of my life.

Millie had begged me to stay for Christmas, but I knew the sooner Nash and I got back to Austin, the sooner our lives would begin.

Twenty-Seven

February~Two months later

NASH

THE SOUND OF laughter filtered through the door as I walked up to it. Unlocking the door, I stepped into the kitchen to see Kaelynn and Morgan sitting at the island.

"You two sound like you're having fun."

When Kaelynn lifted her eyes to meet mine, my heart fluttered in my chest. She smiled the most beautiful smile and rushed over to me. She did it every single day, and it made me feel like the most loved man in the world. I could be gone for an hour or twelve; she greeted me the same way every time. Since Morgan's practice was growing, Kaelynn was doing more volunteer work with another company in Austin that helped widows of veterans. She was passionate about the work, and I loved to see her doing something she loved.

"Hey! How was your day, babe?" she asked, kissing me on the lips and then giving me a hug.

"Long. How about yours?" I asked, kissing her on the forehead before she slipped away and went back to the stool.

"Amazing! Morgan and I have been searching for a playpen for the new baby."

I pulled open the refrigerator and sighed. "We talked about this, Kaelynn. This place is too small."

"Don't be a party pooper." Morgan chuckled.

Leaning against the counter, I stared at the two women. Both of whom were giving me puppy eyes.

"This place is too small for a puppy, and especially for a playpen for a puppy."

Kaelynn jutted her lower lip and pouted. She looked so damn cute; I couldn't help but smile. The moment she saw the boxer puppy two weeks ago on the hike and bike trail, she had been begging me for a puppy. It was something I could actually get on board with, *if* we lived in a house.

After coming home from Utah, I waited until after the holidays and the first of the year before moving in. Kaelynn had gone to the doctor within days of us returning to make sure she hadn't gotten pregnant. I had to admit, when the test came back negative, I was disappointed. Kaelynn seemed to be, as well, but we decided it was for the best. We needed to be with each other before we added a baby into the mix. I put my house on the market, and we had started talking about moving farther out and building a house. Things were moving fast, but neither one of us wanted to waste a moment.

"Don't give me that look," I stated, then looked at my sister, trying to give me her best sad face. "No."

Kaelynn sighed. "Okay, well, what if we looked at getting a bigger place? Maybe even a condo with a yard. They have some."

Taking a sip of beer, I nodded. "Maybe."

"Ugh, you are such a jerk!" Morgan said, closing her laptop. "We even found a puppy who would have been perfect."

I groaned. "You're looking at puppies, Kaelynn?"

She bit into her lip and gave me a little shrug. God, I loved her. She had no idea the surprise I had for her. Two months of living in her little condo had proven to be the push I needed to make this happen.

The knock on the door snapped me out of my thoughts. "That's Blake."

Opening the door, Blake walked in, dressed in a suit and carrying a briefcase. Morgan whistled at him while Kaelynn fanned herself.

"Like what you see?" he asked, walking over and giving Morgan a kiss on the cheek and then doing the same with Kaelynn.

"You look hot in a suit. Why aren't guys my age dressing in suits? Ugh, it's so unfair."

Blake and I both laughed. "Morgan, you're two years younger than us, not ten. It's not like the generation gap is big."

"Still," she stated, packing up her laptop and grabbing her coat. "I don't know when the last time a guy made my girl parts all hot and bothered until just now."

Blake stopped looking at his phone and stared at Morgan. "I make your girly parts hot and bothered, do I?"

I shot him a dirty look as Morgan blew him a kiss and said, "Sad, isn't it? Later, y'all."

Laughing, Blake shook his head and dropped onto the leather chair in the living room.

"Love you, Morgan," I said, walking her out of the condo.

Once she was out into the hall, she leaned in and whispered, "When are you telling her?"

"Tonight."

Her eyes danced with excitement. "I can't wait. The weather is perfect."

I nodded. "Yeah, thanks for helping Charlie and Terri plan it all."

"Of course. I loved doing it for her. She is my best friend and the woman who happens to love my brother. There isn't anything I wouldn't do for either of you."

Laughing, I leaned down and kissed her. "Right. Be careful and let me know when you get home."

"Will do, but I have a date tonight, so I might be late getting home. I'm meeting him for dinner."

"Who is it?" I asked, trying to use my best brotherly tone.

"Rich."

I smiled. "Y'all are dating again?"

She shrugged. "Yeah. I mean, he's a good guy, and I thought maybe we were better off as friends, but we're giving it another go."

Morgan's eyes were saying something different from her lips. She looked lost and confused, but I decided to let it go. She was a grown woman. Her blonde ponytail bobbed on her head as she laughed.

"You're trying to read into it, Nash. Don't. I like him a lot. I may even love him. We're taking it one day at a time, so please don't worry."

"I won't. Is work going good?"

"It's going great!" she said, walking backward. "Stop stalling and go! Love you!"

"Love you, too!"

After shutting the door, I walked into the condo and found Blake arguing with Kaelynn about which channel to put on the TV.

"Why are you here, and why are you arguing with my girlfriend?"

Blake shrugged. "'Cause it's fun."

"Are you ready to go, idiot?" I asked, giving Blake a look that said I wasn't in the mood.

"Where are you guys going?" Kaelynn asked.

"We're all going somewhere," I replied.

"Who's driving?" Blake asked, pulling out an envelope from his briefcase and handing it to me.

Kaelynn looked between the two of us. "The last time you two exchanged an envelope, things didn't turn out so good."

I laughed then kissed her on the cheek. "I have a feeling this time things will be different. Grab your coat, baby, it's cold outside."

❧

"ARE WE GOING to see Charlie and Tucker? I wish I would have known. I had a little gift for Hannah."

Blake and I exchanged a quick look. "No, sorry, babe, not going to see them."

Kaelynn's phone rang. "Crapola, I have to take this really quick. It's a client in New York."

Blake pulled into the gravel driveway as Kaelynn busied herself on the call. She was assisting a small company setting up a fundraiser to send boxes to military men and women overseas for the Fourth of July.

Coming to a stop, Blake and I got out of the truck and started down the path a little ways. I had purchased this land last fall and hadn't told anyone until last week when I told Charlie and Tucker. Blake had been helping with the design of the house for the last month when I stopped by his office and asked him for his input.

"She has no idea?"

"None."

"Think this will be enough land for her?"

"Oh yeah. Kaelynn is a simple woman who doesn't need much. That's one of the things I love about her. She can afford a mansion on Lake Travis, but she'll prefer a country house on fifty acres."

Blake smiled. "You still have those plans for the log cabin in Utah?"

My stomach dropped at the mention of Utah. Kaelynn and I had spent the most amazing week there. One I would never forget. We had talked about building a log cabin on the land that was to be given to her by her parents. Kaelynn said she knew the perfect building site that would overlook the same exact mountains we had looked at day after day when we were stuck from the snowstorm. That was the week that I learned I would never be able to live without this amazing woman in my life.

"Sorry about that, you guys. Lindsey is a bit of a difficult client and thinks I need to drop everything and . . ."

Her voice trailed off as she saw the view in front of us. It wasn't anything like the view she grew up with, but it was beautiful, nonetheless. It faced the west and the sun was starting to set.

"Wow. This is stunning. Blake, did you buy this land?" Kaelynn asked.

Blake laughed. "Kaelynn, do you honestly see me living in the country? There isn't a Starbucks for miles. Where would I go for a quick piece of ass? Not a club in sight."

She giggled and turned to face me. I handed her the large envelope and watched as something in her eyes changed. Her hands shook as she opened it and pulled out the smaller scaled version of the house Blake and I had designed together. It was almost the exact version of the house I had doodled on a piece of paper back when we were in Utah. Kaelynn had added a wish list to the side of the drawing with things she would like in the house, like a mudroom, a laundry room with a big sink, a dog-wash station, as well as a rooftop terrace for us to watch the sunset.

A small sob slipped from her mouth before her hand came up. She stared at the drawing and then looked up at me. "Is this our house?"

I nodded. "I bought this land last fall. You always talk about how much you love the hill country. If you want the house bigger, we can go bigger."

A tear slipped free and she shook her head. "It's perfect. It's beautiful; please don't change a thing."

Throwing herself into me, I wrapped my arms around her and held on to her.

"I love you so much, Kaelynn."

Her body shook as she cried harder. When she finally drew back, I wiped her face dry.

"Nash, I love this so much. And the fact that you designed it makes it all the more special. Will Barrett Construction build it?"

I nodded. "Yeah, I've already got a crew on standby waiting. There's just one other thing I need to do before we can move forward. Two, actually."

The truck and car pulling up behind Blake's was right on time.

"Perfect timing," Blake said, making his way over to Tucker's truck. He opened the back door and Morgan jumped out of the truck.

Then Kaelynn's parents got out of the car and made their way over to us.

"Mom? Dad? What's going on?" Kaelynn asked in a half-sob, half-laugh as her parents walked up and hugged her.

Reaching out my hand to Kaelynn's father, I said, "It's great seeing you again Mr. and Mrs. Whitaker."

"Thank you for asking us to be a part of this darling. It's great to be back in Texas." Mrs. Whitaker said. Kaelynn and I had both flown back up to Utah after Christmas so I could meet her mother and father. They had been to Austin twice since then and had met my parents. I was shocked how well our folks got along. My father and Kaelynn's hit it off instantly, as did the moms.

Turning to face Kaelynn, her mother smiled. "Nash asked us to be here. I'm only sorry to hear his mom and dad were out of town and couldn't be here."

Kaelynn looked confused. "Be here for what?" She turned back and looked at Tucker's truck.

Tucker reached into the back and took out Hannah as Charlie fumbled with something inside the truck.

"I have little surprise for you," I whispered.

"How's it going, y'all?" Tucker said, walking up with a smiling Hannah.

"Hey there, little sweet pea!" Kaelynn cooed to Hannah. She was so wrapped up in Hannah, she didn't even see the puppy in Charlie's arms.

A small bark made Kaelynn jump and then spin to look in the direction of Charlie.

"Oh my gosh! Did you get a puppy?" Kaelynn cried out. "You so suck right now if that is your puppy."

Charlie laughed and handed the puppy to me. Kaelynn looked confused as she watched me drop down to one knee and hold out the puppy. Attached to her pink collar was a white bow with my grandmother's engagement ring tied to it.

Kaelynn broke down and started crying again.

"Kaelynn Shae Dotson Whitaker. . . ."

Everyone laughed, including Kaelynn.

"Would you do me the honor of helping me raise this little puppy as her mother and father, and would you be willing to change your last name to Barrett and be my wife?"

She nodded frantically as she took the puppy from me and hugged her as she pressed her mouth to mine.

"Yes. I will help you raise this puppy. But only if you share poop duties with me."

Smiling, I cupped her face within my hands and kissed her again. "It's a deal."

I took the ring off of the ribbon and slipped it onto Kaelynn's hand as the rest of the gang yelled out in celebration. Even little Hannah got in on it.

"What are you going to name the puppy?" Charlie asked, scratching her under her chin.

Kaelynn glanced down at the puppy, and then back up at me as I shrugged. "It's totally up to you."

Chewing on the corner of her lip, she smiled. "Faith."

Warmth spread though my entire body as I stared into her beautiful, hazel eyes.

"It's perfect," I whispered.

"No, this is perfect. Everything about this moment is perfect."

With a smile, I leaned in and asked, "So, who is in the lead for the romance competition? Me or Jack?"

Kaelynn's eyes beamed with nothing but happiness and love. "Without a doubt you. I'm pretty sure it was the puppy that pushed you into the lead."

"I knew it would," I replied with a wink. "Now, tell me where you want me to build our future."

With a slight twist to her mouth, Kaelynn reached into her back pocket and pulled out an envelope and handed it to me.

"How about we start here?"

Drawing in my brows, I opened the envelope and took out a pregnancy test. Snapping my eyes back to hers, I felt my eyes build with tears. I thought I had experienced pure happiness only moments ago. I was knocked on my ass and proven wrong by this amazing woman.

"A puppy *and* a baby?"

With a laugh that made my knees weak, she nodded. "The plans may need to be changed to include a nursery now. How fast can you build that house?"

~ঞ৽~

The End.

Adore Me

LOOK FOR *ADORE Me*, coming spring 2019!

Morgan Barrett is off limits.

Why?

Because she's my best friend's sister and insists that she isn't interested in a relationship.

That didn't stop us from sharing one incredibly passionate night together. However, one night was not enough for either of us.

I want more. She needs more.

When we give in to the desire, something amazing happens. But can I keep my secret from her? The secret that could possible have her hating me, and worse yet, hating herself.

Thank you

THANK YOU TO Elaine, Hollie, Callie, and Christine for helping make this project the best it can be! I adore each of you.

A huge thank you to my readers, without you, I couldn't follow this dream of mine.

Don't miss Kelly Elliot's *Seduce Me*,
the first book in the *Austin Singles* series!

Turn the page for an excerpt

One

CHARLESTON

HE STOOD ACROSS the room and talked to Angie Reynolds like he had no idea he had shaken my entire world this past weekend. Maybe he did know. The truth was, he'd never know the real reason behind my leaving without saying a word to him. I gave him nothing. Not even, "Hey, thanks for the most incredible weekend of my life."

The only thing I did leave him was a letter because I didn't have the guts to be honest with him.

When his eyes drifted over the room, I looked away before he could see me watching him. I swore my lips still tingled from his kisses. Closing my eyes, I tried like hell to push the feelings away.

I cannot fall for Tucker Middleton.

Who was I kidding? I'd already fallen for him a long time ago.

Peeking toward him again, my breath caught while watching his hand run through his brown hair. My stomach tugged with that familiar desire that Tucker always pulled out of me.

I was struck by Tucker the first moment I ever laid my eyes on him. I turned into a complete mess. He made me feel things I'd never felt before, and that rattled me even more.

My father's voice played in the back of my head over and over. A constant reminder of why I couldn't give in to my feelings for Tucker.

"Charleston, do not be bothered with these boys in college. Focus on your future. Your future is with CMI. You can fall in love later."

When Tucker invited two friends of ours and me to his parents' lake house in Marble Falls, I was foolish enough to think I could resist him.

Yeah, I couldn't have been more wrong. I spent more time in his bed than on the lake.

My eyes closed. I could feel his scourging touch even now. Those magical fingers lightly running over my body. Deliciously soft lips against mine. His hands exploring every inch of my body.

Stop. This. Now. Charlie.

Drawing in a deep breath, I exhaled and glanced around the room. I pressed the beer bottle to my lips and finished it off. It didn't matter how much I drank; I'd never be able to forget the way his body felt. The way he pulled out my first ever orgasm and forever rocked my world.

Ugh, think of something else!

Taking another look around, I found him again. This time he was talking to Lily, my best friend and his sister. My gaze dropped to his soft plump lips. The things he whispered into my ear would replay in my mind for the rest of my life . . . making me feel a high like I'd never felt before.

And therein lies the problem.

I need to stay focused. With Tucker, I cannot focus for shit.

Someday I would be taking over my father's billion-dollar global consulting firm. The last thing I could afford was a distraction. And boy howdy, was Tucker Middleton a distraction.

Feeling someone bump my shoulder, I glanced to my right to see Lily standing there.

Geesh. I was so lost in thought I hadn't even seen her walk over here.

Note to self: Don't daydream about Tucker.

"So, what happened between you and Tucker last weekend?" My heart stopped. With Lily being Tucker's sister, I had no clue what all he told her.

"Why?"

Looking between me and Tucker, who stood across the room, she focused back in on me. "Because he's been pissed ever since he got back. He said something to Nash about you being the biggest bitch he'd ever met. Then he told him if he never talked to you again, he wouldn't lose any sleep over it."

Ouch. I deserved that.

Snapping my head back over to Tucker, I saw he was now talking to a group of guys. I would never admit I was happy to see Angie had moved on and left Tucker alone.

"So . . . are you going to tell me what happened?"

My cheeks heated as I looked at her.

"Oh. My. God. Did y'all sleep together?"

When I didn't answer, she yanked at my arm. "Charlie, wait. I've never seen that look in your eyes before." She gasped then slapped her hand up to her mouth before dropping it again and saying, "You like him!"

With a curt laugh, I rolled my eyes and said, "Please. I do not like Tucker."

Lie. I think I'm in love with him.

She lifted her brow. "But y'all slept together?"

I shrugged. "Maybe."

Grabbing me, she pulled me down the hall and into the bathroom. "Okay, I'm so confused. I know Tucker has the hots for you, but I didn't think you liked him. I mean, you get all weird around him and all but . . ." She gasped again. "Oh no."

My eyes filled with tears, and I quickly looked away. "Charlie, what happened? He acts like he can't stand you now."

I instantly felt sick. "What did he say?"

"Pretty much the same thing he told Nash. That you were cold hearted and didn't care about anyone but yourself. He just told me he didn't care if you ever hung out with us again."

Squaring off my shoulders, I took in a deep breath as I tried to bury the sting of his words. I deserved them, though. "Well then, that's for the best. Takes the awkwardness away from the situation."

Narrowing her deadpan stare, she asked, "What . . . situation?"

How did I tell my best friend I was in love with her brother, had the most amazing weekend of my life with sex that was mind blowing, and then snuck out Sunday morning without so much as a word? Well. There was the note I left, which is probably why he hates me.

"Um . . . well . . . we, ah . . . things got a little . . . you know . . ."

Shaking her head, she responded. "No. I don't know, and you're babbling." Her brows pulled in. "You never babble."

I jumped and pointed at her, causing her to shriek. "See! That's the problem. Your brother brings out this whole other side of me, and I can't think straight when I'm around him. I trip on shit and say the stupidest things. You'd never know I was going to run a huge corporation someday by the way I act when he's near me."

The smile that spread over her face made my stomach drop.

"Oh. My. God. You *really* like him."

I frantically nodded my head. "Yes. No. Oh God, I don't know. No! I don't like him. I cannot like him. We had an amazing weekend with the best sex of my life, but it's over. I told him in my note I wanted to forget it ever happened and that it was best if we were just friends."

Swallowing hard, I looked away as I chewed on my lip. Oh, how I tried to talk myself out of kissing him that first night. We were both a little drunk, and damn it if he didn't look hot as hell in his stupid Dallas Cowboys baseball hat turned backward. *Do guys have any idea how hot that makes them look?*

For the last three years I fought my feelings for Tucker. I had a moment of weakness. Okay, it was more than a moment. It was three days' worth of moments of weakness.

"Friends? So you're saying you're not attracted to my brother?"

Attracted? Pffttt. Boy, was she off. I had fallen for Tucker the first time he grabbed my hand and walked me into a movie theater with our little group of friends. To him it was a friendly gesture . . . to me it made my entire body come to life. I knew then he was going to be my kryptonite.

Innocent touches here and there I could handle, but this past weekend took everything to a DEFCON level 5. All I heard the entire weekend were sirens going off in my head. Not to mention my father's voice warning me to stay focused and not get involved with what could only amount to a fling. After all, college relationships never lasted, he said. It didn't matter he had met my mother in college and married her. Or that they had been happily married for thirty years. He made me promise I wouldn't date and that I would solely focus on school.

I had kept my promise too. Kept it as long as my heart would allow.

Well, until last Thursday night when I let my betraying bitch of a body control me.

But Tucker was different. So very different. He made me want things I never desired before. He was a weakness I couldn't afford to have in my life. Not if I wanted to pursue my dreams. Well, my father's dreams.

"Hello? Earth to Charlie? Are you even listening to me?"

I shook my head to clear my thoughts. "Sorry. Listen, I messed up this past weekend. Things got a little hot and heavy with Tucker. It was a mistake that I . . . that I . . . regret."

I wonder if that sounded convincing to her? It sure as shit didn't to me.

Her mouth damn near dropped to the ground. "Wait, did you say you told him you wished it never happened in the note? The note you left him, Charlie?" Her eyes nearly popped out of her head.

Damn. This is where the shit is going to hit the fan.

"I, um . . . well. I left super early."

The look of disappointment on her face about killed me. I knew if I had waited for Tucker to wake up, I wouldn't have been able to leave. I would have found myself wrapped up in him another day. And that would have turned into another night, which would ultimately turn into more days and nights. There was no way I would have been able to look him in the eyes and say it was a mistake we were together because deep down in my heart, it was exactly what I had been wanting. There wasn't one ounce of regret in my body over the time we spent together, but my mind was flooded with all the whys and hows of why we could never be more than friends.

My blank stare was answer enough.

She closed her eyes for a brief moment before glaring at me with pure anger in her irises. "So, let me get this straight. Y'all made love, you led him on, then got up and left without so much as saying goodbye?"

The way she said it made me feel like such a slut, and truly the world's biggest bitch. Tucker was right when he told Nash I was a bitch. In fact, he was being a tad bit generous in his assessment of me.

Note to self. Sleeping with a guy and then getting up and leaving without so much as a thank you for the multiple orgasms is a bitch move. A total bitch move.

I didn't like the way she looked at me. Anger quickly raced through me. It was the only choice I had. "We didn't make love, Lily. Don't try to romanticize it. We *fucked*. He wanted me; I wanted to see what it would be like with him. Itches scratched. End of story."

Lily slowly shook her head. "You know it was more than that, Charlie. I see it in your eyes. You're just too damn scared to admit it. Maybe next time you want to get laid, go find some asshole who won't care when you get up and leave. Someone who will actually slap your ass on the way out the door. Tucker had feelings for you. How could you do this to him? How could you lead him on all weekend and then leave him high and dry and say it was a mistake?"

My chest squeezed thinking Tucker might no longer have feelings for me. That if he had feelings for me, I'd crushed any chance of ever being more than what we are right now. The thought that I had ruined a friendship I valued so much for a few hours of pleasure was fracturing my already broken heart. I had to keep telling myself it was for the best; it was the only way I'd be able to put one foot in front of the other around him.

Forcing myself to keep a steady voice, I replied, "Tucker wanted in my pants as much as I wanted in his, Lily. I can't help it if he thought there was going to be something more out of it. There were no promises made between us; it was just two adults doing adult things with no strings attached. Plain and simple."

Her head jerked back and she wore a shocked expression before letting out a scoff. "Wow, Charlie. You really *are* a bitch. A heartless bitch with no feelings at all. You've mastered that at the ripe old age of twenty-one. You're going to make a great addition to your father's company with that attitude."

With that, my best friend spun around on her heels and stormed out the door. I couldn't even be mad at her because every single word she said was true.

All of it.

Want more Kelly Elliott?

Check out her *Cowboys & Angels* series